LIVE AND LET CHAI

BREE BAKER

sourcebooks
landmark

Published by Sourcebooks Landmark, an imprint of Sourcebooks, Inc.
P.O. Box 4410, Naperville, Illinois 60563-4410
(630) 961-3900
Fax: (630) 961-2168
sourcebooks.com

Printed and bound in Canada.
MBP 10 9 8 7 6 5 4 3 2 1

NIGHTCHASER

AMANDA BOUCHET

sourcebooks
casablanca

Published by Sourcebooks Casablanca, an imprint of Sourcebooks, Inc.
P.O. Box 4410, Naperville, Illinois 60567-4410
(630) 961-3900
Fax: (630) 961-2168
sourcebooks.com

Printed and bound in Canada.
MBP 10 9 8 7 6 5 4 3 2 1

This book is for my sister, Alexis.

The lights in the night sky aren't the only kind of star. Here on Earth, they don't shine much brighter than you. I love you.

ABOUT THE AUTHOR

 Bree Baker is a Midwestern writer obsessed with small-town hijinks, sweet tea, and the sea. She's been telling stories to her family, friends, and strangers for as long as she can remember, and more often than not, those stories feature a warm ocean breeze and a recipe she's sure to ruin. Now she's working on those fancy cooking skills and dreaming up adventures for the Seaside Café Mysteries. Bree is a member of Sisters in Crime, International Thriller Writers, and the Romance Writers of America.

ACKNOWLEDGMENTS

Thank you, dear readers, for picking up this book and giving Everly's story a chance. By doing that, you've made my dream possible, and I am endlessly, eternally grateful to you.

I would also like to thank my editor, Anna Michels, for seeing promise in my work, and for allowing me to be part of the Sourcebooks team. I'm so proud and honored. Thank you, Jill Marsal, my agent, my Yoda, mentor, and friend. You're changing my life. I can't really thank you properly for that. My critique ladies, Keri and Jennifer, for making my words better. My mother-in-law, Darlene, for all the untold hours of encouragement and babysitting. My parents, for making me believe I could change the world. Noah, Andrew, and Lily, thank you for putting up with a frantic, harebrained, weirdo of a mom. I'm sorry to say, I've rubbed off on one or two of you. *Good luck*.

Finally, my husband, Bryan, who asked a quiet and sensible office administrator to be his wife many years ago. I'm sorry to say she's turned out to be a killer.

*For my sweet mama and her
unending love of the seaside*

CHAPTER
ONE

"Welcome to Sun, Sand, and Tea." I perked up at the precious sound of seashell wind chimes bouncing and tinkling against the front door of my new café. "I'll be right with you."

A pair of ladies in windbreakers and capri pants smoothed their windblown hair and examined the seating options. Sounds of the sea had followed them inside, amplified briefly by the opening door.

I bopped my head to a Temptations song and tapped the large sweet tea jug behind the counter. Until three months ago, owning and operating an iced tea shop on the shore of my hometown had been nothing more than a childish dream. I'd thought being a grown-up meant working a job I hated while wearing uncomfortable clothes, so I'd toed the line for a while, but my looming thirtieth birthday and a broken heart had changed all that.

Now I did what I wanted—in comfy clothes for significantly less money, but at least I could wear flip-flops.

I set a lidless canning jar of Old-Fashioned Sun Tea in front of the man sitting at my counter and beamed. "Let me know if I can fix you anything else, Sam."

He frowned at his phone, too engrossed or distracted to answer. Sam Smart was a local real estate agent. He'd arrived in Charm during the years I'd been away from home, and from what I could tell, he was a type-A, all-stress all-day kind of guy—a little sweet tea was probably just what he needed. I nudged the jar closer until his hand swept out to meet it. "Thanks."

"Everything okay?" I asked.

He flicked his gaze to mine, then back to his phone. "It's Paine." He shook his head and groaned.

"Ah." I grabbed a thin stack of napkins and patted Sam's shoulder on my way to welcome the newcomers. "Good luck with that."

Benedict Paine had been a thorn in my side since the day I'd approached our town council about adding a café to the first floor of my new seaside home. Owning a sweet-tea shop was my dream come true, and honestly, I couldn't afford the house's mortgage payments without the business income. Despite the home's fixer-upper condition, the price tag had been astronomical, making the café a must, and Mr. Paine had fought me the entire way, complaining that adding a business to a residential property would drag down the neighborhood. I could only imagine the kind of headache a man like Paine could cause a real estate agent.

The space that was now my café stretched through

the entire south side of the first floor. Walls had been strategically knocked out, opening the kitchen and formal dining area up to a large space for entertaining. The result was a stunning seaside setup, perfect for my shop.

From the kitchen, a private hallway led to the rest of the first floor and another thousand or so square feet of potential expansion space. A staircase off that hall provided passage to my second-floor living quarters, which were just as big and full of potential. The stairs themselves were amazing, stained a faded red, with delicate carvings along the edges. They were mine alone to enjoy, shut off from the café by a locking door. I could probably thank the home's history as a boarding house for my substantial second-floor kitchen. The cabinets and fixtures were all older than me, but I couldn't complain—the café kitchen was what mattered, and it was fantastic.

Seating at Sun, Sand, and Tea was a hodgepodge of repainted garage sale and thrift shop finds. Twenty seats in total, five at the counter and fifteen scattered across the wide-planked, whitewashed floor, ranging from padded wicker numbers with low tables to tall bistro sets along the perimeter.

The ladies had selected a high table near a wall of windows overlooking my deck.

I refreshed my smile and set a napkin in front of each of them. "Hello. Welcome to Sun, Sand, and Tea."

They dragged their attention slowly away from the rolling waves and driftwood-speckled beach beyond the glass, reluctant to part with the amazing view for even a second.

"Can I get something started for you?"

The taller woman settled tortoiseshell glasses onto the ridge of her sunburned nose and fixed her attention to the café menu, scripted on an enormous blackboard covering the far wall. "Do you really make twenty flavors of iced tea?"

"Yes, ma'am. Plus a daily array of desserts and finger foods." The selection changed without notice, sometimes with the tide, depending on if I ran out of any necessary ingredients.

"Fascinating. I came in for some good old-fashioned sweet tea, but now you've got me wondering about the Country Cranberry Hibiscus. What's in that?" She leaned her elbows on the tabletop and twined her fingers.

"Well, there—there's black tea, hibiscus, and, uh, rose hips, and cranberries." I stammered over the answer to her question the same way I had to similar inquiries on a near-daily basis since opening my café doors. It seemed a fine line between serving my family's secret recipes and sharing them ingredient by ingredient.

The woman glanced out the window again and pressed a palm to her collarbone as a massive gull flapped to a stop on the handrail outside the window. "Dear!"

"Oh, there's Lou," I said.

"Lou?"

"I think he came with the house."

She lowered her hand, but kept one eye on Lou. "I'll try the Cranberry Hibiscus," she said. "What about you, Margo?"

Her friend pursed her lips. "Make mine Summer Citrus Mint, and I'd like to try your crisp cucumber sandwich."

I formed an "okay" sign with my fingers and winked. "Give me just a quick minute, and I'll get that over here for you."

I strode back to the counter, practically vibrating with excitement. After only a month in business, each customer's order was still a thrill for me.

The seashell wind chimes kicked into gear again and I responded on instinct. "Welcome to Sun, Sand, and Tea." I turned on my toes for a look at the newest guest and my stomach dropped. "Oh, hello, Mr. Paine." I shot a warning look at Sam, whose head drooped lower over his tea.

"Miss Swan." Mr. Paine straddled a stool three seats down from Sam and set his straw porkpie hat on the counter. Tufts of white hair stretched east and west from the spaces below his bald spot and above each ear. "Lovely day."

I nodded in acknowledgment. "Can I get you anything?"

"Please," he drawled, giving Sam a thorough once-over. It wasn't clear if he already knew Sam was mad at him, or if he was figuring that out from the silent treatment.

I waited, knowing what the next words out of Mr. Paine's mouth were going to be.

Reluctantly, he pulled his attention back to me. "How about a list of all your ingredients?"

Sam rolled his small brown eyes, but otherwise continued to ignore Mr. Paine's presence.

I grabbed a knife and a loaf of fresh-baked bread and set them on the counter. "You know I can't give that to you, Mr. Paine. Something else, perhaps?" I'd been through this a dozen times with him since Sun, Sand, and Tea's soft opening. Swan women had guarded our tea recipes for a hundred years, and I wasn't about to hand them over just because he said so. "How about a glass of tea instead?"

I cut two thin slices from the loaf, then whacked the crusts off with unnecessary oomph.

Sam took a long pull on his drink, stopping only when there was nothing left but ice, and returned the jar to the counter with a thump. "It's very good," he said, turning to stare at Mr. Paine. "You should try it. I mean, if you'd had it your way, this place wouldn't even be open, right? Seems like the least you can do is find out what you were protesting."

I didn't bother to mention that Mr. Paine had already tried basically every item on the menu as I plied him with free samples to try to get in his good graces.

Mr. Paine frowned, first at Sam, then at me. Wrinkles raced across his pale, sun-spotted face. "It's a health and safety issue," he groused. "People need to know what they're drinking."

"Yes." I arranged cucumber slices on one piece of bread. "I believe you've mentioned that." It had, in fact, been his number one argument since I'd gotten the green light to open. "I'm happy to provide a general list of ingredients for each recipe, but there are certain herbs and spices, as well as brewing methods, that are trade secrets."

"He doesn't care about any of that," Sam said. "He just wants to get his way."

Mr. Paine twisted on his stool to glare at Sam. "Whatever your problem is, Sam Smart, it's not with me, so stow it."

Sam shoved off his stool. "And your problem isn't with her." He grabbed the gray suit jacket from the stool beside him and threaded his arms into the sleeves. "Thanks for the tea, Everly." He tossed a handful of dollar bills onto the counter and a remorseful look in my direction.

I worked to close my slack jaw as the front door slapped shut behind him. Whatever grudge match Sam and Mr. Paine had going, I didn't want a ticket for it. I put the unused cucumber slices away and removed a white ceramic bowl from the fridge.

Mr. Paine watched carefully, teeth clenched.

"Maybe you'd like to try the Peach Tea today," I suggested. "Whatever you want. On the house."

Preferably *to go*.

"How much sugar is in the Peach?" he asked, apparently determined to criticize. "You know I don't like a lot of sugar."

I pointed to a brightly colored section on my menu that highlighted sugar-free options. "How about a tea made with alternative sweeteners, like honey or fruit puree? Maybe the Iced Peach with Ginger?" I turned to the refrigerator and pulled out a large metal bowl, then scooped the cream cheese, mayo, and seasoning mixture onto the second bread slice, turning it face down over the cucumbers. "There's no sugar in that at all."

"Fine." He lifted his fingers in defeat, as usual, pretending to give up but knowing full well he'd be back tomorrow with the same game.

I had quit hoping he'd start paying for his orders two weeks ago. That was never going to happen, and I had decided to chalk the minimal expense up to community relations and let it go. Though if he kept walking off with my shop's canning jars with , he'd soon have a full set—and those weren't cheap.

"Great." I released a long breath and poured a jar of naturally sweetened peach tea for him. He was lucky I didn't serve it in a disposable cup.

"What's in it?" he asked.

"Peaches. Tea." I rocked my knife through the sandwich, making four small crustless triangles.

"And?" Mr. Paine lifted the tea to his mouth, closed his eyes, and gulped before returning the half-empty jar to his napkin. He smacked his lips. "Tastes like sugar."

"No," I assured him. "There's no sugar in that." I plated the crisp cucumber sandwiches, then poured the ladies' mint and cranberry teas, grateful that they were too busy ogling Lou out the window to notice the delay. "Fresh peaches, honey, ginger, lemon, and spices. That's it."

I knew what my tea really tasted like to him: *defeat.* He'd tried to stop me from opening Sun, Sand, and Tea because businesses on the beach were "cliché and overdone." According to Mr. Paine, if I opened a café in my home, Charm, North Carolina, would become a tourist trap and ruin everything he lived for.

Fortunately, the property was old enough to have been zoned commercial before Paine's time on the town council. Built at the turn of the nineteenth century, my home had been a private residence at first, then a number of other businesses ranging from a boarding house to a prep school, and if the rumors were true, possibly a brothel. Though, I couldn't imagine anything so salacious ever having existed in Charm. The town was simply too…charming. And according to my great aunts, who'd been fixtures here since the Great Depression, it had always been that way.

The place was empty when I bought it. The previous owner lived out of town, but he'd sent a number of work crews to make renovations over the years. I could only imagine the money that had been slowly swallowed by the efforts. Eventually it went back on the market.

Mr. Paine eyeballed his drink and rocked the jar from side to side. "I don't see why you won't provide the complete list of your ingredients. What's the big secret?"

"I'm not keeping a secret. The recipes are private. I don't want them out in the world." I wet my lips and tried another explanation, one he might better understand. "These recipes are part of my family's lineage. Our history and legacy." I let my native drawl carry the words. Paine of all people should appreciate an effort to keep things as they were, to respect the past.

He harrumphed. "I'm bringing the ingredient list up at our next council meeting. I'm sure Mayor Dunfree and the other members will agree with me that it's irresponsible not to have it posted."

"Great." He never seemed to tire of reminding me how tight he was with the mayor. He'd used their relationship to the fullest while trying to keep my shop from opening, but even the mayor couldn't prevent a legitimate business from being run in a commercially zoned space. I refilled Mr. Paine's jar, which had been emptied rather quickly. "Let me know if there's anything else you'd like to try."

Mr. Paine climbed off his stool and stuffed his goofy hat back on his mostly bald head. "Just the tea," he said with unnecessary flourish.

"See ya." I piled the ladies' teas and sandwich on a tray and waved Paine off. "Try not to choke on an ice cube," I muttered.

⌒

The afternoon ebbed and flowed in spurts of busyness and lulls of silence. I supposed that was typical of a new business in a small town, not to mention that Sun, Sand, and Tea hadn't had its official launch yet. I was due for a big grand opening, but fear and cowardice kept me from planning it. What if no one came and the whole thing was a flop?

I flipped over the CLOSED sign promptly at five and went upstairs to trade my sundress for exercise gear and hunt for my track shoes. I'd gotten out of shape while I was away, loitering behind a table at culinary school, in a city where I never felt completely safe, eating take-out and every meal on the run because I didn't have time to cook for myself while studying the art of haute cuisine.

Now none of my clothes fit and I wasn't happy about it. Luckily, Charm was a great place to get out and get moving, whether hiking the dunes, playing volleyball on the beach, or swimming in the warm, blue ocean. I hit the boardwalk with a brisk stride.

Waning sunlight glistened on the water, reflecting shadows of soaring birds and the occasional single-engine plane, and the heady scent of home hung in the air. It was the salty, beachy fragrance that clung to my skin and hair long after I'd gone inside, the humidity and seagrass, wet sand and a hint of sun-block. I could never quite put it into words, and my attempts had been wholly lost on the friends I'd made living inland. Maybe rather than just a smell, it was a sensation you had to experience to understand. Kind of like that perfect glass of iced tea. Or maybe it was just me. Some days I wasn't sure if it was sweet tea or saltwater flowing in my veins. Probably a little of both.

I turned away from the beach and headed through the marsh, following the wooden planks beneath my feet. Tenacious green stems poked through stringy bundles of dead seagrass. Spring in Charm was lovely, but soon everything would be in bloom, lush and wild, the way I loved it.

Too soon, the bushy marsh shrank away, revealing a glimpse of Ocean Drive, the main road in town, in the distance. I slowed at the sight of an extra-large moving truck parked across multiple spaces outside the Gas-N-Go.

Was I no longer the newest full-time citizen of Charm? A curious thrill buzzed over my skin. Was the person with the truck new-new, or newly returned, like me? Did I know them from my previous life here? Or was I about to meet a new friend?

Booted feet moved beneath the truck's long metal belly, nearing the back corner at a clip. I nearly held my breath in anticipation.

The boots arrived in full view a moment later, attached to a pair of nicely fitting jeans and six feet of serious.

I gave a low whistle, and the man's head turned sharply in my direction. Keen gray eyes fixed me in place.

"Oh." He'd heard that? My heart raced and my cheeks burned with humiliation. I'd been caught whistling at a strange man. What was next? Catcalls from my porch?

Slowly, he raised a palm in greeting.

I spun on my toes and hightailed it back the way I'd come. I had far too much pride to meet a man who looked like *that* while I looked like *this*—basted in sweat, half-panting, and fully testing the integrity of my outgrown exercise gear. *No way. No how. Nuh uh.* I could only imagine what my crazy brown curls looked like after a couple of miles in a hasty bun.

I didn't slow my pace again until the regal outline of my home came into view. Ocean winds jostled the freshly painted *Sun, Sand, and Tea* sign over my cobblestone walk. The place was historic, majestic, and three floors of much-needed repair. A wide wrap-around porch welcomed guests and stretched into an elaborate deck out back. The backyard had come complete with a picket fence-wrapped garden and small greenhouse overlooking the sea. A lighthouse-like tower rose into the sky with windows on every face and the best views of the Atlantic I'd ever seen. There were decks and verandas at every turn, and I could almost see the faces of aristocrats-past enjoying a party at the owner's invitation. From the rear of my home I had a stunning eastern view of the sea, but the western-facing front of my home had a secret. There was a lovely view of the marsh and boardwalk, yes, but from the front windows of the tower, I could see all the way to the bay.

Unlike the other houses along the seashore, mine had a uniquely Victorian flair and sat at the northern-most tip of our island, high on a cliff, safe from vicious seasonal storms and winds that threatened the town below. The nearest homes were all more than a stone's throw away, but if the old adage was right about good fences making good neighbors, then I supposed a few hundred feet or so between them worked well too. It was the perfect place to show off and make a statement. I thought wryly of whoever commissioned the masterpiece all those years ago and what they might think of a poor pastry-school dropout owning the place today, serving iced tea where they'd once held grand balls.

Despite the home's undeniable grandeur, the place could use a handyman. My windows needed to be replaced, along with the tile in all four bathrooms. Chipped baseboards and dinged walls made regular appearances throughout the house, and almost every step had a little squeak. The hardwood floors were in need of refinishing, and the entire place was drafty. Not to mention the shutters, fences, and exterior railings were all overdue for a fresh coat of paint. It was shabby in the best way, true, but still undeniably worn down—and I had big plans for polishing the old place up. *At minimum.* I couldn't even think about the hours of weeding that awaited me along the garden paths.

A rustling in the weeds drew my attention, and I arced my path as far from the sound as possible without falling off the boardwalk and kept moving. The sun had set while I'd walked, leaving me in the beautiful but useless twilight, squinting against shadows in the marsh. My sincere and lifelong fear of bees was rivaled only by my fear of alligators, and I didn't want to come face-to-face with one if I could avoid it.

Something pale and bulbous on the ground caught my eye. The object was surrounded by smashed weeds and what looked like one of my café's canning jars. Doomed by relentless curiosity—and willing to wash and reuse my jar if possible—I inched closer, hoping I wouldn't meet an alligator.

As I crept over the bank, the mysterious shape registered with a snap: I was looking at the top of someone's bald head! I dashed forward and nearly swallowed my tongue at the sight of his face. "Mr. Paine!"

I scrambled through crushed grass and fell to my knees at his side. "Mr. Paine?" I scanned the scene frantically for help. "Are you hurt?" I asked, patting his cool cheeks. How did a grown man fall off the boardwalk? "Mr. Paine. Wake up," I ordered. "Open your eyes. Can you hear me?" I pressed two fingers to his wrist in search of a pulse, but my own trembling hands made it impossible to locate.

Hot tears swam in my eyes. "Hold on," I begged, moving my hands to his neck and roving inept fingertips over his sweat-dampened skin. Still nothing. "I'm going to call for help." I dug my cell phone from my pocket and dialed 911. "Please nod if you can hear me."

I sent up a thousand silent prayers, but Mr. Paine didn't nod. He didn't move a finger, eyelid, or lip. Something awful had happened to him, and I had no idea how to help.

CHAPTER ❧ TWO

Half the town had turned up with the emergency crews, watching suspiciously from the opposite side of some flimsy yellow caution tape. I was quarantined on the business side of said tape, seated in an ambulance's open doorway and feeling helpless, wrapped in a blanket and waiting to make my formal statement so I could leave. I tugged the itchy fabric more tightly around my shoulders and hunched lower to corral my fading body heat. The temperature had plummeted since I'd left for my walk, and relentless wind had long-since dried my sweaty clothes, leaving my skin covered in goose bumps.

"Tea?" My great-aunt Clara's voice cut through my hazy thoughts. Her long silver and blond hair lashed her cheeks with each gust of wind. I'd called her and her sister, Aunt Fran, the moment I'd disconnected from the call with the emergency dispatch operator. They were my grandmother's sisters, but had functioned more like surrogate mothers than anything else. Aunt Clara moved closer, holding a serving tray loaded with disposable cups of tea in her hands.

A passing EMT accepted her offering with a grateful nod. "Thank you, ma'am."

A fresh gust of wind kicked up, tossing sand and pollen into the air.

Aunt Clara turned her back against the gale, protecting her serving tray and attempting to cover the cups of tea with one arm. The airy fabric of her ivory kimono and ankle-length nightgown fluttered roughly against her narrow frame. While I'd been waiting to make my statement, she and Aunt Fran had been serving my tea to everyone in sight. I tried not to think of it as a massive inventory loss but more of a civic duty, an attempt to console the anxious crowd while we waited for a miracle. Mr. Paine was down, but maybe I had been wrong. Maybe he would be okay.

As if responding to my thought, the paramedics who had been diligently attending to Mr. Paine slowly reemerged from the weeds. They climbed on to the boardwalk with deep regret in their eyes.

One of them lifted his palms and faced the crowd. "I'm sorry."

The night grew silent, save for a few singing frogs and the continuous lull of breaking waves.

I dropped my head to hide my face and stared at my dangling feet. Mr. Paine was really gone. I'd argued with him this afternoon, and now I could never apologize. Tears rolled over my cheeks and dropped onto the sand below.

A pair of brown boots marched into view, stopping in the space before my sneakers. "Miss Swan?"

I raised my eyes at the sound of my name. The man from the moving truck earlier today peered down at me, a look of shock and recognition flashing in his serious eyes. He lifted the shiny silver badge hanging around his neck on a beaded chain. "I'm Detective Hays."

"Everly," I choked out, unsure what else to say.

He scrutinized me. "Did you know the victim?"

"I found him," I said. "And yes, I knew him. Did you say victim?" The rusty cogs of my mind finally creaked into motion. "What kind of detective are you?" I glanced at the grass-lined bank where a black body bag was being loaded onto a gurney. I covered my mouth and turned away.

"Tonight? Homicide."

My mouth went dry. "What happened to him?"

"Looks like poison."

I gasped. The crowd behind me murmured. Phones lit up with fresh buzzes and dings as people texted the news to friends and family.

"Someone killed him? Intentionally?" My chest ached as it was wrenched with grief.

Detective Hays nodded.

Poison. The word rolled aimlessly in my addled mind. "Murder?" I whispered, trying to make the word sound logical. "Are you sure?"

The detective flicked his attention to a white panel van as it rolled into view and parked beside the ambulance. "Preliminary evidence suggests it. We'll know more soon. Meanwhile, I'm going to ask you to accompany me to the police station. I need a written statement from you, and I'd like to ask you a few questions, as well. I'd like to hear the details of the argument you had with the victim today."

I leaned away from him. He said *statement*, but it sounded suspiciously like *confession*.

Panic welled in my chest. I wasn't sure which was more horrifying: the fact that the detective thought there was a murderer in our little town or that he might think it was me. I swiveled my head in search of my great-aunts. Both were already moving in my direction, having handed off the trays of my tea samples to a pair of women who appeared as shocked as myself. They had clearly heard Detective Hays's request.

The aunts shoved past a line of local policemen. "Excuse us," Clara implored, begging their pardon with her signature touch of sweetness. "Move it," Fran demanded in her typical no-nonsense style. Their flowing gowns and long, sleek hair streamed behind them like superhero capes, and their protective eyes were locked on me.

"Darling." Clara patted my cheek and wrapped a bony arm around my shoulders. "This will be fine. I'm sure it's standard procedure."

Fran cocked a hip and narrowed her smart brown eyes at the detective. "Is it?" she asked.

The detective wrinkled his brow. "What?"

"Standard procedure," she clarified. "Are you

taking her in so she can make a statement, or is taking her in *your* way of making a statement?"

"What?"

"She means," Clara interjected, "is there some way Everly can do all that from here? She's been through quite enough already, don't you think? We can go inside and pour some sweet tea, then get whatever protocols and procedures you need out of the way without worrying the girl any more than she already is."

The detective's sharp gray eyes snapped back to mine, clearly unmoved by my aunts' interruption or Clara's request. "Are you worried about talking to me? Any particular reason for that?"

My tongue stuck to the roof of my mouth. I hadn't been worried before, but the way he looked at me implied I might want to reconsider.

A woman in a ponytail and black jacket approached with a clipboard and plastic bag. "Detective?"

He dragged his gaze begrudgingly from mine. "Yep."

She handed him the equivalent of a gallon freezer bag with a yellow label covering most of the front and something solid stuffed inside: one of my tea jars. "We found this at the victim's side."

"Thank you." Detective Hays turned the bag around in his palms and grimaced before facing the contents in my direction. "Is this yours?" He moved his attention from the tea jar in his grip to my eyes, then to the swinging sign above my front door bearing the same logo.

I made a choking sound, unable to speak.

He returned the bag to the woman. "Find out what was in this."

"Yes, sir." She turned and disappeared into the glare of blinding spotlights erected near the crime scene.

Detective Hays pressed wide palms over narrow hips. "I'm afraid you're going to have to come with me to make that statement." He looked at my aunts with a hint of disdain. "And I think I'm going to have to pass on that tea."

Beside us, dozens of people scampered off, all moving double-time to dispose of their tea samples in the garbage cans nearby. The women who had been holding on to my serving trays set them carefully on the ground, then walked briskly away, taking multiple backward glances before breaking into a jog.

My eyes blurred once more, this time with humiliation and rage. "I can't believe you just insinuated that my tea killed Mr. Paine in front of half the town." The words fell like stones off my tongue. "This is my business," I cried. "My livelihood and my entire life savings. How could you do that to me without any proof?"

The white van's headlights flashed on and the engine sparked to life. A small black logo on the rear corner identified it as property of the county coroner.

Detective Hays watched, jaw clenching and releasing, as the vehicle rolled away. "Right now I'm more interested in why someone did *that* to *him*."

❧

The Charm police station was housed in a new brick building on the bay side of town, as far from my home as any place could be without leaving the island. The station faced the mainland, with great views of the bay and the two-mile bridge that carried travelers to and from reality. Until tonight, Charm had always seemed somewhat untouchable by the things news crews covered across the bay. We didn't have crime and corruption. Sometimes there was a bit of litter, but never anything like citizen-on-citizen violence.

Detective Hays opened the station door and held it for me to pass through.

While I'd never been to the police station, I had spent more hours than I could count inside the Nature Preservation Society office next door, volunteering with Aunt Clara and Aunt Fran. They were the only two beekeepers in Charm, and they went to great lengths to educate folks on the importance of nurturing the population of our buzzy little friends. I'd made posters, passed out flyers, and tried desperately not to get stung, never giving the policemen and women next door a single thought.

The building's interior wasn't what I expected. It was laid out in a similar way to the Nature Preservation Society, but it smelled like bleach and air freshener rather than dust and leaves. The white-tiled floor and pale green walls reminded me of a doctor's office, as did the uncomfortable silence. Curious eyes trailed us through the lobby, past a cop manning the front desk and a cleaning crew dusting framed photos and emptying pint-sized trash bins.

"Right this way, please, Miss Swan." The detective led me down a narrow hallway lined with office doors to a little room with a big mirror and no window. "Can I get you anything before we get started?"

"No." Though *legal representation* crossed my mind. I took a seat and avoided eye contact. My scrambled brain raced with too many thoughts, some logical and some not. Everything whirled together into a cyclone of anxiety. I wasn't sure I could answer any questions without crying.

The detective produced a pad of paper and a pen and slid them in front of me. "This is for your written account."

I set one palm on the little stack of items and sniffled. Guilt twisted inside of me. Even if I wasn't a murderer, I'd been mean to an old man on a daily basis for weeks. I'd gotten the café I'd wanted, despite his best efforts to prevent it, and I'd still let him bait and goad me about tea ingredients. And now he was gone.

"Let's start with something simple," Detective Hays said, pulling a chair away from the table and seating himself opposite me. He stripped off his black windbreaker and hung it over the back of his chair. The unassuming gray T-shirt beneath seemed out of place in the sterile room. "Why did you run when I saw you earlier tonight?"

The fine hairs on the back of my neck stood at

attention, and I shivered. His tone and disposition spoke of something more significant than the actual words he was saying. I had no idea what that might be, but my aunts had always said I had a sixth sense about people, and I was certain Detective Hays was about to change my life—probably for the worse.

"Miss Swan," he prodded.

I lifted my aching eyes to meet his measured stare. "What?"

"I saw you on the boardwalk earlier, approximately half an hour before receiving a call that there had been a potential homicide nearby. Imagine my surprise when I discovered the woman who'd found the victim was the same woman who'd taken one look at me and run off only minutes after the victim's estimated time of death."

My mouth opened. Words clogged my throat. I'd run from the cute guy in the moving truck because I was gross and too vain to speak to him in my sweaty condition. "I didn't know you were a cop."

"Then why'd you run?"

I looked down at myself, and a humbling realization set in: I was still in the too-tight exercise pants. Still painted in sweat. Probably covered in bits of marsh weeds now and housing a swarm of gnats in my ratty hair. I dropped my face into waiting palms with a long groan.

"Care to elaborate?" he asked.

I rocked my head side to side. I did not.

"Miss Swan," he began again, shifting in his seat

and resting his forearms on the table between us. "Is it true that you had an argument with the victim earlier today?"

I raised my head and gave the detective my most pleading look. "We fight every day."

"Why is that, exactly?"

I rolled my shoulders and massaged the knotted muscles along the base of my neck, biding time and choosing my words carefully. "Mr. Paine's on the town council, and he didn't want me to open my café. He has a thing about businesses being located inside residences. Had," I corrected myself.

"And you opened anyway."

"Yes." I willed my quivering lips to still. "It was within my rights, but he didn't like it, so he came by every day to complain and drink free tea."

His brows arched dramatically. "You didn't make the man who gave you so much trouble pay for his tea?"

"No."

"Why? You weren't friends. He didn't even want you to have the café. Why would you give him free drinks?"

I worked to settle my breath and folded my hands on the table. Why had I? It was the right thing to do, wasn't it? Under Detective Hays's scrutiny, I was no longer sure. "Once the café opened, Mr. Paine found something new to fuss about—he came around regularly to complain I didn't provide an ingredients list for customers. I thought I could get him to change his mind about the idea of the café if he enjoyed the product. You know. Kill him with kindness." I winced at my word choice. "I didn't mean that."

"Which part?"

I shook off the sarcastic remark. I wouldn't allow him to bait me. "I figured Mr. Paine would eventually see I'm a nice person running a respectable business, making quality products that he and the town could be proud of. It wasn't like I opened a Hooters or had some grand plan to make Charm the next Hilton Head."

"You don't like Hilton Head?"

I rubbed my eyes, beginning to get frustrated. "Hilton Head is fine, but Mr. Paine hated commercialization. That's all I'm saying. And Sun, Sand, and Tea wasn't going to hurt his vision for the town. I thought I could win him over. Show him that my café added to the local charm."

Detective Hays mulled that over.

The silence stretched palpably between us, unraveling my already frayed nerves.

"I would never have hurt Mr. Paine," I pleaded, desperate to convince Detective Hays of my truth. "Even if I had wanted to, which I didn't, I wouldn't have used my tea to do it. A stunt like that would dishonor my family and completely ruin my business."

I'd be lucky to sell another glass all week after Detective Big Mouth's earlier comments. Charm was a fairly superstitious town, with as many legends and tall tales as actual facts, and locals seemed to prefer to former to the latter. I gripped the table edge. I would become a campfire story. *The Sweet-Tea Slayer*, or something equally awful.

I swallowed a boulder of emotion and concentrated on Detective Hays's blank cop expression. "Think about it. No one will want my tea after this. I'll have to close my shop. I won't be able to afford to keep my house, and I've only lived there for three months." Panic replaced the shock and numbness in my limbs. I rubbed a circle on my chest where it was constricted with pain. "I can't go back and live with my aunts again." I launched myself to my feet and paced the floor.

Detective Hays put a hand on the butt of his sidearm and pushed slightly away from the table, as if he expected me to throw myself at him over the table.

His silence unnerved me, and I began to babble. "My aunts are bananas. Kind. Sweet. But totally batty. I just can't." I turned on him. "Why would you hold up my tea jar like that and ask to have the contents tested? You implied that my tea was the murder weapon while half the town was drinking it. They're all probably on their ways to have their stomachs pumped now."

A dark chuckle rolled in my throat, and I dropped back onto my chair.

"What?" Detective Hays relaxed his position, apparently satisfied he wouldn't need to shoot me.

"Irony," I said, dropping both palms onto the table. "He's finally getting what he wanted, and he won't be around to see it."

"Can you think of someone else who may have had reason to hurt Mr. Paine?"

"No."

He shot me a disbelieving look. "So, everyone else in town liked him? He only had an issue with you?"

"Of course not. He was a cranky, crotchety old man who got on everyone's nerves, but he was one of us. Part of this big, weirdo family." I waved my arms around my head like a lunatic.

Detective Hays frowned. Clearly, he didn't understand. Wait until he'd been here a little longer.

A new idea popped into my mind. "Was that your moving truck I saw you with earlier?"

He dipped his chin in silent affirmation.

"You live here now?"

"That's generally what a moving truck indicates."

I was suddenly unsure how I felt about that. "It's not usually like this here," I said, feeling the need to defend my town. "It's usually nice. Quiet. Folks get along. There's an unspoken camaraderie when you share a small space like this island. It's different than anything I've encountered anywhere else. You'll like it, if you don't mind everyone in your business."

"I definitely mind." He tapped the blank paper before me with one tan finger. "I'd like a list of anyone else who you believe might have a reason to harm Mr. Paine."

"Anyone else? Like, besides me?" I scoffed. "I just told you I couldn't have killed Mr. Paine. It's illogical and mean."

"And you're always what?" he asked. "Reasonable and kind?"

"I try to be," I admitted. Though buying a fixer-upper home on a whim and arguing with an old man didn't support either notion. "I'm not writing down a list of people for you to badger, if that's what you're asking. Talk to people. They'll tell you whatever you want to know."

He cocked his head over one shoulder. "Like you're doing?"

I was tired of the sarcasm. "I can't tell you what I don't know. I didn't hurt Mr. Paine, and I have no idea who did. That's all I know."

Someone knocked on the door, then pushed it open. A policeman I recognized from high school gave the detective a pointed look.

"Excuse me," Detective Hays said, rising to his feet. "Write your statement and sign it. Add the date." He strode through the open door and vanished.

He didn't come back.

Eventually, I turned to the notepad and began to recount the events of my evening, logging them as neatly as I could with shaking hands, the memories as vivid and visceral as if I were reliving each awful one. Grief knotted in my throat as I described seeing Mr. Paine in the weeds. Trying to wake him. Thinking he might've had a stroke or heart attack or some other thing that just happened to people all the time. Then learning it was murder.

The paper was stained and spotted with my tears

and bleeding ink when I finished nearly an hour later.

I poked my head through the open doorway, notebook clutched to my chest. "Hello?"

The familiar officer smiled at me from his post beside the door. "All finished?"

"Yeah." I held the paper out to him.

"Thank you. You're free to go. Your aunts are in the lobby to drive you home, and Detective Hays will meet you there."

I blinked. "At my home?"

"Yes." The officer scanned my writing, lifting the pages on the pad one by one. "Judge Helix has issued a search warrant."

Images of dirty dishes and discarded undergarments raced through my head. Detective Hays was putting his hands on my things, searching for evidence that I was a killer, and probably judging my character based on the disastrous condition of my home.

I turned on my heels and made a break for the lobby, half wishing I'd never left my house tonight and half wishing I could shove Detective Hays back into that moving truck and send him home to wherever he came from.

CHAPTER
THREE

Detective Hays was rooting through my café pantry when I got there. I'd passed four other men in official-looking jackets on my way up the porch stairs, who seemed to have finished whatever they were up to. Each man had a little tackle box or clipboard in his hands, and all were headed for the vehicles lining my walk.

"What are you doing?" I asked, horrified, as Detective Hays collected things from my shelves.

"Finishing up." He set the armload of items on the counter between us. "The technicians are finished, but I still have a question. What is all this?"

"Herbs." I eyeballed the tins, boxes, and bags scattered before me. "Rosemary, dill, fennel. Nothing sinister there."

He lifted a finger to the narrow wall of planters opposite us, each one exploding with green leaves, shoots, and sprouts. "I thought those were herbs."

"They are." I went to the hall closet and grabbed

a knee-length cardigan to wrap myself in, then pulled the tie out of my hair. I avoided the mirror and all reflective surfaces on my way back to the kitchen. "Some herbs are best fresh and others are best dried."

Detective Hays had followed me, watching with careful eyes. "Some herbs can be deadly."

So could some women, but I wasn't one of them. "Those," I said, pointing to the mess he'd made on my counter, "are not. I use ordinary, run-of-the-mill plants that won't make anyone sick. And certainly not dead."

"You know which herbs can kill, though, don't you? Which to avoid. How much is safe, how much is too much."

I bit the inside of my cheeks and crossed my arms.

"No answer?"

"Yeah, right," I said. "If I admit I know those things, you'll add it to your case against me, and if I don't, then I'm a poor excuse for an organic Southern chef."

"I'm not trying to build a case against you. I'm just following the evidence. Your tea led me here."

I tied the belt on my cardigan and slid behind the counter. "Can I fix you something to drink?"

The sides of his mouth turned down. "No, thank you."

I shook my head. "If you come into my café and rummage through the kitchen at this hour, you get tea. What kind will it be?" I pointed to the menu board. "I'd recommend my Peach Tea, but it seems to have disappeared."

"We confiscated it for testing," he said.

"Of course you did." I filled a jar with ice and shoved it under the pour spout of my largest tea dispenser. "That's too bad. You would've liked that one. I guess you get the house special instead: Old-Fashioned Sweet Tea."

He eyeballed the drink before lifting it to his lips. "Where are your aunts? I thought they were driving you home."

I rested a hip against the counter and sighed, admiring the quaint, beachy look of my new café and hating that I might be about to lose it all. "I asked them to drop me off. I love them, but I can't take all the fussing tonight. This day has already been too much."

"You lived with them before?" he asked.

I wondered how he knew, but then I remembered my freak-out at the police station and my cheeks heated. "Yeah. I grew up at the family homestead with Aunt Clara, Aunt Fran, and my grandma. And for the record, I shouldn't have been so negative earlier. My aunts aren't bananas. I'm just terrible under pressure."

He lifted his gaze to mine. "Homestead?"

I nodded. "My family has been on the island a long time. My aunts' home and property are handed down." It was strange talking to someone in Charm who didn't already know everything about my family. Unfortunately, I wasn't sure what to share and what to keep to myself.

"Got it." Detective Hays finally took a long sip of tea, eyes widening. "This is good."

"Yeah."

He examined the glass thoughtfully. "You know, my grandma used to tell me not to marry a woman until I knew how she made her sweet tea. I never understood it, but I think of it every time I have a glass."

"Your grandma must've been from the South, because clearly she was a wise woman."

"Charleston," he answered, having another sip, "and she was very wise."

"Is that where you're from?" I leaned slightly forward, careful not to miss whatever he said next.

"Originally. I've lived quite a few places since then."

"Is that what happened to your accent?"

His smile fell. "No. I worked on losing that." He drained his glass and set it reverently aside.

I felt creases gather on my forehead. Why on earth would anyone want to lose their accent? I refilled his glass and returned it to him. "You know," I said, going back to his earlier question, "your grandma knew that sweet tea-making is personal, and if a woman trusts you with her sweet tea secrets, she's not planning on letting you go."

His eyes narrowed slightly, but he didn't respond.

"You seem to have calmed down," I noted. "Maybe my tea *is* drugged."

His chest rose and fell in one long breath. "It's been a long day."

"Do you still think I killed Mr. Paine?"

His pale gray eyes locked on mine for the first time since my return home. "I know you argued with him regularly, and whatever killed him could have been in your tea. That gives you both means and motive."

"No," I corrected. "I didn't have a motive, because I don't believe there are reasons for murder. People are people. We don't have to like them all, but we can't go around killing them, either."

He snorted. "If only it was so simple." He slid off my bar stool and stretched to his full height.

"No more questions?"

"Not tonight, but do me a favor and don't leave town, Miss Swan."

"Detective?" a portly man called from my open front door. "We're ready to go."

Detective Hays nodded to him, then deposited a business card on the counter. "Details have changed, but the number's the same, if you think of anything I should know." He walked away without a goodbye and pulled the door shut behind him.

I flipped the lock, then rushed back to the counter and grabbed the card.

> United States Marshals Service
> Grady Hays
> Deputy U.S. Marshal
> Criminal Investigator

"U.S. Marshal?" I asked the card. When it didn't respond, I turned it over, looking for more information, but found none. I ran to the front window and watched as he climbed behind the wheel of a giant black pickup truck and drove away.

Who was this guy?

∽

I woke early the next morning, having fallen asleep after cleaning my entire house and taking a mental inventory of what was missing. Shockingly, everything seemed to be in its place, minus the contents of my medicine cabinet and a gallon or so of peach tea. I supposed the detective and his crew thought a killer might keep her poisons in the aspirin or cough syrup bottle, but that seemed silly and a little too obvious to me.

I took my time dressing and finding a mental happy place before shuffling downstairs to the café. I'd styled my chestnut locks in barrel curls and dashed a bit of mascara on my lashes, hoping to look as pleasant and harmless as possible for any customers who dared to visit. The vintage floral swing dress I wore was probably overkill, but I figured it wouldn't hurt.

By noon, the silence in the cafe was wearing on me: not a single soul had ventured into Sun, Sand, and Tea since I'd flipped the sign to OPEN an hour earlier.

I took my broom to the back deck and stared at the sea as I swept. Lou, the nosy gull, cocked his head and watched, but didn't offer any help. How was this happening to me? My new start had just gotten started. Words like *unfair, unjust,* and *despicable* came to mind. I threw myself onto a wooden chair and forced the angry thoughts out with the tide. The truly unfair thing was what had happened to Mr. Paine. My perspective was selfishly skewed.

"I wish there was a way to make things right," I told Lou. "And a way to change what people think about my shop before it's too late to recover." I needed to convince people I hadn't hurt Mr. Paine, and I wished there was a way to rewind time and save him too, but there simply wasn't.

Sweat beaded on my brow, so I went back inside, frustrated. I tied an apron around my waist, then grabbed a few colorful sticks of chalk to update my menu board. Assuming no one would request the peach tea for a while, I wrote *Southern Strawberry* in its place.

By two o'clock, when no customers had appeared, my heart had sunk low in my chest. I sliced cucumbers and drizzled homemade ranch dressing on top, then munched mindlessly, silently willing someone to walk through my front door.

At three o'clock, I turned the sign from OPEN to CLOSED and went for a walk to clear my head. A scruffy white cat watched me from the beach until the boardwalk carried me out of sight, walking until I hit Main Street and my aunts' shop came into view.

Blessed Bee was a yellow clapboard house situated between identical pink and blue houses. The pink shop sold ice cream, the blue shop books. My childhood friend Amelia owned the bookstore. I'd yet to meet the owners of the new ice cream parlor, but it was on my to-do list.

Striped honeybees were stenciled over the large window at Blessed Bee, and the welcome mat had a hive on it. The interior was open and equally yellow, though paler inside than out, and featured lots of white shelves and crown molding. A sky-blue ceiling ran overhead, sprinkled with fluffy white cloud shapes. Clara and Fran made everything from lip balm and face scrub to suckers and soap, all with pure, organic honey drawn directly from their own hives. They'd hoped I would join them in their beekeeping adventures one day, but my near-paralyzing fear of bees had eliminated that career choice as an option.

Soft classical music played on hidden speakers throughout the store, and a smattering of shoppers gave me wayward looks as I approached the counter. I forced a tight smile and pressed the little silver service bell with one finger.

"Coming!" Aunt Clara called from the back room.

"It's just me," I answered. "Take your time. I'm only here to pout."

Aunt Fran appeared first, a scowl on her thin, freckled face and looking ready for a tussle. "Who's upset you?"

Clara trotted into view next, following a few steps behind her sister. She waved both hands and smiled. "Everything's going to be fine, my sweet girl."

Fran rounded the counter and gripped my shoulders. "Just ignore those silly gossips and keep your chin up." She released me with a huff and straightened her long silk tunic. "I told Clara I ought to find out who's writing those obnoxious comments and pay them a visit with an angry beehive."

Before I could ask what she was talking about, Clara piped up. "Nonsense," she said. "This too shall pass. Things always do, I promise." She stroked my cheek and beamed. Her loose white frock and blond-gray hair flowed like one moving entity, a direct contrast to Fran's dark tunic and salt-and-pepper braid. You could see the evidence of their different fathers in their hair and facial features—Fran's was an Italian sailor, while Clara's was an Irish salesman—but they moved in tandem, almost like twins.

My mother, grandmother, and I were all leaves on the sailor's branch of our family tree. Dark hair, dark eyes, olive skin, obsession with carbs. I looked more like Fran than Clara, but according to them, I'd inherited my snub nose and giant owl eyes from my dad. I could have done without both of those—though the eyes had come in handy as a teen when I'd needed to beg forgiveness for missing a curfew or dodging my daily chores.

"Wait," I said. "What obnoxious comments?"

"On the blog posts," Clara answered. Confusion wrinkled her brow. "They're just speculative nonsense. Don't give them a second thought."

I stretched my eyes wide and asked my next question slowly, hoping to get an answer I'd understand. "What blog posts?"

My aunts traded meaningful stares. Clara nodded and Fran handed me her phone.

I scanned the little screen. "The *Town Charmer*," I read, setting my jaw. "What's this?"

"Community updates mostly," Aunt Clara said. "Local news. Occasional gossip."

I wrinkled my nose. "Since when does Charm have a gossip blog?"

"A couple of years now," Clara said. "Everyone tries to guess who's behind it, but it's all very hush-hush, and normally the posts are incredibly helpful."

I tucked that information away in my head for later and scrolled through ridiculous comments on a post about Mr. Paine's death. "Seashell 419 says 'Everly Swan clearly came back to Charm for nefarious reasons.' What does that even mean?" The aunts rubbed my back in consolation.

I flipped along, growing more agitated by the minute, utterly shocked as the speculation grew more outrageous with each message. "They're making a big deal out of the fact I want to keep the tea recipes a secret. Why is everyone so bent out of shape about this?" I groaned at the next insane reply. "This one says I won't provide an ingredients list because poison is one of the ingredients. That's completely bananas. Why would I poison my own tea and ruin myself?"

Fran held out her hand, and I returned her phone.

"I can't believe this is happening." I checked around the store for prying ears and found the handful of shoppers had moved conspicuously closer. I fought back tears. "These people know me. They've known me all my life." I shot a pointed look at the various shoppers, mostly women I'd known since elementary school.

The ladies dispersed, cell phones in their palms or pressed to their ears as they headed out the door.

Clara sighed. "But you left, and while it wasn't right, people talked."

"About what? Everyone leaves for college. Culinary school is the same thing."

Fran rolled her eyes, clearly exasperated by the entire conversation. "Yes, but *we* don't leave. Swans never leave."

"It's true," Clara confirmed. "Our roots are here. Jobs. Family. The Swans haven't left Charm since we got here three hundred years ago." She made a pained face. "When we do, people talk. It's the curse, you know."

"That's ridiculous." I loved my family's long lineage and ties to the island, but I hated stories about our alleged curse. *Swan women are cursed in love. We aren't supposed to leave the island. The men who love us will die.* It was all a bunch of hooey. The stories were obviously designed to scare young women into staying where they were hundreds of years ago, when it wasn't safe to leave an established community and the quickest way out of town was with a husband. I could practically hear the mothers warning their teenage daughters: *Can't get married and leave. Swan curse says so. Better stay here where it's safe.* The message to young men getting ideas about my ancestors was even worse: *Love a Swan girl and you will DIE.* No doubt an effective motivation to steer clear in a time when paranoia and superstitions ran the world.

While I appreciated the ingenuity that clearly went into forming these centuries-old safety protocols, the concepts were borderline comical in the new millennium. And got completely on my last nerve. "Lots of Swans have left town," I said, repeating an argument I'd made dozens of times before. "Otherwise the three of us wouldn't be the only ones left."

"Only the men leave," Fran said. "That's how the curse works. Male Swans can't stay and female Swans can't go."

"I went," I argued. "That's the whole point of this."

"Yes, but you came back."

I rolled my shoulders and groaned. "That's how this conversation started." The circular logic would drive me crazy if I tried to untangle it. A new and equally irrelevant question came to mind, but it would bother me unless I asked. "Who was the last male Swan?"

Fran tapped her chin with one thin finger. "I'm not really sure. I'd have to look at the family tree."

"It's been that long since someone had a son?" I asked. It shouldn't have been a surprise, since I couldn't recall any male relatives at the few family reunions I'd attended growing up.

"Seems so," Fran said. "Swan females are dominant. It's genetic." She nodded through the statement, as if it was backed up by facts.

"That's not how science works."

"It's not science, darling. It's our legacy."

It was also our legacy to find husbands willing to take our name and not the other way around.

I rubbed my temple. Fran and Clara were con-
sistently two of the worst historians I'd ever met,
regularly interweaving fact with fiction all my life.
They had some good stories, but tall tales were all
they were.

I changed the subject. "No one came to my café
today. Not a single soul."

"Maybe you should reconsider listing your ingredients," Clara said. "We list everything that goes into
our products. Since it's something folks are worried
about, you can use the gesture to clear the air."

I pursed my lips. Grandma had taken great care
to teach me everything she knew about tea, garden-
ing, and the sea. I choked back a pinch of pride and
a pound of *missing her so much I could die*. "I guess
I could. The ingredient list only takes folks so far,
though." The measurements and brewing process were
what made the teas special.

"Exactly." Clara tugged the ends of my hair. "Our
sister loved you more than anything, and she entrusted
you with all her secrets. We respect that, but honey, it's
not worth villainizing yourself to protect them. She'd
want to see you succeed."

Fran locked her hand over one hip. "What about
that grand opening you've been talking about? Now
might be the perfect time to invite everyone over and
reintroduce yourself. We can print and hang photos of
you growing up here. Remind the naysayers that they
know you, and you are pure goodness."

"Maybe," I said, turning away. I lifted a pint of

beautiful amber honey from the nearby display and examined the comb trapped inside. "Who do you think poisoned Mr. Paine?" Aunt Clara and Aunt Fran had said it themselves: I'd been gone a while. I'd missed things. "And how do the police know he didn't accidently overdose on a prescription or something?"

"We can ask around," Clara offered. "See if anyone has another suspect in mind."

"Okay. Maybe there's someone out there who really did want him dead."

Fran handed me another jar of honey. "Take them both. For your Ginger Tea."

"Thanks." I kissed her cheek, then Clara's. "Let me know what you find out about Mr. Paine."

"Will do," they called after me. "Think about that party."

"Okay." I stepped onto the sidewalk with renewed vigor and a completely different idea brewing in my mind. I knew how I could clear my name *and* get justice for Mr. Paine.

I'd find out who really killed him, and make sure Detective Hays took him to jail.

෨

I hurried home, formulating a plan to covertly survey the town, but stopped short on the boardwalk outside my house.

Detective Hays and his big SUV were situated in

front of my home. "Afternoon," he said, lifting a disposable cup in greeting.

"What are you doing?" I asked. "How long have you been sitting there?"

He shook the cup and sucked his teeth. "'Bout an hour."

"Why?" I cradled the jars of honey against my chest.

"Thinking." He set the cup next to a takeout bag sitting on his truck's hood.

"Do you want to come in?" I asked, hoping he wasn't full and that I could ply him with sweets to see if he'd share some details on how the investigation was going. "It'd be nice to have a guest," I added. "No one came in today. Might've had something to do with your announcement that my products might be poisoned." I bit my lip. I hadn't meant to say that. I got madder every time I remembered why the town was giving me the silent treatment and gossiping about me online.

He tipped his head in what looked like a pitiful apology. "No, thanks. I can't stay."

Yet he claimed to have been here an hour. What was his game? "Well, can I help you with something, then?" I asked. "You must've waited for a reason."

"Not really. I've been exploring the town, but I keep ending up here. I think it's the view." He made a show of looking long and hard in each direction. "It's as if I can see for miles."

"You can," I said. "It's the highest natural point on the island."

He crossed his arms and bobbed his head. "It's beautiful. No lights, though." He shifted his stance and cast his gaze wide, twisting at the waist. "I was out here last night, walking, thinking, and I couldn't see a thing."

I waited for his point. It's dark at night? What could I say to that. "True."

"It seems like Benedict Paine would have known that," he said, turning sharp gray eyes back on me. "Lifelong resident and all."

"So, why was he out walking in the dark?" I asked. "I hope you didn't wait here an hour to ask me that, because I have no idea."

"If you had to guess," he pushed.

I released a long breath. "Maybe it wasn't dark when he started his walk." That was what had happened to me. I'd left before sunset and returned at twilight. "It gets dark fast some nights, especially if there's cloud cover. Maybe the dark came faster than he'd expected, or maybe he got sick and slowed down, and that made the difference."

Detective Hays watched me intently.

I clamped my mouth shut.

"Huh," he grunted.

I fidgeted with the hem of my sleeve, wholly uncomfortable with his prodding looks and the subject matter. "So, what made you choose Charm for your big move?" I asked, praying he'd let me change the subject. Was it pure coincidence that he'd arrived on the night of a murder? Was I overthinking? "It's not exactly a hot spot for someone in your line of work."

Detective Hays looked out over the sandy beach and breaking waves. "I'm not sure why everyone doesn't live here. This place looks like a postcard."

That was true, but his decision to relocate here wasn't that simple. I'd spent some time researching US Marshal Grady Hays last night after picking up his business card. He'd been a big shot in Charlotte before he'd apparently walked away. "Still, it seems odd to leave a prestigious job in the city to play detective to a puny island town."

"I'm not playing." He lifted the badge hanging around his neck. "I needed a change, so I changed."

"Were you fired?" Could he have done something sketchy to collar a criminal and been banished from the agency for it? Seasons of my favorite cop dramas blurred through my mind. What kind of things did a guy have to do to wind up playing Barney Fife to a town of two thousand year-round residents and four thousand seasonal ones? *Assault? Drugs? Case tampering?*

"No. Nothing like that," he said. There was profound sadness in his eyes, and I regretted my implication immediately.

"Sorry." I pushed strands of windblown hair away from my face. "I didn't mean to drag up anything unpleasant."

"You didn't." He cleared his throat. "I looked you up too, you know."

"Yeah?"

"Yep." He squinted against the sun and growing breeze.

I jostled the jars of honey into one curved arm, using the other hand to keep my skirt from blowing over my head. "Find anything good?"

"That's debatable." His lips twisted into a sudden smile that reached his eyes. "Nothing to support my case."

What was that supposed to mean? Fresh alarm shot through me. "What did you read?"

His smile grew, and a dimple sank in, transforming him into someone carefree and youthful, the kind of guy every woman thinks will steal her heart and change her life forever. Basically the opposite of who he was. Dimples were deceiving.

"What is that face?" I asked. "What did you find about me that makes you look like you want to burst into laughter?" My entire life passed before my eyes: an endless parade of goofy island events, college parties for pastry nerds, and my temporary position as Queen Bee to advertise my aunts' honey. "What?" I begged.

He looked me over from top to bottom, then shook his head. "Nothing bad." He collected his lunch trash and climbed behind the wheel of his truck.

So much for feeding him cake and offering to help find Mr. Paine's killer. He'd only stayed at my shop long enough to provoke me and leave, a habit of his I was already learning to hate.

"Chin up, Swan," he said, hanging a tanned elbow through the open window. "I think we're going to get along just fine, if I don't have to arrest you."

I crossed my arms and narrowed my eyes. "You're not going to arrest me."

I was going to find the real killer, clear my name, and save my shop, with or without his help.

Right after I googled myself.

CHAPTER
FOUR

I'd searched my name twenty different ways, looking for what had put that goofy smile on the detective's face, and I'd found all the predictable nightmares online. I'd never been cool, and the internet indisputably proved it. I'd closed the laptop after coming across a photo of twelve-year-old me being sneezed on by a horse at the town fair. The local reporters had found that clip so funny they had run it on the local news for three years in a row.

I spent the rest of the afternoon cleaning tea jars and scrubbing the fridge in my personal kitchen upstairs, puzzling over Detective Hays and his appearance in Charm.

What I needed was a walk to help me think.

I swapped my dress for a belted coral top that accentuated my waist and a pair of white pedal pushers, then grabbed my matching white sneakers off the mat outside my back door so I could get my daily step count in. According to the instructions with my wristwatch/step-counter/fitness gadget, I should walk ten thousand steps a day, though I tried not to take that recommendation too literally. I would probably have to walk all the way to the mainland to reach that number, but that was the Git Fit's preprogrammed goal. Some days, the farthest I walked was around my house nailing down loose boards and puttying drywall holes.

I tied up my laces and marched in place for a few seconds to make sure the counter was working, stepping into the brisk night with my chin up and starting down the boardwalk toward town. The roads and sidewalks would've gotten me to the shops more quickly, but the boardwalk had better views. Plus, I preferred the sound of the retreating tide to that of traffic.

It wasn't long before the evening scents of Charm floated to my nose and made my mouth water: Greasy burgers and salty fries. Rich hot fudge and fresh-baked waffle cones. The after-dinner show was in full swing, serving sweets to those who'd eaten at an appropriate time and deep-fried everything to those who hadn't.

I stepped off the boardwalk with the enthusiasm of Fred Flintstone following a whiff of brontosaurus stew, then floated across Ocean Drive, the main road running along the shore, to stop outside Sandy's Seaside Sweet Shack, the new ice cream shop next to Blessed Bee, inhaling the heavenly scents. The little pink venue was outlined in white twinkle lights and surrounded by couples with children and baby carriages, rocking in chairs on the porch and lining tables on the patio. I'd had a sensible salad for dinner, but that wasn't going to cut it after they day I'd had. I needed comfort food, and the sign inside the window advertised "Free Smiles and Sprinkles." I wanted a little of both.

I followed the steadily moving line to the front of the store. Eventually, the man behind the counter tipped his paper hat at me and smiled. "Welcome to my Seaside Sweet Shack. I'm Sandy. Can I get you something to sweeten your night?" He wiped his hands on a pink and white striped towel and waited patiently while I took in his magical menu.

"Yes, please." I bounced on my toes, feeling ten years younger. "I'd like a scoop of Praline Dream in a sugar cone. And sprinkles." I added the last part in case the free sprinkles were only by request.

"Sure thing." Sandy flipped the curved lid on the freezer and tossed his scoop in the air like a Miami bartender. His smile was contagious, banana-split wide, and already setting me at ease. "My wife and I moved here last summer to open this shop. We've met most everyone, but I don't think I've seen you around here," he said, smooshing praline ice cream into a cone of crispy perfection, the top inch of which had been dipped in chocolate and rolled in jimmies.

I licked my lips in anticipation.

"How long are you in town?" he asked, tidying up the cone and closing the display lid.

"Forever, probably." I stretched to accept the cone over the tall counter.

A familiar silhouette caught my attention outside the giant picture window to my right, and I turned to stare. Detective Hays scooted through the crush of babies and bodies on the patio, vanishing and reappearing several times before arriving at his SUV with a blond woman.

Was he married? I couldn't recall seeing a ring, but then again, I hadn't looked. And I didn't care. Except, if the woman wasn't his wife, then who was she? Surely he hadn't had time to find a date in the day or two since his arrival. He couldn't have had time to unpack, much less ask someone out for ice cream. He didn't even get her door for her. *Rude.*

Sandy punched my order into the register. "Where are you visiting from?" he asked. "You should mark it on our Friends Across the Country map." He nodded toward a giant poster of the United States on the far wall, little ice cream cone stickers plastered all over the East Coast identifying the origins of past customers.

"I'm local," I answered, straining to see over his shoulder as the SUV pulled into traffic. "I grew up here and just moved back."

"Well, that's neat!" He rocked back on his heels and rested a hand on the counter.

I stuffed the top of my cone into my mouth and blamed low blood sugar and a poor night's sleep for my erratic thoughts.

"That'll be two-fifty."

Oops! I'd almost forgotten to pay. I fished a five from my pocket and delivered it to Sandy.

By now, the SUV was long gone. It bugged me more than it should have to know the town's only detective was out having fun instead of investigating Mr. Paine's murder. Didn't these things get more difficult to solve after forty-eight hours? Or was it seventy-two? I took another bite of my cone and contemplated the issue. Maybe I was thinking of the guideline for missing kids. Either way, it had barely been twenty-four hours since I'd found Mr. Paine by the marsh. It hardly seemed like the time for the investigating officer to go out for ice cream.

I gave Sandy a long look. He'd said he'd met most everyone, so did he know Mr. Paine? I took a bite of ice cream to shore up my nerve. "Sandy? Did you know Benedict Paine?" I asked quietly. "Or have you heard anything about what happened to him?"

Recognition lit in Sandy's eyes as he made my change. "I knew him. My wife and I saw him quite a bit after we moved here."

I couldn't imagine Mr. Paine at a sweet shack, considering the level of grief he'd given me about the sugar content of sweet tea, but maybe he'd been involved in the ice cream shop's setup. Probably forcing it into compliance with his vision for Charm.

Sandy glanced over my head at the line of waiting customers, then leaned closer. "I heard he was poisoned. It was terrible." He shook his head sadly. "I read all about it on the *Town Charmer* blog."

I turned to check on the couple behind me. They were still discussing flavors, so I pushed on. "Had you heard anything about him recently?" I asked. "Before the poisoning?" I scanned the crowded ice cream shop, imagining all the things I could overhear if I lingered long enough—pushing a broom or wiping down tables, for example. "Was anyone especially upset with him that you know of?"

Sandy rolled his shoulders back and cocked his head. "Don't you read the town blog? It covered the whole story as it unfolded."

My cheeks heated at the memory of all those mean comments. "I'm just having a hard time accepting his death," I blurted. "Things like that don't happen here."

"I suppose bad stuff happens everywhere, once in a while," he said. "Living here has been a dream come true for my wife and me. What happened to Mr. Paine hasn't changed that. In fact, we feel needed more than ever now. Folks come to our sweet shack for something good and familiar. In some ways, we provide a break from the heartache of losing a community member." He smiled warmly. "What do you do here?"

I rushed through a mouthful of creamy bliss, trying not to choke on a pecan. "My name is Everly Swan. I opened the iced tea shop on the beach last month. Sun, Sand, and Tea."

Sandy's smile faltered a bit before performing a quick recovery. "Of course! Hello!" His sudden and complete overenthusiasm confirmed my suspicions: he clearly recognized the name of my café and my connection to the murder.

"I hope you'll bring your wife by some time for a

glass of tea," I suggested, redoubling the efforts on my smile. "I'd love to meet her, and there's a fabulous view from my café's deck."

"Definitely." He gave the line another long look.

"I think we're ready," the woman behind me said.

I stepped aside and polished off the too-tiny cone, then licked my lips. "Thank you again, Sandy. It was nice meeting you." I smiled and waved at the couple placing their order.

It took all my self-control not to get back in line for seconds.

I picked up the pace a little on my return trip to make up for the spontaneous ice cream. I hadn't come up with any amazing epiphanies on my night's outing, but I had the wind in my hair and the whispering ocean at my side. That was the real prize.

My fitness bracelet beeped and I pressed the button to see what it wanted.

BE MORE ACTIVE.

I loosened my too-tight belt, and I was certain my thighs would start chafing if I went any faster. I'd worn a size six when I left home for culinary school and returned in a size twelve. I was trying not to let the weight gain bother me, but when I tossed in my looming thirtieth birthday and a murder suspicion, I didn't need a Git Fit to remind me I was losing control. Somewhere along the line, my life had stopped being something that happened *because* of me and it had become a collection of things happening *to* me.

I'd had about enough of that.

I took longer, more purposeful strides as I headed home through the waning twilight. The problem was that I'd gotten sidetracked wondering about the new detective when what I should've been doing was asking everyone what they knew about Mr. Paine's most recent complaints around Charm. Sandy didn't know any more than the skewed details the town gossip blog had provided, but someone else might have.

Who had Mr. Paine argued with this week? How about last week? Me and Sam Smart, for starters, but we couldn't have been the only ones. Paine was always miffing someone off.

I wondered idly if my aunts were having any luck coming up with alternate suspects, imagining Clara plying folks with sugar and smiles while Fran pointed a spotlight at their faces and demanded the details.

What I really needed was more than a list of people who had argued with Paine—I needed to know who was willing to kill. In other words, who had motive, and what was it? Why did people commit murder? Love? Power? Money? Mr. Paine didn't seem the sort to care about any of those things. He'd been divorced for a decade and didn't appear to be wealthy. His kids were grown. He'd long ago retired from everything except the town council, which was his sole obsession. So, who would want him dead and why?

I had nothing.

My breaths grew short as my quick steps hauled me farther away down the beach. The sense of freedom was invigorating, but the stitch in my side was not.

I stopped to pant and grip my aching ribs. I'd never been much of a land animal. Put me in a kayak or toss me in the ocean, however, and I was home. Maybe when the weather warmed, I'd trade in my walking shoes for something with fins.

Up ahead, a shadow bobbed swiftly in my direction.

I considered hiding, but there was nowhere to go. I had three feet of boardwalk to get out of the way and zero ability to run. Whoever was headed in my direction was doomed to see me bent at the waist and regretting two-fifty's worth of Praline Dream.

"Everly?" A familiar female voice danced in the darkness. My childhood friend, Amelia, blinked into existence beneath a cone of lamplight, carrying a stack of books.

"Amelia!" I hastened my pace, a wide smile growing on my lips.

"How are you?" she asked, adjusting the tomes against her chest and hugging me with one arm. "I'm so sorry I didn't call or stop by today. I heard about everything that happened last night, but I had ten million things to do and the store was just so busy. Are you doing okay? You should hear the crazy things folks are saying."

I waved her worry away, too thankful to see her face to care what the local gossips were saying. "I'm fine, but I've missed you so much. You look fantastic. And I saw your store today when I went to visit my aunts. It looks bigger. Did you expand?"

Amelia stepped back with a proud smile. "Charming

Reads had a big remodel last summer. I couldn't expand, but I found a better way to use the space. It really made a difference. Thank you for noticing."

A moment later, her smile drooped. "Are you sure you're okay? This town's been so brazen with the gossip."

I puffed out my cheeks, and a deep sigh blew free from my chest. "I'm okay, and I'm going to find out who really killed Mr. Paine." I nodded to encourage myself. I had means and motive for finding justice, but not for murder. "I'll clear my name."

Amelia's narrow brows stretched over wide sapphire blue eyes, and she reached for the headband tucked into her blond hair. "How?"

"I don't know."

She blinked several times. "Okay. Well, when you do, I'm glad to help." She hoisted the load in her arms. "Would you like a book?"

I laughed. "Uh. Sure?" I examined the myriad titles with wonder. "Why are you carrying this lovely selection along the boardwalk at night? Find a lot of readers out here, do you?"

"Don't be silly. I'm only carrying them because the wheel on my wagon broke." She shifted the spines in my direction. "Everyone loves a good book, right?" Her eyes twinkled with pride. Amelia had had her life plotted out since high school, right down to her bookstore on Main Street, where she kept enough literary adventures for all of Charm to get lost in forever. "Go on. Pick your poison." She frowned. "Oh, I didn't mean that. It's an expression."

"It's fine." I took a worn copy of *Little Women* and a hefty-looking recipe book by *Good Housekeeping*, one of those vintage numbers where they instructed you to grease every pan with lard and featured an entire section devoted to Practical Uses of Spam. I smiled as I balanced the books in my arms. The cookbook weighed at least five pounds, or about half as much as any one of the finished Spam recipes.

"How was cooking school?" Amelia asked suddenly. "I feel like I should know this, but I don't."

"I quit." I pursed my lips and focused my attention on the horizon straight ahead. "It was nice, but it didn't work out."

"Sorry. I didn't know."

"Wasn't meant to be," I said. "But I learned a lot about technique and running a kitchen. I'm sure I can put all that knowledge to good use at Sun, Sand, and Tea."

"Well, I'm glad you're back," she said.

"Me too." And it was true, despite the mess I'd fallen into last night when I found Mr. Paine's body.

Part of me wished I'd have finished culinary school, but there was no point in feeling too bad about dreams lost. After all, I had also planned to marry a cowboy, and there was no doubt that would have been disastrous if it had gone my way.

I turned my attention back to Amelia. "Did you say you're carrying these books because your wagon's busted?" I puzzled over the odd explanation. Did she normally take her books for an evening walk? "Are these new donations? Did you just make a pickup?"

"Oh no. These are from the Little Library I put up last week by the beach-access parking lot. I try to switch the inventory every few days for variety and refill when the stock is low. Plus, I make sure there are plenty of my business cards in the little holder."

Amelia's Little Libraries were the cutest things on the boardwalk, and she had several more throughout the town. Some were designed to look like giant birdhouses, others like big wooden tomes. Most stood on a sturdy post, but all were whimsically painted and held a great selection of books. The Little Library concept worked on a need one/take one premise, and seemed like a great way to get readers to stop by her store.

"Smart. I wonder if I should make some business cards or maybe takeout menus for the café." I turned the little rectangle over in my fingertips. "These are really cute. Where did you get them?"

"I made them." She smiled proudly. "They're not hard, and menus won't be, either. I can help you design yours, if you want."

"I'd love it."

A gust of wind whipped our hair and fluttered our clothes. Amelia turned her small face skyward with a frown. "I'd better get going before it gets much later."

"Of course. Hey. You should stop by sometime," I told her. "We should catch up."

"Okay." She beamed. "This week, then. I'll come by for tea."

"That sounds perfect."

Amelia took a few steps backward. "I'd come now

if I could, but I have two more Little Libraries to check in on, and I left Charming Reads open while I ran out. I mean, my dad is there, but he's probably asleep in the archives."

I lifted my books in goodbye. "See ya soon!"

My steps were lighter after running into Amelia, if not faster. By the time the creepy crime scene tape near my house came into view, I'd forgotten about Mr. Paine's murder for a blissful few minutes. The yellow plastic fluttered loosely in the breeze, having been partially knocked away by wildlife or the wind. I tried not to look, but memories of Mr. Paine's slack face forced their way into my head and stalled my antsy feet. Should I fix the broken tape? My gut said to leave it alone, but my head worried that someone might mistake the downed barrier as an invitation to butt in while the investigation was still underway and maybe disturb crucial evidence that could lead to the killer.

I checked over both shoulders for lookie-loos. Amelia's silhouette was nearly invisible in the distance behind me, and a pair of tiny figures near the surf were too far away to identify. I gave myself a pep talk, then reached for the broken tape. It was too short to re-tie easily.

I took another reluctant step forward and yanked one of the little wooden pegs from the ground, then moved it closer by a foot. I jammed it back into the soggy earth and grabbed the loose tape ends. There. Now I could tie the two together and protect the area within.

As I leaned over, my toe caught on an old busted

boat oar and I pitched forward, catching myself with an outstretched hand. "Whoa."

A rustling sound drew my attention, and I righted myself in a hurry, tossing the oar aside. I imagined an alligator lurking in the weeds and swallowing me whole. The entire town would speculate that I'd run away to hide my guilt over Mr. Paine's murder.

"Hello?" I called.

No one answered.

I stepped away from the sound, back toward the safety of the wide-planked boardwalk, when something small and blue caught my eye in the waving grass. Not far, I realized, from where the odd rustling had occurred. I peered down into the darkness, hands on my knees, begging my eyes for better night vision.

"What are you?" I asked the object, creeping back the way I'd come.

Another nearby sound stopped my heart, and I jerked around in a tight one-eighty, sweeping my gaze from left to right and turning my back on the small blue item. I strained to see the source of movement in the darkness, but there was nothing.

Instinct told me someone was near. A shiver of fear ran down my spine and curled my toes inside my sneakers.

What if it was Mr. Paine's killer returning to the scene of the crime?

I'd barely completed the thought before something broad and sturdy collided with my backside. I lurched forward toward the murky water, praying I wasn't met by a hungry gator. A yelp burst from my lips as I fumbled to remain upright, but a half heartbeat later, a second resounding smack sent me tail over teakettle into the marsh.

The scream I let out as I fell into the water was nearly enough to unhinge my jaw. I choked on mouthfuls of duckweed and mud as I jolted out of the marsh, clawing my way back through the crime scene to safety. The muck sucked one of my shoes off in its desperation to keep me, and a cloud of gnats settled around my head like dirt following Pigpen on *Peanuts*.

The worn and busted boat oar rattled to a standstill on the boardwalk, abandoned by whoever had used it against me.

I collapsed beside it in a fit of tears, lungs burning, skin crawling. I swallowed back a second scream and wiped yuck from my nose and eyes. There was no one visible in any direction, save the set of distant figures in the surf, now near enough to recognize as a pair of tween boys, collecting sand and shells in swinging buckets. Whoever had done this to me was gone, and they'd taken whatever I'd seen in the weeds with them.

CHAPTER

FIVE

I was up and dressed in time to watch the sunrise with Lou. I hadn't slept well. Mostly, I relived being whacked on the backside and face-planted into the muck. It was the most humiliating experience of my life. I still wasn't sure if having no witnesses was a blessing or a curse. I'd started to dial the police and report my assault at least a dozen times, but frankly, the only thing injured was my pride, and aside from the pound of cattail fluff caught in my hair and clogging my shower drain, there was no proof the attack even happened. There was, however, an Everly-shaped mud mark raked through Mr. Paine's crime scene.

Besides, I was reluctant to draw Detective Hays's attention again, and any new police report from me would undoubtedly be turned over to the man investigating me for murder. He'd complain that I'd messed with the broken tape and nosed into the restricted area. I had to admit that from his perspective I probably looked more meddlesome than helpful.

Thankfully, that was about to change.

"Everly?" Aunt Clara's sweet voice carried up from the garden to my ears. It was the sort of sound that tamed beasts and enchanted fairies. If she were a vending machine, Clara would dispense hugs. Aunt Fran would dole out sass.

I'd probably provide unsound judgment.

I hopped out of my rocker and leaned over the crisp white deck railing. "Hello! Good morning!"

Aunt Clara was alone. Her pale hair floated in the wind around her shoulders, like clouds against the backdrop of a peaceful surf. She pressed a floppy straw hat to her head with one hand and balanced her vintage beach bicycle with the other. Its wire handlebar basket was filled with fresh flowers wrapped in newspaper and what looked like an old blue watering can.

"Come up!" I ran through the café in bare feet, leaving the glass patio door open behind me to invite the ocean inside, but I'd latched the screen in case Lou got any ideas about becoming an indoor seagull.

I beat her to my front porch and waited on the stairs. "I'm so glad you're here," I called over the railing. "Thank you for agreeing to watch the shop this morning."

Aunt Clara rested her bicycle against my wooden handrail and gathered the things from her basket. "It's no trouble. I brought you some flowers. Every place needs flowers."

I pressed the door wide with one hip and waited for her to pass. "They're beautiful."

She kissed my cheek on her way across the threshold. "I'm sorry Fran couldn't make it. She's elbow-deep in beeswax."

"It's okay. I'll visit her later." I smiled tentatively. "Can we talk?"

"Always."

I didn't want to repeat what had happened at the marsh out loud, but the episode had haunted me all night, and I doubted I'd sleep again until I told someone. I needed to know if I was wrong to worry my attacker might have been Mr. Paine's killer and wanted to hear it was okay to still feel afraid, even in the light of day. "You're not going to like it."

Aunt Clara filled two jars with tea and pushed one in my direction. "You can tell me anything, Everly."

"Okay." I started with the broken crime scene tape, then ended with the abandoned oar and the insanely long shower I'd needed to feel clean again.

"Are you hurt badly?" she asked, eyes wide with fear. "Why didn't you call us? Have you seen a doctor?" She covered her mouth with one hand and color drained from her cheeks.

"I'm fine," I promised. "Shaken, but okay."

"You could've been killed!"

I'd thought the same thing in a moment of panic. "But I was only paddled. Humiliated, basically, and left to cry alone. I kept the paddle."

She wrapped me in her arms and cradled my head to her shoulder the way she had all my life whenever I was upset. "Poor darling." If a thing couldn't be fixed inside Aunt Clara's hug, it probably couldn't be fixed at all.

Too soon, she kissed my head and released me. "What did the police say? They're looking into it, I hope. That's the second act of aggression this town has had in as many days. We can't have some lunatic on the loose attacking people." She returned to her tea and rested her elbows on the counter, setting her chin in her hands.

"Well." I debated how to answer honestly. I'd stayed awake devising acceptable reasons to avoid calling the police, but hadn't made a plan for telling my aunts that I decided against it.

"You told the police," she insisted.

"No."

"Why not?" she cried. "You were assaulted. Someone needs to have record of that."

"I'll report it," I said, unsure if that was true. "I just wasn't up to it last night. I'm still not sure there's even a point."

"There's a point. Wait until Fran hears about this."

"Where did you say she is?" I asked, changing the subject. "Did you say she's doing something with wax?"

Aunt Clara gave me a long look, probably debating how hard to push me on the police report. She relented with a sigh. "Well, I probably shouldn't say," she began, "but Fran met a man last night, and they hit it off."

I steepled my fingers and wiggled my brows in

anticipation of the full story. Knowing my aunts, it could be anything. I prepared to be shocked. "Do tell."

Aunt Clara took a moment to consider my goofy face. "Fine. His name is Henry, and he's a four-star general from the Union army. Everyone knows that Fran is a sucker for a man in uniform, so she's promised to make him two hundred and eighty wax sticks for sealing invitations to the Civil War reenactment down at Atlantic Beach next month."

My shoulders drooped in relief. Henry was a general in the *pretend* Union army. For a moment, I'd thought poor Aunt Clara's mind had finally gone out to pasture. "Well, at least tell me he was handsome," I teased.

Aunt Clara filled the broad metal watering can with cold water and set it on my counter. She unpacked the flowers and arranged them skillfully. "He was, but Fran was never a sucker for a pretty face. That's always been me. She's a shrewd businesswoman who loves a nice-fitting uniform. Their relationship is doomed anyway. He's a Yankee."

"Can't have that." I smiled. "Where's he from originally?"

I watched as she finished the arrangement and carried it to my cozy reading area in the corner. She set the watering-can vase on the wicker coffee table.

"Philadelphia."

"Ah." He was out of luck with Fran, then. Every woman had a line she wouldn't cross when it came to the men her life; Fran's was the Mason-Dixon. "Well,

I'm sorry I missed Aunt Fran today, but I'm very glad you're here. I have a mission."

She returned to my counter and divided the remaining blooms into half a dozen mason jars, then carried those to the café tables. "It's no problem. I was coming by this morning anyway."

"You were?"

"Mm-hmm. I'd already invited some friends to meet me here for tea. Do you think you could say hello and give them a little talk about Sun, Sand, and Tea?"

"Friends?" I wrinkled my nose and tried to recall the last time I'd seen either of my aunts out with friends. A coalition of beekeepers popped into my mind, all arriving in their hooded suits for tea. I smiled. Honestly, I didn't care what anyone arrived in as long as they arrived.

Aunt Clara fluffed and adjusted the brightly colored blooms. "They're fellow historians," she said. "I met them last month when I dropped in on one of their meetings. Their official group name is The Society for the Preservation and Retelling of Unrecorded History. Kitty Hawk Charter," she added. "I've tried to get a group started in Charm for years, but there just isn't enough interest."

"There's a group dedicated to retelling unrecorded history?" I asked. "That sounds like a club for sharing really old gossip."

"Pish-posh," she chided. "Just because no one wrote it down doesn't mean it wasn't true. And just because people do write something down doesn't mean it is true."

"Can't argue with that." I thought of the mean blog commenters. "So what's the temperature on the *Town Charmer* today?" I asked carefully.

"Cold," she answered. "The blogger seems to be covering the situation fairly, but there hasn't been much new information, so the content has gotten…creative."

My tummy rolled. I'd considered reading the blog with my morning coffee, but assumed that would be a terrible way to start my day, and I wanted to stay positive. Still, I needed to know what people were saying about me if I was going to turn the bad press around. "Creative?" I asked.

"Yeah. The charts and graphs don't help."

"There are charts?"

She nodded, flipping one palm out, then the other. "Before you left? No crime. Three months after your return? Murder." Aunt Clara shook her head. "The constant polling keeps it all going. What do we really know about Everly Swan?" she intoned. "Is the Swan family curse growing?"

"Great." Now folks were talking about my family's three-hundred-year string of bad luck as if it really was a curse. "The commenters must love all those opportunities for negativity."

"There are only a few haters," she argued. "You get those everywhere. Most Charmers are reasonable and curious. You just need to get out and talk to them. Pull back the curtain."

I let the subject drop. It only took a few haters to stoke the fire currently destroying my reputation, and I wasn't sure how to mend fences with the public at large. Especially when I hadn't done anything wrong.

Aunt Clara decorated my tables with her usual pizazz and unfettered verve. "I thought this would be the perfect location for the preservation society's April meeting, so I made the suggestion and voila! Plus, I've been wanting to get by and bring you some flowers. The bees are sending our beds into a tizzy. Pollinating everything. I can barely keep up. We'll be overrun in no time at this rate." She placed the final jar, then turned to admire her work. "Now, isn't that nicer? Flowers bring the outside in." She closed her eyes and opened her arms wide, palms up. "Feel that energy?"

"Uh-huh." I went to the café fridge and unloaded several trays of prepoured sweet tea in sample-sized cups. I'd put my sleepless hours last night to good use, slicking Sun, Sand, and Tea stickers onto each unit and sealing them with matching lids. "I made an extra batch of Grandma's favorite recipe, and I'm going to take it to town today. Remind everyone that I'm not a bad guy, and my tea's worth trying."

"That's the spirit." She smiled. "Good for you, but how are you going to get all that in to town?"

I waggled my eyebrows, then went to the closet for my surprise. "Ta-da!" I returned with my childhood wagon, a Radio Flyer that was once red and rusted but now sported a happy coat of aqua paint with bold white stripes and my shop name stenciled down the middle in bright yellow.

"That's adorable," Aunt Clara cooed. She clapped once and leaned in for a closer look.

"Amelia gave me the idea when I ran into her last night hauling books. You left the wagon here when you helped me move in, and I found it again while I was cleaning. I had plenty of paint left over from the café renovation, so I gave it a makeover. You really like it?"

"Like it? I love this wagon. I remember when you used to fit inside it. You, your blanket, and about a hundred sand toys."

The sound of footfalls drew my attention to the front porch.

Aunt Clara perked up. "They're here." She hustled to the door and waved a small crowd of people inside. "Come in!" She hugged the guests one by one, kissed their cheeks, and squeezed their hands. "Everyone, this is my grandniece, Everly Swan. Everly, this is the Society for the Preservation and Retelling of Unrecorded History, Kitty Hawk chapter."

The group seated themselves at my newly decorated tables, filling all but two of the chairs, then turned expectant eyes on me.

"Welcome to Sun, Sand, and Tea," I said. "I'm so glad y'all could make it this morning." I hustled around the counter and lined up some clean jars. "What can I get started for you? Something specific? Just a whole lot of samples? Anything? Everything?"

I hiked up my smile, and hoped they were paying customers.

"Peach tea," one woman called.

"Me too," several voices echoed.

I turned wide eyes to Aunt Clara. Detective Hays and his team of badged thieves had stolen my peach tea, and I hadn't bothered making more, since the whole town thought it was poison.

"Oh." Aunt Clara swept dramatically in my direction, dragging her fingertips over the counter like an actress on stage. "Peach is very good, but you haven't lived until you've tried Everly's"—she turned her back to the crowd and lifted overplucked eyebrows at me— "help me now, sweetie, what was it you named that life-changing blend? It's completely slipped my mind."

"Honey Ginger?" I named the first tea that came to mind.

"That's the one," Aunt Clara agreed, "and the dear uses honey from our hives to make it. It's fantastic. So is the Vanilla and Lavender Tea. That's a longtime favorite of mine too."

I poured a few glasses of Honey Ginger. "The lavender comes from the family homestead, as well." There were acres of every flower and herb I'd ever want at Clara and Fran's home. The land had been passed down for generations, Swan woman to Swan woman, and cultivated by the very best. One sad day, it would all be mine. Given a choice, I'd prefer keeping my aunts forever.

"Do you also raise produce?" someone asked.

"Heavens, no," Clara shook her head vehemently. "For that, Everly calls the Goat Lady."

The group looked at me. I lined up another row of jars and filled them with the various flavors of the day.

"The Goat Lady has the only truly organic farm on the island," I explained. "It's where we get our fruits, veggies, poultry, and dairy. Her real name is Hana, but I think she actually prefers being called the Goat Lady." I smiled. "She moved from Russia to America to study English because she was a teacher back home, but she fell in love and stayed. She's been farming here ever since. Maybe twenty years now."

Hana was one of my favorite people in the world. She raised pygmy goats and made their milk into everything from soap to cheese, and I was pretty sure her garden was tended by fairies. Everything that came from Hana's farm was magical.

I poured the final glass of tea and beamed. "The samples are ready."

I moved through the room, setting an array of teas on each table. "Drink up. Enjoy. Will y'all be doing anything else while you're in Charm today?"

Clara drummed on the counter in a cute little rhythm. "First we're going to enjoy your tea and tour your home. Then, we'll have a quick walk along the beach and boardwalk, a visit to Blessed Bee, and dinner at the homestead tonight, where I can show off the family estate, the bees, the gardens, and Fran's heavenly cooking."

"That sounds like a full day." I eyeballed my wagon

full of sweating cups. "Maybe I should do this another time?" I looked to Aunt Clara for advice. She hadn't said anything about all these plans when I asked her to watch the shop for an hour or two.

"Nope." She waved her fingers at me. "You go. We'll be here long enough for you to deliver your samples and say hello to the locals. Maybe make a stop at the police station while you're out," she suggested. "They'd probably love some tea. If you get caught up, don't worry about it. I'll flip the CLOSED sign on our way out."

"Wait." I worked backward through the conversation. "Did you say you're going to tour my home?" The words had just made it to my brain. I wasn't sure how I felt about it, but at least I had cleaned up after the police had tossed it.

Clara lifted her jar to her lips and smiled behind the rim. She cast her gaze across the crowded tables and addressed her friends, who hung on her every word. "Did you know that this home is more than one hundred and seventy years old? It was originally commissioned by a wealthy businessman up north for an extremely beautiful young woman named Magnolia Baine. A distant relative of ours, if I'm not mistaken." She flicked a glance my way.

The crowd gave a collective "Oooo."

I lifted the wagon handle and started for the door. If I didn't hurry, the ice would melt before I made it to Main Street.

"Her beau was more than twenty years her senior. And married," Aunt Clara said.

"Ahhhh."

"He had children older than Magnolia, but that didn't matter to either of them. Their love was the stuff other women whispered about over cards and toddies. It's said that the affair was torrid and shameless, often resulting in undrawn blinds after dark. They were simply too caught up in one another to care or remember that the man was married, for goodness' sake!" She made eye contact with everyone in the room, giving each listener a moment to let it all settle in. "One night, the man's wife came looking for him, worried his carriage had taken a spill or that he'd been robbed of his escort, and she discovered him in Magnolia's arms. Saw it with her own eyes, right through the open window. His wife was so wretched, she walked straight into the sea, and when the young girl realized her actions had caused the death of another woman, she cast herself from the roof tower. The man was left to grow mad in these very halls, unable to leave the place where his selfishness had ended the lives of the women he loved."

The jaws of Aunt Clara's friends were nearly on the floor as she wound the farfetched tale into something completely salacious and utterly of her own making.

I maneuvered the wagon onto the porch outside the door. I had a killer to catch and wares to peddle. I couldn't afford to be distracted by Aunt Clara's "retellings of unrecorded history," though stories of my new home fascinated me.

I'd dreamed of living here since the first time I'd

seen the property as a child. When it came on the
market the day I moved home, I knew it was fate.
When I realized I could own it *and* open my iced tea
shop inside, I couldn't think of anything else until it
was mine.

"What happened to the man?" a woman at the
counter asked.

Clara hummed softly before speaking, probably
buying time to formulate the best answer. "Some
people still hear him calling for her at night, roaming
the beach in search of his lost love."

"The wife or the mistress?"

"Who's to say?" Aunt Clara answered grimly.
"Though the spirit of one of the women is said to
wander the town as a weathered old cat, ragged from
years of heartbreak and homelessness. Which woman
is anyone's guess—maybe after all these years, she's
become both."

A gasp broke their silence.

I rolled my eyes. "I'll be back. Thank you all so
much for coming, and thank you, Aunt Clara." *For
looking after my fictitiously haunted property.*

I gave the porch stairs a long look, then rethought
my plan. I'd have to empty the wagon and take it
down first, then come back for the drinks and reload
at the bottom.

"It was a sign," Clara's voice carried through the
doorway as I returned from my first trip down the
steps. "Fran and I knew the moment Everly wanted to
come home that this property would show up on the

market, and it did. An anonymous seller asked only as much as Everly could afford to pay, and the deal was taken care of online. Can you believe that? She never even met with the owner."

"Who was the owner?" someone asked.

"All we know is that his name was Lou," Clara whispered.

I stared through the open door, trays of tea stacked two tall in my arms. *Did she say Lou?* Like the seagull? I shook my head. That was probably where she'd come up with the name: she'd stolen it from the freeloading bird who begged for my leftover shrimp and scallops.

"The house is perfect for Everly in so many ways, but historically, there couldn't be a better one," Clara continued. "The Swan women have been cursed in love for centuries. Magnolia Baine, distant relative or not, was no different than the rest of us. Everly will find camaraderie of spirit here, I think."

I rubbed the lines off my forehead and refocused on my mission to drum up some business and find Sam Smart. Sam would know if Mr. Paine had been in a standoff with another business owner, and I could use the lead. I certainly didn't need to hear my family legends recounted to know I was unlucky in love. That truth spoke for itself.

❧

The walk into town was hot. I'd chosen jeans and a T-shirt with the Sun, Sand, and Tea logo across the back, but I should've worn shorts. By the time I reached Main Street, the relentless Southern sun was making short work of the ice cubes in my tea samples and short-circuiting my brain. Everyone I'd met along the boardwalk had declined my offering, and a few had all but run away when they saw me coming. Unloading free sweet tea was going to be harder than I'd expected.

"Sweet tea?" I asked Mrs. Dubiel, my elementary school librarian, as she stepped onto the sidewalk in front of me.

She smiled brightly at my goodies. "Why yes, thank you."

I delivered her a cup and napkin. She shook my hand and savored her drink with a smile.

"Did you know Benedict Paine?" I asked. She was in his age group and had been on the island as long as I could remember, though she didn't seem to remember me.

"Yes." She looked lovingly at her cup, enamored by the tea. "Benedict was a nice man. Shame what happened. This has a lovely flavor. It reminds me of growing up in Georgia."

"Thank you," I beamed. "It's an old family recipe. Had you talked to Mr. Paine recently?"

"No. Not in years. He welcomed my family to town after we moved in and brought a basket of items from the local shops. Let us know where we could buy anything we needed on the island. No need to leave town."

That sounded like him. It also sounded like another dead end.

I offered her a business card. "I'm glad you enjoyed the tea sample. Stop in and see me anytime at Sun, Sand, and Tea. I have twenty signature blends and keep a dozen flavors on tap most days."

The woman raised her drink slowly, twisting the cup until the logo came into view. Her gaze flicked to mine, then back to the logo. Recognition dawned on her face as she aligned my presence with the memory of a sand-covered girl in pigtails, no doubt. Her smile tightened, and she hurried away.

"Have a nice day," I called after her. So far, this hadn't become the fruitful endeavor I'd imagined.

As I gazed after her, a mom and three boys dragged themselves off the boardwalk, heading toward a line of parked cars near the road.

I waved. "Alicia?" I'd played the trumpet beside her little sister in the fifth-grade band. Alicia was in high school then, and she'd seemed so much older than me, but time had closed the age gap between us. Today, she looked my age.

Her boys were covered in sand from their knees down and dripping with sweat everywhere else. She looked like she could use a drink.

"Tea?" I offered. I reached for a cup, certain to make her day.

She put a hand on the smallest boy's shoulder. "No, thank you."

I dropped my hand back to my side, but held the smile. "Okay." I nodded at her and the boys. "It's nice to see you."

"Whoa." The middle-sized child rushed over to my cart. "Is this the stuff from the blog?" He turned crazed eyes on me. "Can I have some?"

"Yes?" Suddenly I wasn't sure. My new confidence began to shrink beneath Alicia's wide-eyed stare.

"Here." He gathered three cups in his hands and gave one to each of his brothers. "You first," he told the smallest one.

The boy removed the lid and sniffed the contents curiously. "No way. You."

Panic and humiliation flooded my chest. "You don't need to drink that," I said. "It's fine. Not everyone likes tea."

The oldest lifted his tea and smiled bravely. "I do." He shot his younger brother a look. "Man, don't be dumb. She's not planning to take out the town. You think she's going door-to-door in broad daylight delivering poison?" He removed the lid and gulped his cup dry.

Alicia made a strangled sound. "I am so sorry," she said to me, finally snapping into action. "We're late for something. I'd stay and visit, but I really have to go. Come on, boys." She took the other two cups away and hurried her children toward the public parking lot, tossing the tea into a nearby garbage can. "Hustle," she growled, as they piled into the car. "You're all grounded forever."

The oldest kid tipped his head back and laughed.

I tried not to stare as they drove away. My eyes stung as if I'd been slapped. *Is this really where I stand with the town?* Barely home three months and already I was a joke? All because someone killed a local outside my shop, and I'd found him?

That wasn't fair, and it wouldn't do at all.

I spent the next hour walking the blocks of storefronts, looking for someone in need of refreshment or willing to talk about Mr. Paine. It wasn't easy. The streets were as still as a Wild West town when a gunslinger rode in. Most of the stores were empty and a few, like Sam's realty office, were closed, with a clock sign in the window. *Be Back Soon.*

Where was everyone?

I stopped at the corner of Main and Middletown, deciding where to go next, or if I should give up. Middletown Street acted as the island equator, stretching from Bay View, the street that faced the bay, all the way across the island like a belt, concluding at the ocean on the opposite side of town. The street along the ocean was appropriately named Ocean Drive, and it paralleled the boardwalk for several miles, separating town from beach. Whoever had been charged with naming the streets had been fairly unimaginative. Personally, I appreciated that fact. It made giving directions much simpler.

The same white cat I had seen at the beach sat in an alleyway between two shops, watching me and rotating one notched ear as if she could hear something I couldn't.

Aunt Clara's story of my allegedly distant relative, Magnolia Baine, and her married lover came to mind.

The spirit of one of the women is said to wander the town as a weathered old cat. "Any chance you're inhabited by the spirit of a heartbroken mistress?" I asked.

The cat flicked its tail.

"That seems like a yes to me," I said. "So, I'm going to call you Maggie, and we'll be friends. How does that sound?"

Maggie turned and walked away.

"See you soon," I called to her retreating frame.

I cracked the top off a disposable cup and sucked down a tea sample, then gathered my wild, sticky hair into a ponytail and piled it on top of my sweaty head. Even with the melted ice watering it down, Grandma's sweet tea was delicious.

The sounds of hammering and power tools filtered into my consciousness as I moved up Middletown Street toward the bay. A crew of construction workers had torn the roof off a large waterfront home and were working to build a new one under the blazing sun. If *they* wouldn't take my free tea, I was in worse trouble than I'd realized.

I jogged across Bay View with my wagon, careful not to spill the goods. The men in hard hats and work belts were quick to notice my approach.

I waved. "Sweet tea?"

The answer was a resounding yes.

The men swarmed me. Some tried to pay me. I gave the money back, along with my business card and directions to my café. Turns out, the crew wasn't from Charm, so they didn't read the local gossip blog. They also didn't know Mr. Paine or have a clue that he'd died suspiciously. Best of all, they expected to work six-day weeks through the summer and it was only late April.

Maybe I'd be able to pay my mortgage next month after all.

Fresh out of supplies and business cards, I dragged my empty wagon back down Middletown Street through town. The streets had begun to fill since my first pass, and a light was on inside Sam's office.

I parked the wagon and went inside.

"Sam?" I approached the reception desk and tapped the little silver bell. "Sam Smart?" The office was business-bland. I wrinkled my nose against the stink of new carpet and fresh paint. A section of blue faux-leather seats broke up the tan carpet and cream walls and a television in the corner played the company's commercial on a loop. "Sam?" I tried the bell again.

Sam scuttled into view from somewhere in back. His cheeks were flushed, and his eyes were wide. "Oh, hello, Everly." He broke my name into three separate syllables and spoke it loudly.

"Hi." I glanced around. "Everything okay?"

He drove a handkerchief over his dewy forehead and met me on my side of the counter. "Yes. Fine. How are you? What brings you in? Ready to move so soon?" He laughed awkwardly.

"No. I've been thinking about what happened to Mr. Paine, and I hoped you might be willing to tell me what was going on between the two of you that day at my shop. It was obvious that you weren't happy with one another."

Sam tugged his ear and crossed his arms. His foot tapped nervously. "I don't know what you mean. Paine and I were fine. You were the one who argued with him. What was that about, exactly?"

I made a face as Sam picked lint off his rumpled dress shirt and straightened his tie. "You know what it was about. He wanted an ingredients list, and I wouldn't give it to him. We said as much while we were fussing. Everyone heard it, and you were sitting right there. I want to know what the two of you were up in arms about."

He settled into an overly casual stance, one hip against the desk, hands in pockets. "I don't know what you mean."

I cocked my head and tried not to call out *liar-liar pants on fire*. "Fine. Let me jar your memory. First, you were trading dirty looks and thinly veiled accusations with him, then he started in on me, and you interrupted him. You said"—I lifted my fingers in air quotes—"'I know what your problem is, and it's not her.'"

Sam's fake orange tan paled.

"So, I ask you. What was Paine's problem?"

Sam pulled his hands from his pockets, bringing them to the back of his neck. "I was just trying to rile him up. Push his buttons."

"Why?"

"I don't know. Maybe because he gave everyone else such a hard time. But I didn't hurt him."

"Oh-kay," I drawled. The idea that Sam had hurt him hadn't occurred to me before that moment. It was still too unreal to think anyone on our island would kill another human being.

But I couldn't help wondering why Sam had made such a declaration when I hadn't even asked. Did he have a reason to announce his innocence in Paine's death? A reason like guilt?

I stepped a little closer to the door. What if I'd cluelessly waltzed into an office devoid of witnesses and confronted a murderer?

"I believe you," I gushed, suddenly unsure that was completely true. "Do you have any idea who might have? Because the new detective is looking at me, and I'd like to make some secondary options available."

Sam's eyes slid hard to the right before he pulled them back to my face. "Have you taken a look at Paine's gold-digging ex-wife, Lucinda?"

"No."

"She's a class-A nightmare. Always on the take. I wouldn't put anything past her."

"Two cranky people in one marriage probably explains the divorce," I murmured.

Sam mopped his forehead again. "I don't know what else to tell you, but I'm in the middle of something, so…"

"Sure." I moved toward the front door, thankful for an exit cue and already determined to meet Paine's ex-wife. "One more thing," I said, realizing I had no idea who she was. "Does Lucinda live in town?"

"No, but she's got a gaudy bauble store in Duck."

"Thank you," I said. "Come back for tea sometime. Don't be a stranger."

He lifted a hand in goodbye, but the gesture felt more like *get out*.

I dragged my wagon home with a skip in my step. I'd found a construction crew to woo with my tea, and I'd gotten a lead on my investigation: Mr. Paine's pain in the behind ex-wife.

Not too bad for a lady with no idea what she was doing.

CHAPTER

SIX

I dialed the police station from the boardwalk. Sam's strange behavior had given me the willies, and I couldn't stop thinking about what had happened on the boardwalk the night before. Much as I hated to relive it, Aunt Clara was right—the people should know there had been another attack by the marsh. I put my pride aside and waited for the call to connect.

Yes, being swatted paddle-style with an old oar was humiliating, but I wanted to know who had hit me and why. The cops couldn't find my assailant if I didn't report the crime.

When an officer finally answered, I unloaded every detail I could recall and was thrilled to learn they would accept a verbal report, though the officer told me to make a trip to the station at my convenience and sign the official document. Peace washed over me as we disconnected. The truth was out there, and I wouldn't have to think about it anymore.

My shoulders sagged in relief when my home came

into view a few minutes later. I parked my wagon at the bottom of the steps and tucked the stack of empty trays beneath one bent arm. With any luck, Aunt Clara's group of faux historians enjoyed their tea and ghost story enough to spread the word and come back with friends. Then again, if the café failed, I could always open my home as a haunted house and charge for tours. One way or another, I needed an income to afford the enormous place. Currently, every stick of furniture I owned could fit into any one of the massive rooms, but I'd chosen to spread the pieces throughout the second floor as the layout dictated—a couch here, a table there.

I leaned against the handrail to enjoy the moment, and it swayed against my weight. Well, that wasn't good. I couldn't have folks falling off my porch on the way in for tea. I stepped back onto solid ground and gave the rail a shake to test the integrity.

Weathered paint stuck to my palms, along with a handful of rotted wood flakes and dirt. *Jeez.* I kicked the base of the railing lightly with my toe, and the bottom support bumped loose, revealing a rusted nail and oversized hole where the wood had aged to the opposite of perfection.

"Good grief!" I forced the beam back into place and sat on the bottom step, settling the empty trays on my lap.

The sound of footfalls drew my attention to the boardwalk. Detective Hays walked toward me, his lips puckered in a whistle. "That handrail is in bad shape."

"No kidding," I murmured, stretching my hot, jean-clad legs into the sun. "I was having such a good day too."

He dropped onto the step beside me. His knees poked up in front of him and his arms hung loosely across them, leaving big tan hands to dangle over his feet. Authority oozed from him in a near-tangible aura.

I leaned away so I could squint up at his face. "What do you want? Not tea, I suppose."

He shrugged. "I could use some information."

I made a face. "What?"

He flicked his wrist toward the length of crime scene tape, fluttering in the breeze twenty yards away. "I got a call this morning from a man who says he heard a woman scream out here last night just after dark. Didn't call till this morning because by the time he got over to where he thought the sound had come from, there was no one there. Woke up feeling like he still ought to say something, so he did."

I wrenched upright. "Who?"

"A night fisherman. He was down by the public bathrooms. I was just out this way talking to him when I got a call from the station."

My cheeks flushed. I'd barely hung up the phone and Detective Hays already knew I had filed a report. "You're here looking into that?" I asked.

"Yep."

My tummy grumbled. "You might as well come inside." I had a feeling this wouldn't be a short conversation, and I was starving.

Detective Hays levered himself off the step and went to roll a big rock against the base of the broken handrail post. "I wasn't kidding about fixing that. It's a safety violation."

"Fine, I'll fix it today."

He followed me onto the porch, still eyeballing the busted rail. "You'll need new wood and hardware. You can't just go pounding the same rusted nail into a different place on an already decrepit board and call it fixed."

"I have wood," I said, unlocking the door and stepping inside. I flipped the sign to OPEN. "I have nails. I have all sorts of building supplies left behind by the previous owner. I guess he had big plans for renovations but changed his mind." My thoughts drifted to Aunt Clara's strange story from this morning, but I pushed that nonsense away.

I flipped the lights on and the café lit up with a warm glow. "Make yourself comfortable."

Detective Hays took a seat at the counter and I poured two glasses of sweet tea and set one in front of him. "Do you like tomato, basil, and goat cheese salad?"

"Got any hamburgers?"

"No." I perused my refrigerator for inspiration and decided paninis seemed like former-U.S.-marshal-turned-small-town-detective food. I filled my workspace with ingredients and plugged in my panini press. "What do you usually eat for lunch?" Whatever it was, mine would be better.

"Antacids."

Yep. Definitely better.

I cut two thick slices of bread so soft I could use them for pillows, then stacked one piece with thinly cut apples and smoked ham. I topped that with a stubbornly sticky slice of brie and smothered it all in my homemade honey mustard.

"There." I put the sandwich into my heated press and popped a slice of apple into my mouth.

Detective Hays folded his hands on the counter, watching. "You really enjoy that."

"Eating?" I gave myself a lighthearted glance. "Obviously."

He let his gaze drift over my figure with a strange, pained expression. "Agree to disagree."

The press dinged and I jumped to attention, plating sandwich halves and scooping tomato, basil, and goat cheese salad onto mismatched dinnerware from my family's estate. The plates had been passed down like everything else the Swans had, including tall tales, legends, and recipes. "Here you are."

I took the stool beside him at the counter and dug in immediately. Best to keep my mouth busy before I put my foot in it.

He sighed into his first bite, eyes briefly rolling back.

My heart fluttered. If I could create and serve food that made folks look like that every day, I'd exist in a perpetual state of bliss. "Good?"

"Unreal." He took another bite. And another.

I smiled through half my sandwich and most of my

salad before the button on my jeans protested, and my fitness band beeped. **BE MORE ACTIVE**.

I pinched the acknowledgement button until my fingers hurt.

Detective Hays wiped his mouth on a napkin. "Now. Are you ready to talk about what happened last night?"

I sipped my tea and searched his face. He wouldn't be here if my little marsh mishap wasn't a big deal.

"I already have the basics from the report you called in. To someone else." He ground out the last three words, as if I'd somehow offended him.

I inhaled deeply to settle my nerves, then blew the details out all over again. "The crime scene tape was broken when I came back from my walk. I stopped to tie it back together, and I saw something in the weeds. When I sneaked down there for a better look, someone whacked me with an old oar, and I wound up face-down in the yuck."

Detective Hays dropped his napkin on the counter and frowned at me. "Why didn't you call the station immediately? There might have been a patrolman in the area. Someone might have seen something."

"There was no one. Just a couple of teenage boys in the distance, way down by the surf."

"Can you identify them? Maybe they saw more than you think."

"No." My shoulders slumped. "They were barely more than silhouettes against the ocean."

He pressed his lips into a thin white line. "You

still should've let someone know. You should've let *me* know. We are in the middle of a murder investigation."

I bristled. I knew he meant well, but I didn't like being scolded. "I was afraid, but I wasn't hurt, and I had no proof of the attack. Except the paddle, but how could I prove I'd been hit with it? I didn't even see who did it. And it was humiliating."

He didn't look convinced. "Well, what was in the weeds that got you over there to start with?"

"I don't know. It was gone when I climbed back onto the boardwalk. I kept the busted boat oar, but I'm not sure what good it'll do."

Detective Hays swore under his breath. "It was the weapon used in your attack. Where is it?"

I left him alone in the café and went to retrieve the dumb oar. I hated carrying it. Hated touching it. It looked even worse for wear in the light of day.

I huffed back into his view and thrust the paddle at him. "Here."

"Thanks." His grouchy expression turned sour at the sight of it. He took the thing from my hands and gave it a thorough once over. "Well, I guess your story explains why my crime scene looks as if a swamp monster crawled through it."

I frowned.

"Anything else you want to tell me?" he asked, an edge of a dare in his tone.

"Yeah," I blurted. "I don't like being referred to as a swamp monster, and you should know that Mr. Paine has an opportunistic ex-wife who might've had a reason to cause him trouble. If not, then she might know who did. Maybe you ought to talk to her."

The detective's mouth formed a little O before he snapped it closed and clenched his square jaw. "And where'd you hear that?"

I crossed my arms and kept my mouth clamped shut.

"Talk."

I raised my eyebrows.

"Don't make me threaten you with an obstruction charge."

"Obstruction," I huffed. "At least I'm out there asking people questions, rather than focusing on one innocent bystander. Trying to find out what really happened. That's called investigating."

"It's called obstruction. Now, who were you talking to?"

I pressed my lips together. Whatever I told him was likely to make him madder, and I was still unsure why he was mad to start with. I was *helping*.

Detective Hays shook his head at me, as if *he* was the one utterly exasperated. "I know you think you're being useful, but what you're actually doing is undermining my investigation, and I can't have that."

I slid off my stool and onto tired feet. He didn't want to hear my ideas, and I couldn't just wait around for him to get started actually looking for who might have killed Mr. Paine. That put us in a predicament. "What do you expect me to do?" I asked, "because frankly, it feels as if your 'investigation' is moving slower than molasses and it's still pointed alarmingly in my direction. I can't sit by and do nothing while my reputation is ruined, while my business is buried by rumors and lies. I've poured every ounce of my life savings and inheritance into this place." My determined tone turned slowly into a whine and made me want to cringe.

Moving back to Charm was supposed to have been a fresh start for me. A chance to heal my broken heart. A do-over. But without the café, I couldn't afford to stay, at least not in this house. "I have to do *something*. You would too, if you were in my shoes."

He climbed off his stool and lifted his empty plate. After a brief staring contest, he carried the dirty dinnerware to my sink behind the counter and ran water over it. "You think I'm being mean, but I'm telling you what's right. This is what I do, and I'm good at it. I don't need any help, and I don't want you putting yourself in harm's way. That's just more paperwork for me."

"Stop that." I beetled around to his side and shooed him out of the way. "Get."

He sucked his teeth, but retreated. "Who all did you talk to today?"

I stuck our plates in the dishwasher and snapped the door shut. "Just Sam. He's a real estate agent."

"I know who Sam is," Detective Hays grumped. "He's the one who pointed you in Lucinda's direction."

"Yeah. How do you know Sam already? Was he your agent?"

He tapped a smug finger against the badge on his hip. "This ain't my first rodeo, Swan."

The word rodeo twisted like a corkscrew in my belly, reminding me of the cowboy who'd recently broken my heart. "Why'd you say that?"

"What?"

I marched toward him, and he retreated. "The rodeo thing. Why'd you say it?"

An uncomfortable laugh changed his grouchy face. "It's a saying. People say it."

"You meant something by it."

He shook his head. "What I meant was for you to stay out of my investigation. That's all, and nothing more. I won't hesitate to haul you in if I have to. Better to have you in jail than out there getting yourself killed."

"Killed!" I squeaked. "Was that meant to scare me, or is it an actual possibility?" I trailed him to the doorway. "What kind of maniac are we dealing with here?"

The detective walked right out the door, toting the oar. "Thank you for lunch," he called over one shoulder, "and the evidence."

I stared, fuming, as he strode away, wishing I'd had the chance to use that big paddle on him.

‿

I spent the afternoon familiarizing myself with power tools. I replaced the handrail and all the questionable boards on the front steps with sturdy new pieces. Then

I sanded everything nice and smooth. A fresh coat of white paint would pull it all together, but that was a job for tomorrow. I gripped the now-unshakable handrail, proud of my work. So what if it had taken me four hours? The next time it would only take two.

I wiped the sweat from my brow with the back of one arm and envisioned something different awaiting my many new and prospective customers. Like a pint-sized chalkboard outside the front door, listing the daily specials or just welcoming folks inside, and a big vase of my aunts' wildflowers with their load-lightening scent charming guests. I could line the outside decks and railings in twinkle lights like Sandy had done at his Seaside Sweet Shack, so people would see my café from the beach. My cliff-top location would make it impossible to miss after dark. A bevvy of new ideas danced through my mind, buoyed by hope.

Maybe it was time for that grand opening after all.

I put my tools away and headed onto the beach to watch the sunset across the island. Sunrises over the Atlantic were magnificent, but there was something to be said for the arrival of twilight. Street lamps and house lights snapped on, illuminating my hometown. The first smattering of stars peeked their faces into view, and soon our local herd of wild Colonial Spanish mustangs would wander out for their evening run through the surf.

I had always loved the horses. I shuffled along the darkening beach, through thick grasses and around tiny inlets, until I found the perfect spot to wait for a glimpse of the mustangs. I kicked off my shoes and climbed onto a giant hunk of driftwood.

Our town wasn't the only one in the string of narrow North Carolina islands to have wild horses, but ours were indisputably the best because they were truly free. Charm wasn't overrun with big-money companies driving air-conditioned caravans of tourists onto the beaches for an intrusive look at the horses' lives. The people in Charm left our horses alone, aside from a handful of scientists who observed from a cautious distance and reported their findings for education. For most Charmers, the horses were just another component of our town's robust wildlife, not a spectacle to be exploited.

I, on the other hand, was obsessed. Always had been. And I didn't care if I was usually alone in the fixation. I'd spent years of my adolescence seated among the dunes, waiting for the mustangs to appear. Once I'd learned their patterns, I'd returned every night and waited for them to arrive. I'd bided my time, moved one step closer each night, using a heavy chunk of driftwood as my seat and placeholder, until eventually the horses became comfortable enough to ignore me at about thirty yards. I hadn't expected more, and I'd stopped creeping closer at that point. To my sheer delight, they had started moving closer to me, freely using the space all around me so long as I stayed still and quiet. We'd had a companionable relationship until I left for culinary school.

Now I wasn't even sure where to look for them. I

hugged my knees to my chest and rested my chin on them. The gentle hush of the sea and the dimming light coaxed piles of painful emotion to the surface, and heartbreak crawled all over me.

This was how I'd met Wyatt, my ex-boyfriend. He was a college student and aspiring cowboy who'd come to Charm to study the horses, heal from a recent bronco-riding injury, and save money for his next rodeo. I'd left town with him three months later.

Stupid.

There was no way to know if Detective Hays had meant anything by his rodeo comment, but it had felt pointed and painful at the time. Most of my thoughts having to do with Wyatt still were. I'd loved him with every ounce of my soul and every fiber of my being. It had been the heart-crushing brand of first love that some people never got over. Some days I had literally ached from it.

I liked to tell people that I'd left Charm for college, but the truth was I'd left for Wyatt. I'd studied in Kentucky instead of New York for him, staying away from Charm much longer than I'd ever intended, chasing my cowboy across the country. I'd remained by his side until the very end, when a devastating injury and a stint in traction removed him from the show, possibly forever.

I'd given up everything to follow Wyatt's dreams, but he couldn't ride, and I only had one year of culinary school left, so I'd asked him to follow me back to Kentucky while he healed.

He said no.

I blinked against the waning sun as a predictable round of tears fell.

In the distance, a line of mustangs filed cautiously onto the sand and watched me cry.

CHAPTER
SEVEN

I woke with a punch of adrenaline the next morning. Coming back to Charm was supposed to be my new start, a chance to follow *my* dreams, live *my* life. And I was going to do it. I was going to make my business a success, fix up the incredible house I had the unbelievable fortune to own, and prove to this town and Detective Hays that I wasn't a killer.

At six o'clock, I cocooned myself in a blanket and carried my laptop out to the deck to watch the sunrise. By eight, I'd finished a kettle's worth of tea and bookmarked a dozen websites with tips for inexpensive but clever ideas to make my grand opening a success. I also bought a book on public relations. Given the recent murder and poisoning insinuations thrown my way, I figured it couldn't hurt to memorize and live by it.

First order of business: win back the affection of residents of my sweet town. If the year-rounders loved Sun, Sand, and Tea, they'd eat here *and* spread the word about my café when tourists asked for recommendations for a good glass of sweet tea or a place for lunch. According to my research, word of mouth was the cheapest and most effective marketing tool, so I needed to get the local tongues wagging—in a good way.

My printer rocked to life in the next room, and I ran to evaluate my efforts. I'd mocked up five-by-seven flyers to announce my big party. The images fit side by side, two per page, saving me money, ink, and paper, plus they were the perfect size for customers to put up on their refrigerators at home. I made a mental note to order cheap magnets with my logo and contact information. I could offer carry-out for people who wanted to call and order in advance.

I snagged the next paper coughed out by the aged machine and lifted it into the air. Tiny yellow suns created the perfect border to frame my announcement. A cartoon glass of sweet tea sat in a little hill of clip-art sand beside the text:

You're invited to the Grand Opening
of
Sun, Sand, and Tea!
Sample the selection! Enjoy the view!

"Perfect!"

I cut the papers down the middle, into two thick stacks of half-sheet flyers, then headed for the door. If my efforts paid off, I'd be making mortgage payments in no time.

I bounced down the front steps and across the

soft grass to the old carriage house, a storage space that most folks would use as a garage. My wagon was parked in the center, handle up, ready to roll. "Rise and shine," I told the wagon. "We've got work to do, baby."

Once I got my life together, I would need a vehicle. A bike like my great aunts rode was all I needed for summer travel in Charm, and a golf cart would be perfect for winter. I couldn't be expected to walk my supplies home in a wagon when it was thirty degrees outside.

Getting a car wasn't even an option. Cars were too expensive, from the initial cost to the insurance and upkeep. *Forget it.* I'd never needed a car before, and I doubted that I ever would. I'd walked everywhere on campus while I was away at school and rode in Wyatt's truck from rodeo to rodeo. I'd never gotten my driver's license either, though I'd acquired a learner's permit in a few different states in case I needed to drive Wyatt to the hospital after his shows. We'd never stayed anywhere long enough to justify the time and effort to get an actual license.

Besides, a bicycle or golf cart would let me enjoy my beautiful town far better than any car.

The sunshine and ocean breeze worked in tandem to lure me back to the beach as I headed toward town along the boardwalk. A family with brightly colored blankets, bags, and buckets had claimed a spot near the water, a little girl sitting atop her dad's shoulders, controlling the string of a frog kite soaring proudly in the cloudless blue sky. The mom patted sand cakes with a shirtless toddler in a red sun hat. They were making memories that would last a lifetime. That was what I wanted to do with my café: I wanted people to come and make memories. I needed to think more carefully about how I could do that—I'd realized this morning that I hadn't given any thought to a business plan before opening my doors, naively running on the idea that *if you build it, they will come*. And some did, but not enough of them, and maybe the setback I was experiencing now could actually help me do a better job in the long run than I would have without it.

I stepped onto Main Street with purpose. This time, I'd paired my Sun, Sand, and Tea shirt with a long gauzy skirt and flip-flops. I'd painstakingly piled all fifty pounds of my dark curls into a whimsical and effortless-looking bun, then secured it with a tray of bobby pins and hair-sprayed the creation to within an inch of its life. All in the name of looking deceitfully carefree.

First stop: the community bulletin board on the square. I pinned one of my flyers to each corner, then walked methodically up and down the grid of business streets at the center of town, leaving copies in windows and near cash registers when possible. If anyone was brave enough to make eye contact, I handed them a copy directly and invited them personally to attend. If that didn't scare them off, I asked whether they knew anything about Mr. Paine. A teen couple in beach gear said I should ask the gossip blogger "because that dude knows everything." Unfortunately, neither kid knew who ran the blog.

A man reading the paper said Paine was a pain, which I already knew, and a lady wearing yoga gear and Birkenstocks told me his death was probably karma, then offered to clear my aura.

Charm had either gotten stranger while I was away, or I'd simply never paid enough attention before.

About thirty minutes later, a suspicious number folks started avoiding my eyes and staring down at their cell phones. The town blogger must've gotten wind I was out harassing the people again and updated his or her post. I kept my chin up and my smile on as I entered Molly's Market for my grand opening décor needs.

"Hey, Everly," Mr. Waters called from the register. Fifty years of chain smoking had whittled his voice into a windy rasp.

"Hello." I stopped at the counter with a flyer. "It's so good to see you. How's Molly?" Mr. Waters had named the store after his daughter, my former babysitter.

"She's good. Four kids now." He pulled a framed family photo from behind him.

"Nice. What a beautiful family!" I pushed away any thoughts of Wyatt and the adorable kids we would have made together.

"What can I do for you today?" he asked.

"A couple of things, actually." I showed him a flyer. "I'm hosting a grand opening and need to pick up a few things."

He put on his glasses and smiled at my handiwork. "Will you be at the street party this weekend?"

I'd nearly forgotten about the annual street party. It was Charm's last quiet hurrah before tourists made their way across the bridge for the summer. We didn't get nearly as much traffic as other nearby favorites like Corolla and Nags Head, but there were enough rental homes in town to change Charm's quaint dynamic from May through September.

In a way, the street fair also kicked off the money-making months for many hometown businesses. Mr. Paine had hated the influx of tourists, but for many people, the money they made each summer was enough to keep their lives afloat the rest of the year, and everything else was just a bonus.

I could only imagine.

"I wouldn't miss it. Do you mind if I leave a couple extra flyers on the counter?"

He took a generous stack and winked. "Absolutely not, and you can count on the missus and me to be at your party. Now, what else can I do for you?"

I checked for listening ears, leaning against the counter. "Do you know if Mr. Paine had anything unusual going on recently? Like an abnormally big fight with someone?"

Or an ongoing beef that could've made the other party homicidal from sheer frustration?

Mr. Waters rubbed his chin. "Not that I've heard, and I hear a lot. Only market in town and all."

That was exactly why I'd asked. "Okay," I said,

"How about his ex-wife, Lucinda? Can you tell me anything about her?"

"I didn't know Lucinda well, but I remember her. She always seemed a little too fancy for Charm, so I wasn't shocked when she left Benedict. He was Charm through and through."

"Were they getting along lately?"

Mr. Waters rubbed his eyes beneath his glasses. "I suppose. They've been divorced a few years now. Not much to argue about anymore. What makes you ask?"

I gave him a sad smile. "I'm just trying to figure out who could've hurt him that night. The ex-wife is probably a stretch, but if they were still in touch, she might know if there was something big going on with him."

He smiled brightly, apparently pleased with my quest. "I've always liked a go-getter. Tell you what, I'll keep my ears open and let you know if I hear anything."

"Deal." If only everyone in town were so quick to believe I was innocent and offer their help.

I filled my wagon with plates, cups, and bowls that looked fancier than they were, then went to get some toothpicks for hors d'oeuvres and sandwiches. I found some foam boards for displaying photos and added them to my growing pile.

"What's this?" A thick Russian accent turned me on my heels.

"Hana!" I crushed her in my arms.

We rocked side to side in our embrace, stiff-legged and jubilant, like a pair of eighth graders during their first slow dance.

She stepped away first, eyeballing my wagon. "What's this?" she repeated, stealing a flyer from the stack I was carrying. "You're going to have a party without me?"

"Of course not!" I laughed. "I planned to come see you tomorrow and invite you myself."

Hana was closer to my age than my great aunts, but the three of them ran in the same circles. Holistic, tree-hugging, naturalist circles. Today, she wore a silk headband with a Patsy Cline T-shirt and cutoff jeans. Her petite build and girlish figure was deceiving. I'd seen her carry feed sacks I wouldn't have been able to budge with a dolly.

"What do you need?" she asked.

"I don't know yet. I'm going to put together the menu tonight, then come to your place with a list of ingredients. Is that okay?"

"Mm-hmm." She tugged the ends of her dark pixie cut. I could practically see the delight in her eyes at the idea of getting to provide fresh goodies for the party. She looked me up and down. "So, what's new with you? Besides, you know…" She wiggled her phone, having clearly gotten all the *Town Charmer* details about my poisonous ways.

"Oh, not much, just trying to solve a murder and launch an iced tea shop."

She nodded, as if this was a normal set of goals.

"Did you know Mr. Paine?" I asked.

"Yes. He didn't like me selling produce from my home. He said to go to the farmers' market. I said I *am* a farmers' market. End of story."

I gave her a sympathetic smile before hugging her goodbye and promised to get my produce order to her as soon as I could. A few minutes later, my wagon was four shopping bags heavier and my wallet was sixty-three dollars lighter, but I had gobs of disposable cups and plates for my party, and I'd chosen the beachiest of decorations to up my shop's already great look—shells, starfish, sand dollars, and buckets. It would be a party no Charmer would soon forget.

Maggie, the scruffy white cat, tailed me back down Middletown to the boardwalk, trotting stealthily alongside me in the tall grasses.

"I can see you," I said, turning to look at her. "It's okay to like me. I'm a nice lady."

Maggie froze.

I smiled. "You're white, and you're trying to hide in the very green grass. Come on out here," I urged.

She didn't budge a muscle.

I squatted and clucked my tongue, wiggling my fingers as if I had something in my hand she might want to see.

She didn't.

"Fine." I dropped my hand and straightened to my feet. I'd wear her down eventually. She was already interested, so I had that going for me.

Amelia was peering into one of her little libraries when I lifted my eyes back to the boardwalk. She brushed sand from the top and inside shelves, then lifted books from a pile stacked on the ground into the tiny structure. When she glanced up at me, I was struck by the sadness in her eyes. She looked as if someone had stolen her puppy.

"Hey." I let my wagon roll to a stop. "What's the matter?"

"Oh, you know. Everything." She wound a length of stick-straight hair behind one ear. The rest hung loose in a chin-length bob. "How much time do you have?"

I smiled. "Are you going my way? Maybe I can keep you company."

"That sounds really nice." She stared along the boardwalk toward my home and her next Little Library. "My ex-husband is a total creep, and he lives in town, and he remarried last weekend. They're home from their honeymoon now. You know where they went? Hawaii. You know where he took me? The B&B on Bay Street."

"You were eighteen," I said, rubbing her back as we began to walk. "Do you still love him?" I couldn't even think of Amelia's ex-husband's name. They'd had a whirlwind romance our senior year, then married that summer. I remembered a bonfire on the beach and some underage drinking, but that was all. I was home before curfew, playing cards with Aunt Fran until dawn, marveling over how two people my age had agreed to such a commitment when I'd had trouble committing to a summer lifeguarding job.

"I don't love him anymore," Amelia said. "The divorce is just a point of failure that I'll always have to live with. Like a black mark on my record or something. Being young and stupid is awful. His new wife will always think of me as the loser who couldn't keep him."

"You don't want him."

"Not the point!" she growled.

I pulled my hand back so I wouldn't lose it. "Sorry."

"It's fine. I think I'm just extra irritable because someone keeps filling all my Little Libraries with sand at night. People open the doors to see what's available and get five gallons of sand dumped all over them. It's wrecking some of the books. Makes me so mad."

I had no idea who'd want to vandalize a place to get free books, but her story about her ex-husband reminded me of my quest. "Did you know Mr. Paine's ex-wife?"

Amelia raised her brow. Her pale blond hair nearly matched her fair skin. "No. Why? You think she's doing this to my books?"

"What?" I looked at her sand-dusted sundress. "No! Not at all. I spoke with Sam Smart yesterday about Mr. Paine, and Sam said Mr. Paine's ex-wife was a real pill. That maybe she had reason to hurt him, or she might be able to tell us who did."

"Oh." Amelia's narrow lips pulled low into a frown. "Well, have you talked to her?"

"Not yet. I don't know her or where she lives. I still need to look her up. Sam said she has a jewelry store in Duck."

Amelia's downturned mouth flipped up. "I love Duck. We should take a road trip as soon as possible. We can use my car."

I smiled. "Yeah? How about tomorrow? We can leave early and spend the day."

"And shop?" She clutched her hands to her chest.

"Sure."

"Yes, please!"

I wasn't sure I had the funds for shopping, but I definitely wanted to take a girlfriends' road trip and question my newest lead in Mr. Paine's murder investigation.

Amelia spun, skirt flying out around her, one palm raised for a high five. "That's a date."

We clapped hands, then parted ways at the next Little Library. I went home to work up a menu for my party and list of questions for Paine's ex-wife. All the good questions had to come first, in case she wasn't cooperative and decided to throw me out.

Just before sunset, I changed into the outfit I'd worn to paint the inside of my house and stuffed my messy bun into a ball cap. I needed to paint my newly repaired steps, but success was in the timing: start the job too early, and be burnt to a crisp, wait too long and ten thousand nighttime bugs would be dried to the paint before dawn.

I moved the brush expertly along the new handrail, rehearsing my questions for the ex-Mrs. Paine and rethinking my desserts for the party. An easy whistle lifted from my lips as I worked. For the first time in a long time, I had abundant purpose and renewed hope as a restaurateur.

Even if local kids were daring one another to try my samples.

CHAPTER
EIGHT

Amelia was on my doorstep at 8:00 a.m. with a cheery smile and two iced coffees. "Ready?" She nearly vibrated with enthusiasm as she passed me a cup.

"Thanks."

The scruffy white cat watched us from the edge of my wide-planked porch.

"Hi, Maggie," I said to the cat. "Would you like some milk before I go?"

She arched her back and darted away with a loud hiss and complaint.

"That's my cat," I told Amelia.

She laughed. "She seems lovely."

I'd put food out for her last night after she'd followed me along the boardwalk. The bowl was empty in the morning, so it was official: I'd claimed her. She just hadn't reciprocated.

I stared at the steps and willed my feet to move, but second thoughts had been my morning companion. I knocked wild curls away from my face and squinted indecisively against the balmy ocean wind.

Amelia's smile fell. "What's wrong?"

"I'm about to drive to another town to badger a grieving woman. Is this such a great idea? Maybe we shouldn't go."

"No," she dragged the word out for several syllables, then hooked one hand under my elbow and hauled me toward her car. "*I'm* driving. *You're* in pursuit of justice."

I laughed. "My mistake." I stopped short of opening the car door, finally noticing Amelia's adorable ensemble. "You look amazing." I plucked the flowy fabric of my peasant top away from my midsection. "I look like I'm going to hunt seashells."

Amelia's black capris and white sleeveless blouse were classic and sophisticated. She'd tucked her sleek blond hair beneath a silk polka-dotted scarf and hung a huge leather hobo bag from her shoulder; I'd dressed in worn cutoffs and a shapeless top with flip-flops. Her pumps matched her bag, lips, and nails; my lips and nails were the color God made them, and my bag was a wallet with a leather strap that hung from my wrist. "I should change," I said, stepping back toward the house.

Amelia wrenched the passenger door open and nearly shoved me inside. "If I could pull off youthful and sporty, believe me, I would. My style has been stuck somewhere between *I Love Lucy* and librarian-chic since middle school. I finally quit fighting it."

I climbed into the passenger side of Amelia's red convertible, wrangling my untameable locks into a ponytail before buckling my seat belt—otherwise my hair would've become the size of an orbiting satellite before the first stoplight. "I didn't know you had a convertible."

Amelia eased the sporty little car onto the road and slowly picked up speed until the tails of her silk scarf whipped behind her like a banner. "I bought it last month on a whim. I thought it'd make me feel like a movie star."

"Does it?"

She pushed large, white-framed sunglasses over her bright blue eyes. "Sometimes."

"I'm going to buy a golf cart," I told her. "Hopefully it won't make me feel like a retired dentist."

I stuck my hand into the whipping wind, enjoying the beat of it against my palm and inhaling that indescribable island scent. Salt and sand. Sun and seagrass. "Thanks for doing this with me."

"Glad to," she said. "I haven't made spontaneous plans like this in a long time."

I bit my tongue against the oxymoron of spontaneous plans. Amelia had always loved lists and order. I'd bucked the concepts for nearly three decades, but lately I was seeing the benefits of having some kind of life plan.

"I found the perfect place for lunch," Amelia said, "and there's an iced tea shop we should probably check out."

"Duck has an iced tea shop?" That was bad news. Sun, Sand, and Tea was supposed to be one of a kind. "I didn't know that. Maybe it's just a café that happens to serve sweet tea."

"It's not in Duck," Amelia corrected. "Kitty Hawk."

"Kitty Hawk!" I squawked. That was worse. Kitty Hawk was ten miles closer. "And you want to go there?" Personally, I kind of wanted to go home and breathe into a paper bag. I had no idea there was another iced tea shop so close to home.

"It's good research," she said. "You should know your competition and how they compare."

I let that thought settle in. "Do you know anything about market analysis?" I'd just read about the concept online yesterday.

"I have a business degree." She smiled. "It was a condition of my parents cosigning my first business loan. They wanted to be sure I knew what I was getting into. I paid them back in a hurry, but the student loans are another story. I'll probably die with those. What about you? Is culinary school expensive?"

"I had a scholarship." I rubbed my forehead a little too roughly, annoyed at the reminder of another thing I'd thrown away to follow my heart. The logical move would have been to finish school no matter what, but the sting of Wyatt's rejection had sent me running home to lick my wounds. Now that I was here, I couldn't imagine leaving.

"Hey." Amelia batted at my shoulder as we slowed for a stop sign. "Whatever happened to that cowboy?

Remember him? The two of you practically lived on the beach the summer he was here."

Amelia glanced over and the look on my face must've said what I couldn't.

"Oh." She honked and waved at a carload of men with surfboards tied to the roof. "Changing the subject, then. What's the new detective like? Besides tall, dark, and mysterious. And handsome. Those dimples." She sagged into a dreamy sigh.

I pulled my lips to one side, unwilling to respond. I'd already given Grady Hays more of my thoughts than I should have. And I refused to think about the dimples. They distracted me from my mission.

"Is he nice?" she asked. "No one seems to know, but you've been seen talking with him a *lot*."

"That's because he thinks I'm a murderess," I grumped. "A dumb one too. Why would I kill someone with my tea? Could I pick a more obvious murder weapon?" It made me mad every time I thought about it. I couldn't decide what was more offensive—the fact that he thought I would kill an old man, or that he thought I was stupid.

"Who knows why people do the things they do?" She shrugged. "Besides, he doesn't know you very well yet. For all he knows, you could be crazy."

I was getting there.

"His eyes are pretty," Amelia went on. "Pale gray, like the moon on the sea."

Along with being super smart, Amelia was dramatic. Four years of high school theater club had clearly left their mark. I shut my eyes to keep them from rolling, but now I was thinking about the infuriating detective again.

"He told me to stay out of his investigation. Can you believe that? He called it *his* investigation. Who's more motivated to find the killer than me? It's not like I'm showing up at his office in a trench coat and Columbo hat. I'm doing my own thing and reporting back. Completely out of his way."

I stretched my neck and shook my hands out at the wrist, trying to release the sudden knots of tension that had appeared. I didn't like thinking of Detective Hays's unfair assumptions or twenty-five to life, so I changed the subject.

"I did a little research on Mr. Paine's ex-wife last night. Lucinda Paine kept her married name, and she seems like a sweet old lady. Our trip is probably going to be a bust. Aside from the shopping, of course."

"Shopping is never a bust. Plus she'll be a wealth of knowledge. They were together for fifteen years, according to my dad. He didn't know much about her when I asked, but then again, he avoided Mr. Paine like the plague. Dad hates when people harsh his mellow. He might have had two knee replacements, but he's still a surfer at heart."

I'd always liked Amelia's dad, who was a lifetime Charm resident. "Well, according to the handful of local news articles I could dig up, Lucinda opened her jewelry shop after the divorce. She told the reporter covering her grand opening that she'd always dreamed of owning her own business, and that she'd grown up making things with sea glass, so she started designing earrings and the whole thing took off from there. Apparently, it's been fast-growing, because she's moved her store twice in seven years, both times to a larger venue."

"Consider me jealous," Amelia said. "I couldn't afford a bigger space, even if I needed one. I actually met Mr. Paine a couple years ago while I was securing permits for renovations to Charming Reads. I turned a storage closet into an alcove to add more retail space. He was so fussy, I'm shocked he was ever married."

"Lucinda's name showed up in the Duck *Daily Chronicle* a couple times, without a photo. A charity chili cook-off at her church and some other nice old lady things. Makes me wonder what Sam had against her. Mr. Waters said she was fancy, but that's hardly a reason for Sam to think she might've hurt her husband."

"Sam's pretty uptight," Amelia said. "He probably has something against all of us."

"Maybe," I agreed.

"Only one way to find out about the ex, though." Amelia hooked the next left past a carved wooden sign welcoming us to Duck. "Let's start with her and get it over with. Then we can spend the rest of the day outlet shopping in Nags Head."

"Deal." I smiled. "Thanks again for this."

Amelia coasted into a long, narrow parking lot lined with boutiques. "What are friends for?" She parked in the far corner, under the shade of a massive kite-shop sign. "There. Now we won't burn our bottoms on the upholstery when we come back."

Lucinda's shop was across the way. Ocean Dreams had a wooden mermaid suspended in the front window, surrounded by bits of floating sea glass. If I had to guess, I'd say there was some clear fishing line involved in the effect, but we were too far away to tell.

I stepped out of the car as Amelia swung her feet out the driver's side door and took her shoes off one-by-one, shaking them upside-down. "I can never get all the sand out. That little library bandit has had me coated in it for a week. It's like high school all over again, except I didn't used to mind the sand."

"Yeah." I sighed. "That was before we became the ones who have to clean it up." I watched as she dusted the bottoms of her feet with baby powder, then knocked the sand off with an easy swipe of her palm. A handy beach trick. I smiled, glad to spend the day with someone who knew it. "Have you had any luck figuring out who's harassing you?"

"No." She slipped her pumps back on and stood. "It could be anyone. Dad could've ticked someone off while he was watching the store for me, or maybe I did and didn't know it. Sometimes I wonder if my ex would do something so juvenile, or his new wife. Then I remember they're happy and don't think about me at all."

I twisted my mouth in a sympathetic look. "No enemies? Archrivals? Personal nemesis?"

She shook her head sadly. "Usually people love me. I run the only bookstore in town. I have an open-mic night for would-be poets and authors, story time for children, general interest speakers for adults, and the Sassy Sixties Book Club meets at my shop every Tuesday. The ladies always bring snacks. I make coffee. Dad covers the register, and he even wears aftershave. Everything was great until this started. Now I wake up in stress hives."

"I'm so sorry," I told her.

She started across the parking lot, and I followed.

"I can't understand who'd want to bully me like this. It's making me crazy. I'm losing sleep over it, and I think I lost a little extra hair in the shower this morning."

"Yikes." My heart ached for her. "I had no idea the sand bandit was getting to you like this. I can see why it would, I just didn't know."

She puffed air into long, side-swept bangs, setting them aflutter. "I'm trying to play it cool, but truthfully, I want to cry every time I think about it. The police have put the situation at the bottom of their priority list, and I can only be in one place at a time, but I have four libraries to keep an eye on, plus the store." She tipped her head back and groaned.

"Tell you what," I said. "I'll help. We can divide and conquer. I'll take the two Little Libraries on the boardwalk as soon as I get through my grand opening party. With two of us on the job, we'll catch whoever is doing this in no time."

Amelia stopped outside the door to Ocean Dreams.

"You don't have to do that. I didn't mean to make you feel like it was your problem. You've already got a mess of your own to sort out."

I wrapped an arm around her shoulders and dug up my best mobster impression. "Hey. If you've got a problem, then I've got a problem."

She opened the glass door with a wide smile. "Fine. I accept."

I smiled back. I was officially assisting in two local crime investigations. Detective Hays would hate it.

Now, to confront Lucinda Paine.

A blast of cold air from the vent above the door shot goose bumps down my spine. I tried not to think of it as an omen.

The store's interior was pale blue, lined in silver shelves and glass cases. I dragged a fingertip across a display filled with jewelry. Amelia stopped at a shelf full of seashell and sand sculptures. Everything was very pretty and smelled like patchouli.

"Welcome to Ocean Dreams," a charming female voice called.

"Hello," Amelia answered.

I turned my eyes from a gorgeous sea-glass necklace to the sexagenarian woman in a black pantsuit greeting my friend.

"Looking for anything in particular?" the woman asked. *Lucinda* was written on her name tag. "A gift, perhaps?"

"Just shopping," Amelia said. "We're having a girls' day out."

"Oh? Where are you from?"

I zipped over to Amelia's side. "Charm," I answered with a smile. "Do you know it?"

The woman's smile drooped. "Quite well. Excuse me." She drifted away without further discussion, off to help a man inspecting a delicate-looking glass figurine. Her white hair was gracefully looped into a chignon, and her gait screamed poise and self-importance. I struggled to reconcile the image before me with her goody-two-shoes portrayal in the local paper. I supposed someone could be a bit of a snob and still believe in volunteerism and community outreach.

I grabbed a sandcastle paperweight and went after her. "How much is this?" I interrupted her chastising the man for handling the figurine.

She frowned at my rudeness, and the man took the opportunity to escape her scolding.

"Sorry," I said. "I thought you were finished."

Lucinda crossed her arms. "That sandcastle was handmade. I collected the materials from the beach myself, then sculpted them into what you see there. An authentic product of this island, and I'm asking one hundred seventy for it."

"Dollars?" I asked, mystified. "You just told me you made it from our sand. There's an infinity of that right outside the door."

She narrowed her eyes. "Why are you really here?"

"What?"

"Do I look like I was born yesterday?" She stomped back toward the counter, and I followed with Amelia on my heels. Lucinda stopped beneath a massive sea-glass mosaic on the back wall and turned to us. "You're from Charm, so you know about what happened to my ex-husband. Is that why you're here? You're what? Reporters?" She looked us up and down. "You don't look like cops. Are you the ones who write that blog Benedict was so up in arms about?"

"Of course not," I protested. "Let me explain."

She parked her hands on her hips and tapped her foot. "I ought to call the police. This is harassment."

I pulled my palms up and took a step back. "We knew your ex-husband, and we're very sorry about what happened. That's all."

Lucinda gave us another appraising stare. "How did you know him?"

I forced a tight smile, prepared to skirt over the details about how Mr. Paine hated me for going against his wishes in opening Sun, Sand, and Tea. "We own shops in Charm, and we got to know him through his position on the council. We really are sorry about your loss."

Her shoulders relaxed and the anger drained from her face. "Benedict was a good man," she said, a tremor in her voice. "He was what a man should be. Confident. Steadfast." She pressed her lips into a tight line and her cheeks flushed. "I loved him so much."

Amelia glanced my way.

I stood helpless and frozen as she swiped falling tears off her wrinkled cheeks. They were divorced, but she still loved him.

"Do you have any idea who might've wanted to hurt him?" I asked, hoping the question sounded less awful to her ears than mine. I'd come all this way for the answer, I had to know.

"No." She patted her cheeks and took a steadying breath. "Benedict was opinionated and he wasn't shy about it, but people respected him. Except that lunatic of an iced tea-maker. She's the one who killed him."

I gasped. My heart jumped into third gear, and I checked my proximity to the nearest exit. Amelia curled a hand over her lips and her cheeks lifted in a smile.

Lucinda lifted her eyebrows. "What? Hadn't you heard who was responsible?"

"Um." I chewed my lip, unsure how to proceed. "People are saying the tea-maker has an alibi. Maybe Mr. Paine had been arguing with someone else lately. Do you know if there was anything unusual going on in his life?"

She seemed to consider the question. "Benedict's entire life was unusual. He was a busy man in love with an island." She gave a soft laugh. "He cared about everything that went on there, and he strived to preserve the place he'd fallen in love with. I always said that place would be the death of him. I'd just assumed it would be figurative."

"Was he butting heads with anyone in particular lately?" I prodded.

"He worked on the town council. He was continuously at odds with someone. Trying to keep things in Charm the way he liked was a real drain. Real estate developers hated him. Homeowners weren't much better. Everyone wants to add a business to their private residence these days. It was a pet peeve of Benny's. And anyone trying to open a franchise…" She did a dramatic head roll. "Forget about it."

I chewed my lip, wishing I wasn't so out of the loop on local drama, and trying to get over anyone calling Mr. Paine *Benny*. "Did you say the gossip blogger had him worked up? Why?"

"You're certainly asking a lot of questions for someone who claims not to be a reporter." Lucinda narrowed her eyes at me. "What did you say your name was?"

The room seemed to grow smaller under her heavy gaze. "I'm…" I began, then trailed off.

I looked to Amelia for help. Giving out our names seemed stupid. If I got reported for bothering her, Detective Hays was sure to lecture me again.

Amelia fluttered her eyelids dramatically, then stumbled against my side, the back of one hand pressed to her forehead like a fainting Southern belle. "Goodness, I feel ill. Is it hot in here? I'm afraid I've gone woozy."

I gripped the display case to steady myself under her weight. "Oh dear." I shot Lucinda an apologetic look. "I'd better get her something to drink and find her a cool place to rest. This happens to her sometimes."

"Ohhh," Amelia moaned. "Do you see the spots?"

I darted for the door while Amelia clung to my side and we staggered down the street as fast as I could move while supporting her weight. We didn't stop until I smelled waffle fries. "Here." I pulled her into a shop with shave-ice posters on the window. The smells of hot fudge and fruit smoothies wafted over me, and my mouth watered.

Amelia righted herself with a smile. "I have to tell you, those years of theater have paid off tenfold since becoming an adult." She got in line and ordered a frozen lemonade.

I bought a bottle of water and a small sweet tea. The first was to quench my thirst. The second was reconnaissance. Amelia was right—I might as well try all the sweet tea I came across so I knew what else was out there.

The waitress typed our order into a tablet. "Those will be ready for you at the end of the counter."

I connected to the free Wi-Fi while we waited. "Lucinda asked if we were from the blog that Mr. Paine was so worked up about. She had to mean the Charm gossip blog, right? Maybe he uncovered the identity of the person stirring up trouble, and the blogger wanted to silence him. I should probably also see if someone from the town council will talk to me about whatever Mr. Paine had been working on for them. Maybe one of those pesky entrepreneurs did him in."

"It's worth a try," Amelia said, "but I like the blog, and it isn't always making trouble. The blogger's identity is a secret, which irritates some people, that's all. I go on there once in a while to check the local calendar and read funny recaps of events I attend. I've never been offended by what I've seen, though I'm admittedly not a regular reader. You should check it out. See what you think. The articles are a little sensationalized, and the photos are never flattering, but the information is rarely wrong."

"I'm going there now." I typed the URL into the web browser on my phone. The page loaded at a snail's pace. There was a scrolling weather report, a sidebar with water conditions, a tide schedule, coupons for local businesses.

I sucked in air as my senior high school photo appeared beside a shot of the outside of Sun, Sand, and Tea. "That's me!"

"Yeah," Amelia said. "You've been a hot topic for a while now, as I'm sure you've noticed."

"Good grief." I tucked that in my mental files for later. "If Lucinda reads today's post, she'll know I'm the lunatic iced tea-maker."

Amelia giggled. "That was funny."

I scrolled past the photos, afraid to read the latest article, written yesterday morning.

"What does it say?" she asked, peeping over my shoulder.

"Sun, Sand, and Tea: It's to Die For." I tried not to have a stroke. "I can't read it." I shoved the phone into Amelia's hand. "Detective Hays already made it sound as if Mr. Paine died drinking my tea. I won't survive another hit, especially not like this. Wide-scale. And memorialized forever on the internet." I covered my face with both hands. "Read it."

"'Charm, North Carolina, is known for many

things,'" Amelia began. "'Wild horses, amazing sunrises, and a rich and storied history, to name a few. The natural treasures, from our shores and bays to our preserves and people, are unrivaled anywhere in the world, and believe me, I've been everywhere. Our humble town is just far enough off the beaten path to be a true hideaway and close enough to the mainland bridge for folks to return year after year. And what says Southern summer days louder than a clean, sandy beach and a jar of good old-fashioned sweet tea?'"

I lowered one hand. "This doesn't sound like a slander piece."

"Shh." Amelia waved her fingers at me. "'A few things happened last winter that got our little town excited for spring. One was the rousing tour of birders, but that's an article for another time. Second was the return of our own Miss Everly Swan. For those of you who are unfamiliar, the Swan family has been a part of our town since the land was settled in 1702. Swan women are a staple in our society, and when we discovered her intentions to open an iced tea shop this spring, we were thrilled. Needless to say, it was a long winter.'"

My eyes stung with relief, shock, and pride.

Amelia went on. "'Everly's Sun, Sand, and Tea is everything we'd hoped it would be. As it should be. Everly was trained at the skirt-tails of the very best. Her grandmother, Hazel Grace Swan, knew how to make simple things magical, and she has undeniably passed that gift to her granddaughter.'"

"Grandmama," I whispered.

"That's it for today. A nod to Grandma Swan and cheers to you." Amelia returned my phone, and I shoved it in my pocket. "See, no trouble brewing at all."

"Thank goodness." Especially for the absence of goofy charts and calls for commentary. Just something *nice*.

A college-aged woman in pigtails and short-shorts appeared at the counter. "Sweet tea, frozen lemonade, bottled water?"

"Thanks." We accepted the order, and headed for the door.

"I can't believe the blog mentioned my grandma," I said, nostalgia tickling my nose and making me sniffle.

Amelia held the door while I passed through, balancing my water and tea. "Everyone knew your grandma. We all know your great-aunts and we know you. Swans are like unspoken island royalty or something."

"Since when?" I hugged the bottled water to my ribs and popped the top off the tea for a sniff.

"Since always." Amelia raised her eyebrows. "Are you kidding?"

"No." I lifted the tea to my mouth without interest. I could tell by the smell and color that it was a powdered mix plus approximately ten pounds of cane sugar. "No one's ever said or done anything to make me believe they think our family is more than a little weird, definitely not special in any particular way. In fact, I always liked how everyone was treated the same in Charm."

"Hmm," Amelia pursed her lips. "Maybe you never noticed because you'd never been treated any differently before now." Amelia pumped her straw up and down in her drink. "This blog coverage will go a long way toward helping all this blow over, plus I saw you talking to people in town yesterday. They'll like that too. It was hard for them when you came home and kept to yourself for the first month or so. Confusing. Like, were you glad to be here, mad about being here? Leaving? Staying?"

I'd had no idea anyone cared. I was so wrapped up in trying to fill the hole left in my heart, buying my dream house and launching a new business. "Yeow." I smacked my lips. "Now, this is some *sweet* tea."

"Good?"

"Nope. This is definitely not my competition, but now I'm interested in visiting that specialty shop you mentioned. That could be fun."

"Perfect. It's on our way to the outlets."

I tossed the tea in the trash. Too much sugar made me break out, and frankly, I didn't need anything else to worry about.

Amelia wrapped her lips around the straw of her drink. "This is so good. What was wrong with your tea?"

"It was just sweet. No real flavor and no depth."

"Sounds like my ex."

I laughed as we rounded the corner back toward Amelia's car, gulping water between giggles. Maybe it wasn't such a bad thing that Wyatt had gotten away. Things would've been monumentally worse if I'd figured out where I stood with him *after* an engagement, or worse, a wedding.

I took another chug of water, washing the taste of sugar out of my mouth. My attention drifted back to Ocean Dreams. A yellow sign on the door read OUT TO LUNCH.

Strange. We had just come out of there.

Amelia shrieked and I followed her gaze to her pretty red convertible, whose windshield was spattered with white goop.

"Oh no!" She jogged toward her car. "What the heck do they feed the birds around here?"

I stopped at her side, about ten feet from the vehicle.

"Is that sun tan lotion?" she asked. The familiar scent of coconut and palm oil drifted on the breeze. Then I saw that someone had used the lotion to scrawl letters on the windshield of the car.

Stop snooping. Or else.

I pressed the cold water bottle against one temple. "Yeah, and I don't think that message is from the birds."

CHAPTER

NINE

The threat put a damper on our trip, so we called for a rain check on the shopping and rode home in silence. The coconut scent of *or else* wafted over me for the full twenty miles, despite a thorough scrubbing at the closest gas station and a drive-through car wash. The sunblock had slid off Amelia's windshield with ease, but it had seeped into my mind, and I doubted I would be able to wash it away anytime soon.

I had to tell Detective Hays about this, and he would hate it.

Amelia made the turn into Charm with care, her hands at ten and two, her eyes glued to the road as if she anticipated danger ahead.

"Can I make you some lunch?" I asked. "It's the least I can do. My snooping wrecked our day."

"You already paid for the car wash. Don't worry about me." She pried her weary gaze off the road and gave me a quick once over. "How are you doing?"

"Fine," I lied. I'd rationalized my way into

acceptance during our quiet drive. "It's not as if I was ever in danger," I said. "Whoever left that note knew where I was. They could've made a move to hurt me, but they didn't."

"I don't understand how anyone knew we were in Duck," she said, clearly as baffled as myself.

"Not just in Duck," I added. "Someone knew you'd parked in the lot outside Ocean Dreams."

Amelia chewed her bottom lip. She flicked her gaze in my direction before fixing it quickly back on the road. "Do you think Lucinda could have snuck out and left that message on my windshield while we were getting drinks?"

"I don't know." I'd considered that scenario when I first saw the writing on the glass, but it seemed impossible. Lucinda would've had to have been watching when we arrived, but she was nowhere near the front when we first walked inside.

Amelia frowned, then her eyes went wide. "What if someone followed us there from Charm?"

I pressed tired fingertips to throbbing temples. "I hope not." The last thing I needed was a killer following me everywhere I went to go with the rest of my bum luck. "Sam Smart was the one who'd pointed his finger at Lucinda, so he could have linked me to her or even to her store's parking lot, but I didn't tell him when I planned to talk to her. In fact, he was acting so weird that day, I barely got her name and location before he rushed me off."

"Did you tell anyone else about our trip?" she asked.

"Just my aunts. How about you?"

Amelia's cheeks darkened. "I might've told a few people we were going to the outlets today, but I never mentioned Duck, Lucinda, or her store. I swear."

"It's okay," I said, dropping my hands from my temples. "Going shopping shouldn't have to be a secret."

She looked my way again, sincere blue eyes drowning in apology. "I'm sorry you're going through this," she said.

"I'm sorry you got dragged into it this time," I answered.

Amelia gave a small smile. "I'm still really glad you're back."

"Me too."

Amelia snuck glances at me as we rolled slowly through town. "I can't believe no one saw anything. Everyone we asked about the vandalism looked at us like we were crazy. How did they all miss a person writing on my car with a bottle of sunscreen?"

"I don't know." I sighed. "Duck is pretty touristy. Chances are that everyone we talked to was from somewhere else. Distracted. Focused on their vacation and family. They probably wouldn't notice anything that didn't whack them on the head."

"I'm glad you thought ahead enough to take a couple of pictures with your phone. All I could think about was getting the sunscreen off my window."

I knew Detective Hays would want to see the note, but I couldn't bring myself to call and drag him out to Duck, so a picture seemed like a solid compromise.

The midday sun beat against my head, lifting a line of sweat on my brow. "I'm exhausted."

Amelia parked in the sand and grass lot beside my place. "So am I. It's the stress."

My café door was propped open. Laughter and Beach Boys music spilled through the screen. "What on earth?" I said, leaning over the dashboard for a better look.

"Looks like you're going to have to put a pin in that nap. You've got guests."

I squinted up the steps toward the buzzing of voices. My aunts had keys to the place, but they'd never used them. "If this is a break-in, the burglars are pretty obnoxious."

"Everly!" Aunt Fran appeared and picked her way over the sand, barefoot and slowly navigating the incline to my yard from the beach. "There you are."

A man in round glasses followed her, one hand at the small of her back.

"Here I am." I nearly fell over in shock. I hadn't seen either of my great-aunts with a man since I was a child and they were still married. Since then, both uncles had succumbed to separate unique and untimely demises.

Happily-ever-afters simply weren't in the cards for Swan women, it seemed. Sometimes the men died and the women lived long, lonely lives without them. Other times, the men died and the women followed soon after with a broken heart—like my mother. Either way, it stunk.

This guy had rolled the sleeves of his dress shirt to the elbows and the cuffs of his slacks were bunched above his knees. His suit jacket hung neatly over one crooked arm.

I dragged my gaze back to Aunt Fran. "What's going on?"

"This is Henry, a new friend of mine."

Ah, the Civil War general Aunt Clara had told me about.

Henry extended a hand to me. When I accepted it, he lifted my fingers to his lips and kissed them instead. Fran watched with obvious approval.

I took my hand back and pushed it into my pocket, certain I'd never get the feel of his mustache off my knuckles. "Nice to meet you, Henry. This is my friend Amelia. Aunt Fran, you know Amelia."

Fran marched to Amelia's side and squeezed her in a one-armed hug. "I certainly do. I attend her Sassy Sixties Book Club on Tuesdays. How was Duck? Did you have a nice time?" She frowned, then checked her watched. "Wait a minute. It's barely lunchtime. I didn't expect to hear from you until late tonight. What happened to shopping?"

Amelia made a deep, throaty noise. "Something crazy happened. You'll never believe it."

I lifted a finger, requesting a hold on that particular conversation, preferably until I was somewhere else. "Aunt Fran, you haven't told me what's happening up there." I pointed to my café. "Please tell me there aren't more people touring my home."

Aunt Fran shook her head. "Nothing like that. A

few folks at the town meeting seemed to be on the fence about your innocence in Mr. Paine's murder, so Clara and I are putting their minds at ease. Apparently there's a rumor saying you came back from college a little cuckoo." She circled a finger around her ear and crossed her eyes.

"I'm not sure that's a rumor," I said, rubbing my painfully tense neck and shoulders.

Aunt Fran snorted. "They think you set up your tea shop to exact revenge on the town in some sort of ill-conceived notion."

"Jeez."

Henry chuckled. "I guess you aren't very good at mass revenge. Only one victim."

I looked to Amelia for help. Was this supposed to be funny? "So, people are up there sampling my tea to see if it kills them?"

Fran waved a hand between us, unable to speak through a bout of giggles. She turned me around by my shoulders and steered me toward the steps.

"Hey." Something else registered in my cluttered mind. "What town meeting?" I craned my head for a look at Fran's red face. "Is that where everyone was while I was in town with my wagon trying to give away my samples?"

Amelia mounted the steps behind us. "There was a blog notice to meet outside the Nature Preservation Society yesterday."

My heart pumped erratically. Darn it, I had to start checking that blog. "Was the meeting about me?"

Fran squeezed my shoulder as we arrived outside the party. "I don't think so. I was a little late. I had to help Henry with his Civil War invitations, and Clara was here with her group from Kitty Hawk. We missed the beginning."

"I went," Amelia said reluctantly. Her voice was a shallow whisper. "I should've said something sooner, but it was so ridiculous."

"What did they say?" Panic rose in my chest and throat. Why did I feel like a mob was about to light torches and run me out of town?

"The meeting was about Mr. Paine," Amelia said. "They needed to pull together some details for a town-wide memorial. You were just a side topic. Some of the older folks believe that thing about it being bad luck for Swans to leave the island. That's why they wondered if you came back a little wackadoodle."

"The curse," Fran said.

My mouth fell open. *Again with the curse.*

I wiggled free of her grip, my frustration boiling to a head. I needed time to think about the threat on Amelia's windshield and to pull my thoughts together. More than that, I needed to make a good impression on the people in my café despite the fact that I was dangerously close to a nervous breakdown.

The café door sprang open, and Clara waved us inside. "Wonderful," she cooed. "You're here." The brim of her large white hat bounced gently with each step.

A dozen semifamiliar faces turned to stare as I entered. Everyone seemed a little overdressed for an iced tea shop: beach casual was the whole point, but I tried to just be happy they were willing to give me a shot.

I lifted my hand hip high and smiled. "Hello."

Aunt Clara ushered us to the counter. "When our usual customers stopped coming to Blessed Bee, I made a call or two," she said. "I wanted to be sure they weren't ill, that they didn't need anything. As it turned out, they simply had a few concerns about what you do here at Sun, Sand, and Tea."

I blinked through the sting of her words. "People are boycotting your store now? Because of me?"

"No, no. Not at all," Clara soothed. "Grown people make their own decisions. Anyway, when I heard about their questions, I offered to bring them over and show them around your café so they could see for themselves. I hope it's okay we let ourselves in. I was just about to set out a selection of your teas."

I forced a perky smile to cover my frustration and anger. They were avoiding the aunts' store now too? For what purpose? I imagined the ridiculous blog content posted before the lovely piece on my grandma. It probably examined my diet or upbringing. Something polite but pointed enough to make anxious folks fear shopping or eating honey. *Raised by beekeepers, and a man died outside her home. Coincidence, or something more? Charmers, chime in! How much honey do you eat?*

"It's so nice to see y'all," I said with as much forced merriment as I could muster. "Thank you for coming. I hope you're having a good time so far. Have you seen the view from the deck? It's a great place for a glass of tea."

Most folks managed a smile. All looked expectant and curious.

I slipped behind the counter and grabbed my left-over flyers. Aunt Clara had told me once that locals just wanted the truth. I hadn't been very social in the month or so after I came home, before opening Sun, Sand, and Tea, more like broken-hearted and mopey. Then Mr. Paine died, rumors started, and the only ongoing news source was an anonymously run blog. I almost couldn't blame them for their confusion.

"I'm having a party here tomorrow night, and everyone is invited. A grand opening. I want a chance to reconnect with Charm and introduce you to some more of my family's best recipes. I hope you'll come." I moved around the room with my most congenial smile, putting paper into each hand. *Pull back the curtain*, I thought.

Amelia took a flyer. "Thank you. I'll be there. Right now, I'm going to go home and take that nap for you."

I clapped her on the shoulder, wishing I could go too. "You're a true friend."

The music grew louder behind me, and I turned back to find Aunt Fran and her friend Henry dancing to "Kokomo." For a lady who thought the Swan women were cursed in love, she certainly didn't seem concerned about Henry's impending death.

"Here you go," Clara called. She lined my counter in clusters of iced tea jars. "Samples! Help yourselves." She moved little paper tepees in front of each bunch. The flavors were written neatly in purple ink.

The group silently exchanged glances.

Her smile slowly faded. "Well, help yourself. Don't be shy."

When no one moved, Clara looked to Aunt Fran.

My tummy churned. After the day I'd had, I really needed a thread of hope. People couldn't seriously think I'd hurt someone—could they? Until that moment, I'd hoped the town's standoffish behavior would soon pass, that it was no more than the grown-up equivalent of *Everly has the cooties*.

Tears stung my eyes at the realization that this was so much worse than I'd imagined.

Hurt crossed Fran's pretty face. She marched to the counter and grabbed the nearest jar. "This one has always been my favorite." She sucked down several gulps, then smiled at the group. "Mmm."

The guests traded strange expressions. When Fran didn't fall over and die, a handful of them moved in her direction, mumbling under their breath to one another and carefully selecting a sample for themselves. To my great relief, they sipped, then smiled.

The rest of the guests inched toward the door.

Clara's brows furrowed, her angelic face uncharacteristically forlorn. "You don't have to go," she called. "We can play Yahtzee! Or bridge! Sit out on the deck?"

Henry went to Fran's side and grabbed a jar of tea.

He tapped his glass to hers and drank it straight down. "This is fantastic." He eyeballed the empty jar. "Really, really good. Have you thought of bottling for retail?"

I slumped onto a bar stool and dropped my chin into my hands. "No."

A man in a black jacket and tie took the stool beside mine. "Don't worry about them," he said. "They'll come around."

I gave the lone encourager a closer look. "Mr. Blackstock?" My ninth grade history teacher smiled warmly at me, empty tea jar in hand. "What are you doing here?"

"I came to see your café. It's very well done." He patted my shoulder. "And for the record, it's nice to have you back. Not just for the tea."

"I wish everyone felt that way." Seeing him again brought a true smile to my lips. Mr. Blackstock had opened my eyes to the history all around me. As a teen, I'd barely thought beyond the present moment, until I took his class. He gave me an appreciation for my aunts' cuckoo obsession with passing family stories along. It didn't matter if I believed them, or even if the stories were true, only that they were part of my legacy, formed in the minds and spoken from the lips of ancestors who couldn't possibly know we'd still be repeating them two centuries later. The concept was pretty cool if I remembered to think of it that way. "I don't suppose you know what Mr. Paine was working on lately?"

He made a face. "I do, actually. It's funny that you ask, because I rarely had reason to speak with him."

"Really?" I'd started to feel like a pest for asking everyone I met the same question, but it had finally paid off. "Go on."

He chuckled. "My wife is on the town council. She handles the calendar, scheduling, that sort of thing, but she attends all the meetings and hears all the drama. She's nicer than me. She calls any issues that come up 'dilemmas.'" He made air quotes. "One of the council's biggest dilemmas involved Paine battling a local real estate developer over turning multiple historic homes into bed and breakfasts."

"Yikes."

"Yeah, and here's the kicker, this guy wanted his B&Bs to share a name."

My jaw dropped. "A dreaded chain." Good grief. It wasn't exactly a set of golden arches or a Hilton, but if the poison hadn't killed him, and the B&Bs went forward, he might've had heart failure instead. "Who was it?"

"That I don't know, but I can ask." He stretched and got to his feet, checking his watch. "Good news. All the suspicion and funny looks? I've got a great historic quote for you: 'This too shall pass.' Everything does. Meanwhile, I've got to go. I came to say hello, but most of the folks who left just now were probably here killing time before the funeral. I'm sure there was no offense intended by their sudden departures." He patted the counter and waved goodbye with a jaunty whistle.

Funeral? The word bumbled around in my brain. "There's a funeral today?"

Aunt Clara put Mr. Blackstock's glass in the dishwasher. "Mr. Paine's, dear."

"That's today? Right now?" An image of the silent, staring crowd popped back into mind. Now that I thought of it, I realized an unusual number of people had been wearing black. No wonder everyone had seemed so dressed up. "They came to the place where they think he was poisoned ten minutes before his funeral? Amelia was right. People are strange."

Aunt Clara came around the counter and slid a soft palm over my hand. "I'm sorry that didn't go better. I wanted them to come by, try the teas, and remember who you are—not just the fact that someone poisoned a man's tea which you happened to brew."

Aunt Fran stood at her sister's side and wrapped an arm around her back. "They're warming. Give them time."

"How did I not know the funeral was today?" I rose to my feet, feeling frustrated but energized. "Never mind." I'd missed the town gossip meeting, and I hadn't kept up with the blog. "I remember: nobody tells me anything anymore."

I paced in a small circle, formulating a new plan. "Aunt Clara? Aunt Fran? I have something to do. Would you mind locking up when you leave?" I needed the name of this bed and breakfast developer.

They smiled. I kissed their cheeks and shook Henry's hand, then darted upstairs to look for something black to wear.

I had a funeral to attend.

CHAPTER
❧

TEN

I speed-walked through town in a simple black dress with matching flats, forgoing the boardwalk for the sake of time and heading for Boardman's Funeral Home as quickly as I could without breaking a sweat. There were three locations for an eternal send-off in Charm, but Boardman's was the most popular and almost double the size of our other two options.

The breeze grew unseasonably cool as dark clouds rolled onto the horizon and snuffed out the blistering sun. The proverbial April showers had loomed for a week, threatening in spurts but without making good on their promise. I just hoped the storm would hold off until I reached my destination.

Outside the local resale shop, I eyeballed a rusty old Schwinn. It was pink beneath the corrosion, with faded letter decals and a filthy white woven vinyl basket that was partially coming undone. The price tag said ten bucks, quite a deal for a woman racing the rain to a funeral. Unfortunately, I didn't have time to stop.

The funeral home parking lot was full, and Detective Hays's SUV stood sentinel at the curb.

I detoured to a side entrance to avoid him. Was he there as part of his investigation? As a caring new local? Or as security? Hopefully, the first option. He needed to figure this thing out before I got another threat; I was already nervous to be home alone as it was.

I followed the sounds of doom and gloom to a door marked "Paine Celebration," then took a seat in the back. The bleating organ easily covered the soft snick of the door behind me.

I crossed my ankles and tried to look as if I'd been there all along.

Lucinda was in the front row, leaning on a younger woman. Dozens of Charm families filled the seats, mixed with a sprinkling of strangers I assumed were Mr. Paine's family, or folks who'd moved to town while I'd been away. The remaining members of the town council filled the second row. Mr. Blackstock sat beside a small brunette.

Detective Hays was nowhere to be seen.

I slouched in my seat, searching each face for someone who looked suspicious, keeping myself on high alert in case the cranky detective appeared and busted me. He'd definitely think it was inappropriate for me to be at Mr. Paine's funeral, given that he seemed to suspect I'd killed him, but imagine the gossip if I didn't come. People would think I'd stayed away out of guilt.

It was hard to guess who would approve and who

wouldn't, so I had to lay low, do my reconnaissance, and make sure a couple people saw me so they could spread the word later that I'd come to pay my respects.

A man in the middle section across the aisle took notice and smiled at me. His bushy salt-and-pepper hair looked premature against his youthful face, but I'd have recognized Martin Paine anywhere—Mr. Paine's nephew had been a man in demand on the beach every summer when we were teens. He'd lived up north somewhere but spent the weeks between each school year in Charm, making my town his annual playground.

I waved in a silent greeting. His smile grew and I flipped my gaze forward before he drew more attention my way.

"Excuse me," he whispered, rising to a hunched position and shuffling past the others seated in his row. "Pardon." He held his jacket together with one hand and guided himself with the other, using the seat backs as balance.

He ducked across the aisle and parked himself on the empty seat at my side. "Hi." He shook my hand.

"Hi." I forced my attention back to the preacher.

Martin crossed his legs and settled in.

Twenty long minutes later, after some rambling remembrances of what a dedicated man Mr. Paine had been, the mourners were excused. Folks stood and filtered toward the front, congregating around Lucinda.

I headed for the hallway, followed closely by Martin Paine.

"Quite a turnout," he said, once we'd broken free.

"Quite," I agreed.

His smile remained easy and true as he gave me a long look. "I can't believe how little you've changed since high school."

I guffawed. That was a total lie, but nice of him to say anyway.

"You remember me, don't you?" he asked.

"Who could forget?" Martin had left for college and stopped visiting Charm the year I became a junior in high school. Girls had flocked to him back then, and time had been good to him, so I imagined not much had changed. Personally, I'd always preferred rough and rugged to clean and shiny. "I'm so sorry about your loss," I said. My heart ached for him.

Martin's smile turned slowly downward. "I know you didn't kill him," he said. "I hate that he's gone, but please know I don't blame you. I've seen you rescue crabs and worms drying out on the sand or sidewalk— there's no way you could hurt another human being. You jumped in on an escalating argument between me and Ned Kester my senior summer here, remember?"

I scrambled backward mentally in search of the fuzzy memory. "Oh, that's right. I hate bullies."

Martin's brows rose over his forehead. "You thought you were saving me from a bully? Ouch." He patted his chest.

"I wasn't?" Confusion muddled the memory. "That guy had fifty pounds on you. What did I walk into, then?"

"He'd just caught me kissing his girlfriend. In my defense, I hadn't been here since the previous summer, so I had no idea she had a boyfriend, and she didn't offer up the information." Martin rubbed a manicured hand across his lips to contain the smile.

Clearly, I'd defended the wrong guy.

I chewed my lip and weighed my options. I could ask Martin what he knew about his uncle's death and risk offending him in the process, or I could keep my mouth shut and lose a golden opportunity.

Curiosity and the need to end this whole mess opened my mouth. "Have you heard anything more about what happened to your uncle?" I lowered my voice to a whisper, then checked for prying ears. "The detective thought someone had put something in the tea."

"Mom said it was a prescription medicine of some kind. I don't remember what. She was crying. I was shocked."

"Sure." I nodded. "I can't imagine getting news like that. Losing one of my aunts would be devastating. Knowing someone had killed her..." My throat tightened until I couldn't finish the sentence.

My addled brain struggled to make sense of the new information. Who would have had access to him like this? Someone had been close enough to overdose him with a prescription. I lifted my gaze to his. "Martin, how well do you know Lucinda?"

"Aunt Lucinda?" he asked with a slight laugh. "Pretty well."

"Oh. Right."

"Why? Are you looking for her?" He twisted and peered over the crowd still clustered in the viewing room. "Do you want me to find her for you?"

"No," I yipped. "No, no." I shook my head. "I just wondered if you knew how well she and your uncle got along. Someone said they were still in contact, and she wasn't very nice."

Martin blinked. The intent behind my questions seemed to register, and his jovial expression faded. "Aunt Lucinda had no reason to fight with Uncle Benedict. They've been divorced for years."

"I wasn't trying to be rude," I said. "I'm just trying to figure out what happened that night. Someone knows, but half the people I talk to treat me like I have the plague and the other half literally run the other way when they see me coming."

Martin watched me with furrowed brows. He tipped his head sharply over one shoulder, then moved in that direction.

I followed him around the corner to a quiet hallway with a love seat anchored beneath a seascape oil painting.

Martin took a seat, hiking one ankle onto the opposite knee and blowing out a long, weary breath. "I appreciate that you're trying to find out what happened to my uncle, but you don't need to. There's a detective assigned to the case. From what I understand, this guy's the real deal. He's very good."

I bit my tongue and nodded.

Martin stretched forward, balancing his elbows on his thighs. "I can tell you're going to push, so let's get it over."

"Thank you."

He shook his head sadly. "Uncle Benedict had his own ideas about how life in Charm should be. I'm sure you know that. He loved his life here and his position on the town council, but I think the job made him as many enemies as friends."

I lowered onto the cushion beside Martin, unable to disagree. "He made me half batty wanting ingredient lists for everything in my café, but I can understand why he was so adamant. He wanted things done right, and he wanted the best for this town."

Long, dark lashes cast shadows across his smooth cheeks. Indecision played on his features. "This is probably nothing, so if you follow up on it, leave my name out of the conversation, okay?"

I leaned closer in anticipation of whatever news he had to share. "Of course."

"There's an entrepreneur in town named Metz. Uncle Benedict said he was a greedy, obnoxious putz who wanted to rezone an historic colonial into a commercial B&B with a gift shop. I guess he's had a construction crew out there on Bay View for a couple of weeks, pointedly ignoring Uncle Benedict's protests against the requested zoning change. I'm not sure how that works, but it was making my uncle crazy."

I made an *uh-oh* face. That sounded a lot like my situation with Mr. Paine and even more like the guy

Mr. Blackstock had told me about. "Your uncle fought me on opening the café at my place too. When we dug into the records, I learned the property had been rezoned during the Great Depression to allow home-based businesses as long as the owner resided on the property, which I do. So his hands were tied, and I opened Sun, Sand, and Tea six weeks ago."

"This guy doesn't even live in Charm," Martin said. "And the property is strictly residential. Always has been."

Which meant Paine would've gone to battle to keep it that way. But how hard was Metz willing to fight back? "Do you know if Metz was working on more than one renovation project here?" *A chain, perhaps?*

Martin rubbed his palms against the fabric of his black slacks. "No. Maybe. I don't know. I still can't believe Uncle Benedict is gone."

I set a gentle hand on his. "Me either." I offered a tight smile when he looked my way. "I'll find out what happened to him. I promise."

Emotion glistened in Martin's eyes. He lifted his gaze over my head.

The low buzz of a crowd filtered to us, echoing from the main hallway. A few mourners looked our way as they dispersed toward the parking lot and Lucinda came into view, her gaze locked on me.

I bounced to my feet and shook Martin's hand overenthusiastically. "I'd better get going. You should stop by Sun, Sand, and Tea sometime," I told him. "I'd love to make you lunch, maybe a glass of tea."

He smiled. "I'd like that."

"There!" Lucinda's voice sliced through the soft murmur of the crowd. "She's with my nephew. Stop her!"

I snapped my head in the direction of her voice, but Lucinda was invisible, swallowed by the mass of mourners.

A familiar set of steel-gray eyes nearly leveled me. Detective Hays was moving in my direction.

Holy teacups! Lucinda had sicced the law on me!

I tossed Martin one last wave and made a run for the emergency exit sign at the end of the empty hall. I didn't slow down until I hit Bay View, the newest destination in my mission log.

It didn't seem like I'd been followed, which probably meant that Lucinda and Detective Hays were hounding Martin for information about my presence there, and I was sure to hear about it later.

The steady pounding of hammers and whistling of drills drew me to my destination like a tractor beam. Soon, the historic colonial came into view, covered in the construction crew I'd shared my tea samples with.

"Hello." I waved one hand overhead while shading my eyes with the other.

A few men took notice, one met me on the sidewalk. "No iced tea today?" His congenial smile was a welcome sight. "That was good stuff."

Something crashed in the distance, and I winced. A string of curses rose from within the regal structure.

"No tea today," I said, "but I'm glad you enjoyed it."

He jutted his bottom lip in a playful pout. "Then

what brings you by?" He rocked on his heels and gave me an appreciative look. "You on your way to a party?"

"Funeral." I hooked a thumb casually over my shoulder. "I don't suppose your name is Metz, by any chance?" I forced a smile, hoping this was the man I'd come to see. The fact we'd already met would make it easier to ask him about his feud with Mr. Paine.

"Nah."

Another round of blatant profanity flew through the air. Two men in drooping tool belts bustled out of the home's front door and disappeared into the side yard, hard hats sliding over their heads. A third man emerged with vengeance in his eyes. His high-end suit was a contrast with the dusty work zone.

The man before me ducked his head. "That's Mr. Metz. Good luck." He followed the other workers around the corner, leaving me to face off with the pathological cusser.

I squared my shoulders and shored up my nerve. "Mr. Metz?" I used my most pleasant voice in an attempt not to be yelled at. "Hello."

He slid a linen suit jacket on over his pit-stained shirt, then smoothed a hand through his thinning hair. "Hello." His shoulders were broad and his legs were long. He was over forty, but had clearly been an athlete. "I'm Leo Metz." He smiled. The tip of a gold-capped tooth twinkled in the sun. "Can I help you, Miss—?"

"Swan." I reached for his hand to shake. "Everly Swan. I knew a friend of yours, I think. Benedict Paine."

Metz's face morphed from confusion to shock

before landing on distrust. He slid his gaze over my ensemble. "I suppose you came from his funeral?"

"Yes, sir."

He choked out an ugly sound. "You here to accuse me of riding him too hard? Being too disagreeable? Rude? Greedy? Successful? Handsome?"

That had taken an unexpected turn.

"Actually, I was wondering if you'd tell me about your dispute with Mr. Paine. I hear he'd taken issue with your renovation of this property."

"Yeah, so?"

"So, now that he's gone, how will it impact what you're doing here?"

He barked a humorless laugh. "How will Paine's death impact me?"

I nodded my head too quickly. "Yes."

"Well, for starters, now that Paine's out of my way, I'm ecstatic. Thrilled. Saving money and moving along as planned." He opened a palm and gestured to his colonial as if he were a middle-aged game show host. "What about it?"

"I'm just trying to figure out who hurt him. Trying to track his actions those last couple of days."

Metz grimaced. "Who cares? Paine was a crotchety old fool who wanted to preserve his notion of what this town was rather than embrace the possibilities of all it can be. This bed and breakfast is going to make us a lot of money. Me *and* your town. This one and the others I've put bids on are going to bring folks across that bridge who never would've come otherwise.

Paine should've been shaking my hand and singing my praises instead of fighting me every step of the way. His death was a blessing. I'll save a fortune in attorney fees by not having to fight him on his nonsense. I'm glad he's gone. Now I can get stuff done. Goodbye and good riddance!"

I sucked in air as my feet carried me back a step. The construction site had gone silent around us.

Mr. Metz seemed to return to himself with a start. His cheeks went ruddy as he took in the gawking faces. "Back to work!"

I opened my mouth to excuse myself, but the words didn't come. Instead, I crossed the street at a jog and kept going. Anyone who would yell at a total stranger like that, in broad daylight, with a dozen witnesses, was someone I didn't trust, and I couldn't help worrying that Mr. Paine's determination to preserve Charm had gotten him killed.

I collapsed on a bench behind a thick oak tree on Main Street and tried to slow my panicked heart. Mr. Metz hadn't given a confession, but he'd made it clear he was glad Mr. Paine was dead. That felt like a lead to me, and I had witnesses who had heard his cold-hearted statement.

I dug my cell phone from my purse and dialed the number I'd saved under *Detective Meanie*.

A blustery wind whipped over me, tossing hair into my face and flipping the hem of my skirt over my knees. "Goodness!" I wedged the phone between my ear and shoulder, then scanned the street for signs of

Mr. Metz, Lucinda, or anyone who looked like they might want to shove me in a marsh.

The bizarrely attentive white cat from the beach and alleyway caught my eye. Her sharp green eyes locked on mine. "Hello, Maggie." I waved.

"Detective Hays." A deep tenor cracked through the phone.

"Hi," I said, pulling my focus off the kitty. "This is Everly Swan." I forced wads of windblown hair away from my face. "Can we talk?"

He groaned. "Where are you?"

Something rubbed against my legs and I screamed.

"Everly?" he barked. "What's wrong?"

"Just a cat," I panted, pressing a palm to my aching chest. I hadn't even seen her cross the street.

The ratty-looking feline stared up at me and meowed.

I stroked her head and worked my heart rate back toward normal. "Detective?"

"You know the lighthouse on the peninsula?" he asked.

"Yeah. Why?"

"Meet me there in thirty minutes." The line disconnected.

I pulled the phone away from my ear and made an angry face at it. "I can't walk to the peninsula in thirty minutes," I complained.

Maggie rubbed her face against my leg, then darted across the street at an angle and leaped onto the narrow window ledge outside Finders Keepers, the resale shop.

"The bike!" I jumped up and followed her lead. "Brilliant!"

Five minutes and ten bucks later, I was the proud owner of a fixer-upper Schwinn. I walked the bike to Molly's, three doors down, for a packet of tuna. The kitty followed, clearly anticipating my next move.

"Here." I tore the packet open and emptied the tuna onto the sidewalk, then tossed the container into a garbage can. "Thanks for reminding me about the bike." I rubbed the top of Maggie's head and scratched behind her notched ear. "Meet you at home later?"

She gobbled the tuna without another look in my direction.

I fit my backside onto the narrow bike seat and started pedaling. Fifteen minutes later, I'd made it to the lighthouse, where Detective Hays walked toward me at a leisurely pace on the long gravel lane beside the lighthouse.

I hopped off the bike, checking to be sure my dress was back in place.

The detective had changed clothes since the funeral, trading the stuffy suit for fitted jeans, a simple white T-shirt, and sneakers. There was a ball cap over his wavy brown hair, and he carried a child on his shoulders, cowboy-booted feet bouncing against his chest as they moved. Detective Hays gripped the boy's calves with both hands, and pinned me with his stare. "You okay?" he asked.

"I'm okay." I tried not to stare at the tiny, gray-eyed human he wore around his head, but it couldn't be helped. The wavy brown hair, the mischievous smile, and that dimple—I struggled to swallow the block of surprise wedged in my throat. "Who's this?"

I asked as a formality. There was no denying this boy was Detective Hays's son.

CHAPTER

ELEVEN

Detective Hays swung the pint-sized version of himself off his shoulders and set him on the gravel. "Denver, this is Miss Everly."

I leaned forward, struggling to add a new adjective to what I knew about Grady Hays. He was a *daddy*. "Hello, Denver."

The boy lifted one dimpled hand to me.

I shook it gently. "It's nice to meet you."

"It's very nice to meet you, ma'am," he said, dropping his hand back to his side. Denver raised his eyes to his daddy.

The detective nodded. "All right."

Denver turned on his dusty boots and ran back the way they'd come. His thin arms and legs pumped as he raced off the gravel and into the field.

A moment later, a pair of ducks took flight; Denver squealed in delight.

"Leave the ducks alone," Detective Hays called. "They lived here first."

Denver chased them into the weeds, then set them off again.

The detective smiled. "He loves the ducks."

Confusion coiled my brain into a knot as he watched Denver running through the field. There was a kindness in his eyes I'd never seen before. It was a side of him I hadn't imagined, and I liked it.

I blinked through the haze of shock. "He's handsome," I said. "Looks just like you."

The detective's gaze heated my cheeks. I ignored the warmth rushing through me. I hadn't intended to call him handsome, but there it was. I watched intently as Denver raced in circles, arms wide like airplane wings. "How old is he?"

"He'll be five next month."

"Wow." According to the internet, Detective Hays was thirty-four, so he'd had Denver at close to my age. What would I do with a baby? I barely remembered to feed Lou.

Denver's small frame ambled toward the lighthouse at the end of the snub peninsula, and I cast a sideways glance at Detective Hays.

The sound of tires on gravel drew my attention.

Detective Hays's SUV bounced up the worn and pitted lane, the young blond woman I'd seen him with outside the ice cream shop behind the steering wheel. She powered the window down and pushed large designer sunglasses onto her head. "Hello," she said congenially to me before swinging her gaze more pointedly to the detective. "I got that call we were waiting for. Company's coming in two weeks."

He gave a curt nod. "Denver's headed for the lighthouse."

Her eyes scanned the horizon, sticking on something midsweep. "Chicken for dinner."

"Yep."

She powered the window up and rolled on, heading for the little boy and the lighthouse.

I dragged my attention back to Detective Hays, forcing my gaping mouth shut. She'd said "Company's coming in two weeks" as ominously as if that would be the last day of the world, then simply added "chicken for dinner" like it was a completely sensible follow-up. My mind overflowed with questions, none of which had answers that were any of my business. Like, how old was she anyhow? She looked like a baby. Very early twenties, I guessed, which would have practically made her a child when they'd gotten married, *if* they were married. My gaze slid down his arm in search of a wedding band on one of his long tan fingers. Nothing. Not even a white line to suggest a ring had ever existed.

"She's not his mother," he said, following my gaze.

"What?" I jerked my head up.

His eyes were already on mine. "Denise." He nodded in the direction of the SUV. "She's not Denver's mom."

"Oh." A nonsensical wave of relief washed over me. "It's none of my business."

He locked his hands over narrow hips, fingertips resting on a gun holstered on his belt. "Denver's mom died three years ago."

I kicked the stand down on my Schwinn, captivated by the unexpected peek into his private life. "I'm so sorry."

"Yeah, me too." Profound sadness pooled in his eyes. "Cancer. I know people are going to ask."

"I wasn't."

He nodded. "We came here for a fresh start, but it feels a little like losing her again every time I have to say she's gone."

I forced a tight smile. "Well, if it makes you feel any better, you'll probably only have to say it once or twice around here. The town gossip will take care of the rest."

He chuckled softly. "It helps."

I knew I shouldn't pry, but my insatiable curiosity reared its rude head once more. "Is that why you left the marshals service?"

He didn't answer.

I kept babbling on. "It sounds like you had an impressive career." According to the articles I'd binge-read that first night, he'd been a local hero in Charlotte. "You led a violent fugitives task force, a successful one that landed your name in the papers a dozen times in the past five years. You apprehended more than a hundred known criminals and reduced crime by twenty percent." My voice rose with enthusiasm on each new count.

"You've done your research."

"Yeah, but I couldn't figure out why you'd leave success like that behind." I'd assumed the reason was something bad that he'd done.

"Amy died," he said. "And suddenly I couldn't go undercover anymore. I couldn't work unending hours. I was a widower with a toddler. The grieving father to a confused kid who didn't stop asking for mama for four months." Emotion glossed his eyes, and he lowered his gaze from mine. "For weeks, all I wanted was for him to stop calling for her, and the minute he did…" He pinched the bridge of his nose.

My heart clenched, waiting for his next words.

Instead, the crunch of gravel returned and the SUV passed us, Denver and Denise waving from the car.

When the vehicle was nothing but taillights, he turned to me as if he hadn't just shared his heart-wrenching truth. "You and I have some ground to cover," he said. "I just can't decide if we should start with what brings you here, why Lucinda wanted to have you removed from the funeral home, or why you ran away when you first saw me on the boardwalk the other night."

I had no idea. I was just thankful, if we were talking about me, that he didn't want to hear my sob story about a cowboy who didn't return my affections. Knowing what Detective Hays and Denver had been through put my mess into perspective, and I decided right then that I wouldn't let my past hurt me anymore. I'd shed enough tears for the loss of a dead-end relationship, and it was time I started looking forward again. If the man beside me could carry on, there was no reason for me to wallow.

I took a deep breath, letting the excessive drama of my day snap back like a rubber band. "I'm here to report a threat," I said, "and I have a new lead for you in Paine's murder. Maybe two."

His eyelids shut and he murmured for several long beats.

I inched closer, trying to understand the words. "Are you counting down from ten?"

He opened his eyes, spread his fingers wide, and exhaled. "Go on."

"Wait a minute. What was that?" I said, motioning between us. "What did you just do?"

"It's a relaxation technique. I looked it up online after meeting you."

"Ha, ha."

His cheek ticked up. "I'm not kidding. Start at the beginning and don't skip any details. I need to know everything you've been holding back."

"Okay." I mimicked his relaxation technique, then I let him have it, unloading it all, from the strange visit with Sam and his finger-pointing at Lucinda to my trip to Duck and the sunscreen threat left on Amelia's windshield, all before stopping for a breath.

"Anything else?"

I nodded. "I was just catching my breath. I also spoke with Martin Paine at the funeral and he pointed me to Mr. Metz, the guy renovating the colonial on

Bay View. So, I talked to him too. Oh wait, Martin asked that his name be left out of this, so that last bit is off the record."

"Uh huh." He pressed the heels of his hands against his eyes. "And what about Metz?"

"He's a major jerk. That's really why I'm here," I admitted. "Metz is the new lead I mentioned. Everything else is unsubstantiated, but Metz is awful. He said he was glad Mr. Paine died, that his death saved him tons of time and money in legal fees—and there were witnesses to the statement. That's got to be motive, and he's been here every day for two weeks, according to Martin, so there's your means."

"Being a jerk doesn't make him a killer," he said, "And being in Charm doesn't give him means— otherwise you could accuse the whole town. The killer needed access to both Paine's drink and his pills. There's no evidence to suggest Metz had either."

"So, the prescription was Mr. Paine's," I whispered. That explained why I hadn't been arrested. Martin's mom had told him there was a prescription medication of some kind found in Mr. Paine's tea. I hadn't considered someone might have used Paine's own medicine against him.

"Are you sure it wasn't an accidental overdose?"

"Yes." Detective Hays mashed his lips into a thin white line. "You need to stop this. Now." He ground the last word between his teeth.

I raised both palms over my head, then let them drop. "I want to. I really do, but how can I stop looking for the real killer when someone is clearly after me? They pushed me into the marsh, followed me to Duck. What's next?"

"Nothing," he said. "If you'd let me handle this."

"It's not that simple." I hated the desperation in my voice. "The poison was in *my* tea. Now no one wants to come to my shop, and they're boycotting my aunts! Can you believe that? This thing is out of control. My aunts' livelihoods shouldn't be damaged for their kinship with me, and I can't afford my house without the café. I don't want to leave Charm again, or move back to the family homestead. I know this town has been a mess since you got here, and some folks are being real dumb right now, but I love this place." My heart dropped. "I have to straighten this out, and I have to do it before the damage to my reputation is irrevocable. Shoot. I should've asked Metz's crew if he'd been there all day. Then I'd know if he'd had time to follow me to Lucinda's shop and leave a nasty message."

Detective Hays leveled me with his business stare. "Look. I like you. I think you're a nice lady and probably not a murderer."

I rolled my eyes. "Oh, stop. Sweet-talker." I removed my phone from my purse and brought up the photo of Amelia's windshield with the threat. "Here."

He gave it a dirty look, then tapped my screen for several seconds, presumably sending a copy to himself.

"I don't want to see you hurt. So please let me handle this. The more you interfere, the more of a distraction you become. Do you understand what I'm saying?"

I made an angry face.

"Imagine someone hired you to cater their wedding, but you had to babysit that day. How much more difficult would it be to do your job if you were constantly sidetracked by people calling to tell you the toddler under your care was getting into trouble? Or hurt? Or lost. Whatever. Bottom line is that the toddler would make doing your job very difficult, and even if you got the job done, it would take twice as long."

I grabbed the handlebars of my new old bicycle and kicked the stand up. "I'm not a toddler, and I didn't come here to be called one."

"Where are you going?"

"Home." Today had been a terrible, horrible, no good, very bad day, and I was done. There were too many things ping-ponging around in my heart and mind. I just wanted some sweet tea, my favorite rocker, and a view of the ocean to help me think.

The detective followed me down the gravel drive, closing the distance between us faster than I could create it without actually getting on my bike. "At least let me drive you. I can toss the bike in my truck." His hand stretched out to cover mine on the handlebars and a powerful jolt of electricity pulsed through me.

My mouth opened and my gaze flicked to his.

The detective's eyes narrowed. Confusion and

curiosity crossed his rugged features. He jerked his hand away from mine and stuffed it into his pocket.

I climbed on my bike and rode away, the full weight of his eyes on my back as I made my way to the main road.

So far, my fresh new start stunk.

CHAPTER

TWELVE

I pedaled back down Bay View to Middletown Street, avoiding eye contact with shoppers and pedestrians on retail-heavy streets and focusing instead on getting home before the storm hit.

I hopped off at the boardwalk and checked on Amelia's Little Library. No added sand. Either Amelia had cleaned it up on her way home from my place earlier or the hooligan had taken a day off. Maybe the sand bandit had even gone to Mr. Paine's funeral and opted to stay for the obligatory meal served in Boardman's adjacent reception hall.

My tummy groaned at the thought of food.

I borrowed a tattered hardcover copy of *Body Language: Unspoken Cues to Know If He Loves You* before I shut the library door. I didn't care if he loved me, but I thought the book might help me figure out when I was being lied to. Probably a good skill to have while interviewing potential killers. I tossed the book into my derelict basket and made plans to fix the filthy vinyl after a bite to eat and a refreshing shower.

I wasn't sure there was enough soap and hot water to wash the ick off from my day. Being threatened in sunscreen had gotten under my skin, and I'd felt watched every moment since. The paranoia was thick around me as I walked my bike along the familiar wooden planks. *Someone had followed me to Duck.* How could anyone have known I was there unless I was being watched or eavesdropped on when we'd made plans last night? Who could do that without me noticing?

Sam Smart had pointed me in Lucinda's direction, but he couldn't have known when or if I'd visit her— could he? I needed to talk with Sam again. I'd like to know why he hadn't told me about Mr. Metz's feud with Mr. Paine. As the town's most popular real estate agent, Sam must've known about it. The memory of Mr. Metz's red face sent ice into my gut. He was scary, angry, and a bully.

Thunder grumbled in the distance. The rain wasn't far away.

I climbed back onto my bike and pedaled, trying to outrun my problems and the rolling storm clouds at my back. The daylight seemed to dim, then vanish ahead of me, vacuumed away by the brewing storm.

I squinted from the low throb beginning in my head. I couldn't remember eating anything after the honey toast I'd had for breakfast. After my shower, I was absolutely raiding the fridge—a perfect yellow-and-white frosted lemon cake came to mind.

My fitness band made a strange trumpet sound, and I nearly ran my bike into the sand.

"Good grief!" I struggled to control the handlebars as I released my grip with one hand, determined to push the little rubber button and see what the problem was now.

YOU'VE TAKEN MORE THAN 8,000 STEPS TODAY!

Well, what do you know? No sand in the Little Library. My digital trainer was happy. Maybe my day was finally taking a positive turn.

The Sun, Sand, and Tea sign came into view as the first fat drops of rain burst around me. Another dose of good luck. I hurried into the carriage house and parked the bike beside my wagon and a pile of partially used spray paint cans. "Your makeover is scheduled for tomorrow," I told the Schwinn. "Right now, my pajamas are calling."

Maggie appeared just outside the open door, mewling and rubbing her arched self against the doorway.

"I knew you liked me. Feel like a little dinner?" I took a step in her direction.

She took three steps away.

"Well, you can't stay on that little strip of dry cement. It won't last. Why don't you come inside?" I went to her. "I've got more tuna upstairs."

I was close enough to feel the whisper of her fur on my palms when she ran around the corner toward my home.

I followed. "Where are you going? You're getting soaked."

The front door was open. The cat was gone. I hustled toward the porch, hoping this meant Aunt Clara or Aunt Fran was still around, maybe cleaning up after their impromptu gathering of unsupportive locals.

"Aunt Clara? Aunt Fran?"

Lightning zigzagged across the sky as I reached the open door. Surprisingly, the lights were off inside.

My heart stopped.

The next blast of lightning flashed and blinked my café into view before leaving it in darkness once more.

I poked an arm inside and flipped the power switch, praying that the strobing light had played a trick on my brain. It hadn't. My stomach plummeted in shock. The room had been tossed: My tea vessels were overturned. The pantry door was open, its contents spilled onto the counters and floor. Cupboard doors were swung wide, dishes broken and shattered. The flower arrangements Aunt Clara had brought over were crushed on the floor, as if someone had taken the time to grind them into the floorboards.

I crept inside, crunching over broken glass and pressing trembling fingertips to quivering lips. Why was this happening? My vision blurred with tears and my need for oxygen.

A pair of birds flew in from the open deck door and helped themselves to the buffet of toppled breads, crumbled sweets, and plethora of nesting materials. Maggie crept into position behind them.

I turned in a small circle, taking in the chaos. Even my giant menu chalkboard was face down on the floor.

The cat pounced. Birds scattered.

I stumbled back onto the porch with a scream lodged in my throat and dialed Detective Hays.

√

Detective Hays arrived five minutes later, a cruiser with two policemen pulling in behind him.

I was in the carriage house, huddled near the beach gear, when their vehicles rushed into view. Unwilling to check my freshly burgled house for killers—even if I could have put on dry clothes—I'd unloaded a beach bag instead and wrapped myself in a towel.

"Everly!" Detective Hays shouted on his way up the front steps, long legs easily taking them two at a time.

The officers fanned out, flashlights in hand.

I crept into view with a small wave.

Their lights trained on my face in an instant, hands jumping to their holstered guns.

"It's the homeowner," one officer said. "Everly Swan."

"Hello," I said shyly. "Yes, it's me."

They dropped their hands.

"Detective Hays," I said, pointing cautiously toward my still open door, asking if I could go in.

"Go on."

"Thanks." I hustled up my front steps. "Hey." I rounded the doorway on the detective's heels, out of breath. "Thanks for coming."

He frowned. "Where were you?"

"Just…you know…" I wrapped my arms around my middle, ignoring the odd look on his face and trying to settle my breath. "Hiding."

He made a face. "Where?"

"In the carriage house."

His gaze fell to my shoulders, then rose to the top of my head.

I'd draped colorful sea horse-and-starfish-printed beach towels over my hair and shoulders. "I was caught in the rain on my way home—then this happened and I was afraid to wait inside. I keep beach gear in the carriage house."

He closed his eyes for a quick beat, and I imagined him counting silently. He turned away. "Is this what it looked like when you went back outside?"

Honestly, it looked even worse on second inspection. "I think so. Yes."

He exhaled long and slow. "Are you okay? Are you hurt?"

"No. Just shaken."

He circled the room. "Anything taken? Money, maybe? Do you have a cash register?"

I shook my head. "This wasn't a robbery, and it's not a coincidence."

He cocked a brow, as if he wasn't quick to agree. "Did you go into any other parts of the house?"

I made my most elaborate *yeah, right* face, then flapped my beach towel covered arms. *Obviously not.*

He fought a smile. "Come on."

I followed him from room to room, waiting

at the door while he checked closets and alcoves before returning to ask the same thing. "Anything missing?"

The answer was always, "No. It doesn't look like anyone was up here."

"So they focused their aggression on the tea shop." He gave my living space a long look. "I sure admire that view."

The back wall was mostly windows, just like in the café, also with a partly covered deck.

Below us, the officers' voices carried through the floorboards and up the staircase.

I drifted to my bedroom doorway. "Do you mind? I'm soaked."

"Nah. Meet me downstairs when you're ready. I'll see if the officers found anything."

I took my time, drying off slowly as I processed the night's unbelievable events. Even fresh clothes and some quality time with the blow dryer did nothing to alleviate the residual chill of fear on my skin.

The officers were gone when I arrived in the café.

Detective Hays strode across the cluttered floor, surveying the mess.

"What do we do now?" I asked.

He pulled a broom and dustpan from the utility closet. "We clean up. I've got all the photos I need, and the report's been made. You can make a written statement when you're ready. For now, I say we fix this mess and get you set up for tomorrow. Maybe make a list of the things you need replaced. That goes with the report, and your insurance will want a copy if you're filing a claim."

I deflated against the wall. "That's it? I write down that someone trashed my café, make a list of broken things, and you're done? No fingerprinting or evidence collection?"

Detective Hays rubbed his brow. "The officers dusted for prints on the pantry and cabinet knobs, but the results weren't great. We'll hear from the lab in a day or two. It's the best we can do in a public area like this one."

I harrumphed.

"How many people would you say have touched these things today?" He motioned to the overturned tables, chairs, and tea jars. A thin line of patience threaded the words. "This week? This month?"

I looked at the disaster zone around me. There had been a dozen guests, plus Amelia, Henry, my aunts and I, just today. Yesterday the group from Kitty Hawk was here. "A lot, I guess. And my aunts did take a group on a tour of the whole house. I don't know what they touched."

He dipped his chin in affirmation. "And whoever did this didn't go into your private quarters. It'll be tough, but we'll try. Okay?" He turned to the open door. "I didn't notice any signs of a break-in."

I took the broom and started sweeping. "My aunts have a key, but they might've left it unlocked, or put the key under the mat."

Detective Hays looked at me as if I'd grown a

second head. "You can't leave the key to your home under a mat. I don't care where you live. That's naive at best. Reckless at worst." He crouched with the dustpan while I pushed piles of broken glass on it.

"I'm not naive."

He puffed out air, but kept whatever he was thinking to himself.

"This place isn't always like this," I said. "I know I sound like a broken record, but I don't know what else I can say."

"Say you'll keep your doors locked, and no more hiding the key on your property."

I ignored him, concentrating instead on the work, glad to have a partner in it without having to tell my aunts just yet. I didn't have the energy left for that.

"Sorry I unloaded my life story earlier." He broke the silence, but kept his eyes on the work.

I filled the tray, then grabbed a trash bag from the pantry and fanned it into life. "I didn't mind."

He dumped the glass into the bag. "You caught me at a tough time. It was unprofessional and out of character. It won't happen again."

I stopped sweeping, unable to imagine what he was going through and wished, pointlessly, that we could be friends. *It would help if he had someone who knew his story.* Someone he could talk to.

Then I remembered there was already someone in his life who knew his story. Probably more of it than I did. "Who's Denise?" I asked.

"She's the au pair." He crouched near another busted tea jar and waited, dustpan in position.

I shoved more broken bits into the pan, shocked at his willingness to answer me.

He rolled sharp gray eyes up at me. "No follow-up questions?"

"Well, I'm stunned you know what an au pair is," I said. "I'm downright floored you have one in your service, but no—no more questions. And so you know, folks call those nannies."

"Denise prefers au pair."

"Ah."

We repeated the process of dump and fill until my floors were free of debris.

He rose to his feet and gathered ruined food from the counters, stuffing that into the bag with the broken glass and dishes.

I leaned my broom against the wall. Behind the counter I restacked unopened boxes into the pantry. "I'm glad you decided to come here for your and Denver's fresh start. It's a great place to grow up. Usually," I amended.

"That's what folks keep telling me." He went to deal with the fallen chalkboard.

"That's heavy. Let me help." I set the last tin of herbs and spices on the shelf and dusted my palms against my shorts. "I hope it didn't crack."

He slipped his hands under one side.

I put mine under the other. "On three?"

His brows pulled together before he raised his eyes

to mine. "I hate to ask this because I know it's going to make you mad all over again, but is there any chance this particular crime is unrelated to the others?"

"What do you mean? Why would you ask that?"

He made a pained face. "Two acts of vandalism in one day is a lot of activity for someone who should be laying low and hoping this whole thing blows over unsolved. Every new crime creates the potential to be caught. Any decent criminal would know that. Whoever it was that killed Paine ought to be making his way across the country, not hanging around here messing with a wannabe sleuth."

I tried not to get stuck on the insult and concentrated on the larger implication instead. "You think I have two enemies mad enough to threaten me and destroy my business?" I snapped. Was he kidding? "Or maybe this is my doing. I'm a nut creating crimes against myself to divert your attention and make me look like the victim instead of the killer?"

"I didn't say that."

"You implied it, one thing or the other, and both stink." I dropped my end of the chalkboard. "I'm a nice lady!"

The menu slapped against the detective's feet. "Hey!"

"I am not the one doing these things, and I don't have multiple enemies. That's ridiculous." I grabbed a rag and took my rage out on the counters and sink, before righting the tables and chairs.

I forced myself not to look at him.

"You're inferring things on your own, you know," he said. "I'm just gathering information. For example, how was your last breakup?"

I flipped the final bar stool, shooting him the stink eye. "Why?"

"Is there any chance that an ex-boyfriend is behind this? Maybe some former date or a jaded lover?"

"No." The word was barely a whisper on my tongue. My only former lover was Wyatt, and he couldn't have cared less that I'd left him.

Humiliation colored my cheeks the way it always did when I thought of the way I'd chased a man around the country, giving up everything I cared about to be with him, like a big, blind dodo.

"Okay." He relented. "I had to ask. If you think of anyone else who might have a beef against you, let me know. An old rival or nemesis, maybe. Someone less than happy to see you come home. I know you've been gone a while, but people can hold grudges. Sometimes they don't even remember why."

"There's nothing like that for me," I said, evaluating my progress.

Aside from the fallen menu board and full bag of trash, the café looked good. I'd have to mop in the morning to be sure no shards of glass lingered on the floor. And I'd need to replace the busted jars and dishes.

"Come back here and grab this," he said, moving into position at the chalkboard. "Don't let go this time. I think you broke my toe before."

"You're wearing steel-toed boots." I took hold of the massive menu board and counted to three.

He hefted it back onto the hooks while I helped keep it balanced.

"Detective Hays?" I blinked at the huge jagged letters etched into the board where my daily specials used to be.

YOU WERE WARNED.

"What?" He stepped back once the board was secured. "Well, hell."

"Yep." I stumbled backward until the counter stopped me, grabbing the edge to keep from flopping onto the floor. My second threat of the day. Dizziness swept over me and I blinked.

Detective Hays took a picture of the message, then tapped his phone screen for several seconds while I debated getting back on my bicycle and pedaling to the safety of the mainland.

He pushed his phone into his pocket, then poured a glass of ice water. "Let's go." He led the way to my covered deck, handing me the water. "Sit."

I dropped into my favorite rocker.

"I've got local officers coming to collect your menu board. They'll run it for prints. I assume you're the only one who normally handles that."

I stared at the rushing waves, white and frothy from the fading storm. Rain had streamed over the glass as we cleaned, but now it seemed we were both done.

"I'll bring a new chalkboard by in the morning. I know your big party's tomorrow."

Surprise turned me in his direction. "You do? Are you coming?"

"Wouldn't miss it." He pulled the screen shut behind him on his way inside.

I turned back to the water and let my head rest against the chair back. My eyes drifted shut and tears rolled down my cheeks. The day seemed to slowly slip away.

"Everly?" The detective's voice roused me.

"Hmm?" The sweet, zesty scent of lemons and sugar assaulted my senses. I shot upright in my seat, suddenly aware I'd fallen asleep.

He handed me a plate with a fat slice of my lemon cake at its center. "Hungry?"

"Famished." I accepted the offering as my brain sloughed off the fog of sleep. "How long was I out?"

"Not long. Maybe twenty minutes. I didn't mean to wake you or leave you out here so long," he said, "but your chalkboard is officially on its way to evidence. Bad news is that the lab wasn't able to pull a decent print from that busted oar. Good news is that Denise swung by with a replacement chalkboard. We hung it before she left."

I sank the tines of my fork into soft lemony bliss. "She runs errands too?"

"Sometimes, under special circumstances," he said around a mouthful of cake. "This cake is unreal. I think I'm having an out-of-body experience."

I laughed, savoring the first bite, knowing it was always the best, before my mouth and brain became desensitized to the magic. "I made this for tomorrow. It's an old family recipe." I pushed another bite between my lips, trying not to dwell on the number of things I'd have to remake for tomorrow's grand opening party.

He pointed his fork at the tiny remains of his slice. "I'm trying to feel bad for stealing it, but I can't. This is too good. I'm not sure you should share it. I think maybe it would be a great secret just between us." He moaned as he finished it off. "Phenomenal."

I smiled wider. "It's another one of Grandma's secret recipes. Though it probably originated with another Swan woman from even further back."

He held my stare. "You were raised by your grandma."

"Correct. And her sisters, Clara and Fran."

"Why?"

I hated answering this question, it made everyone uncomfortable, and I suspected, given his situation, he wouldn't be any different. "My parents died when I was young."

The expectant look fell from his face. "Both?"

"Both."

A pained expression bled over his features, and he shifted his gaze into the distance.

I couldn't help wondering if he was thinking of his son and what it might be like for Denver to grow up without a mother. It's what I would have been wondering in his situation. "Denver's going to be okay," I said.

Detective Hays turned questioning eyes on me.

"All he needs is unconditional love and acceptance. It doesn't matter if he has a mom and a dad, just one of those, or three old ladies."

"How can you be so sure?" he asked. "You only met him once."

"You're forgetting—I know his daddy."

His sudden, thankful smile lit my heart. A moment later, he dislodged his phone from one pocket. "Sorry. Give me just a minute." He checked the screen with a frown. "I've got to get going. I want you to lock your doors behind me. Don't leave this place unlocked for a while. Okay?" He set the plate aside.

"Okay."

Maggie appeared at the closed screen door.

"There you are," I said. "Where have you been? No cats in the café."

Detective Hays reached back to open the door and set her free. "I wasn't sure if the cat was yours, but I managed to get the birds out."

"She's mine now," I said. "I think she used to live here." I polished off another bite of cake, then set my crumb-strewn plate on top of his. "Thanks for helping me tonight. Sorry I fell asleep. I haven't been sleeping well. The fact that I conked out sitting up is a testimony to your reassuring presence."

He rubbed a palm over his stubbled cheek. "You'll always be safe with me. You can count on that."

I nodded, a knot forming in my throat.

"I want you to be careful, though," he said. "Drop your amateur investigation, and let me do my job. I'm excellent at my job." He got to his feet and carried our plates to the sink.

"Lock up behind me. I'll add your place to the nightly patrol list. Be safe." His eyes turned soft and pleading. "I don't know what I'd do if anything happened to you."

My heart picked up speed. "Oh yeah?"

"Sure. I can't go through life without another slice of that lemon cake." He flashed a cheeky smile and his dimple caved in.

I smiled back, and he winked before disappearing into the night.

Flipping the dead bolt behind him, I tried not to think about that flirty wink or his blasted dimple.

I marched across the room and opened the refrigerator in search of my lemon cake. "You're coming with me," I said and carried the rest of it to bed.

CHAPTER
THIRTEEN

I didn't sleep well after Detective Hays left, and it turned out that I wasn't hungry for the cake without him. Instead, I tossed and turned, rehashing the day and making mental lists of all I had to accomplish before my grand opening party, an event that was beginning to feel more like a please-believe-I'm-not-a-killer party.

I gave up on sleep at five thirty and went to make coffee and watch the sunrise. Lou met me on the deck, perched at the far corner of my railing.

"I've got a big day today," I told him. "There's too much to do, and I'm not in the right mind-set, but there's no going back now." Lou's tiny gray eyelids slid shut.

I sipped my coffee and basked in the soft amber and tangerine light creeping over the horizon. Maybe if I got to the market when it opened and Mr. Waters had everything I needed, I could run home, drop off my packages, start brewing the tea, and head out again. I could call an order in to Hana while I was prepping the tea, then make a quick trip to pick up the meat, cheese, and produce before coming home to make the food.

My heart sank at the complete impossibility of getting everything done. I'd still need time to shower and get myself ready for the shindig, not to mention mop and decorate the cafe. "I need a clone."

Lou cocked his head and eyeballed me. He puffed the feathers of his great white chest and ruffled his sleek gray wings.

"I don't suppose you can transform into a footman until midnight. I could really use the help."

He bent his sturdy legs and plunged into the air, as if to give an emphatic no.

"Figured."

I finished my coffee and enacted my usual plan for handling the impossible. *Just get started.* I set several teas to brew, mopped and scrubbed everything in sight, then made inventory replacement lists and an order for Hana. Two hours later, I broke down and called my aunts.

They assumed my anxiety stemmed only from the pressure of holding a grand opening party in nine short hours, and I let them. If I told them about what had happened to the café last night, I'd wind up crying again, and there was no time for that. I couldn't put it off for long, though—I needed to tell them before someone else did, or I would be in big trouble. On the up side, very few people knew what had happened and you would think you could trust the police to keep quiet. On the down side, I still had no idea who the mystery blogger was or how the writer seemed to know so much about the things going on in Charm.

Aunt Clara agreed to take my list to Hana and deliver my ingredients before lunch. She also promised more flowers and extra plates from the family collection and said she'd decorate for the party while I showered and prepared for guests. All I had to do was hit up Molly's Market to replace what had been ruined in the break-in.

I stacked my thick brown curls on top of my head and dropped a shapeless floral sundress over bike shorts, heading for the market. My big canvas shopping bag was secured cross-body-style, and my favorite pink sneakers were laced up tight.

I was halfway down the boardwalk to town before I remembered I had a bike and a wagon, and either one would make this easier and faster. My continued lack of sleep was killing brain cells.

The day was humid but beautiful, and it felt good to get out and walk. I admired the beach in all its glory. The evening storm had pushed boatloads of seaweed and shells ashore, the receding tide displaying it all. Sandpipers raced the outgoing waves for a quick snack of bugs and biofilm before barreling back over the water-packed sand, outrunning the next blue wave.

Low tide had always been my favorite as a child: so many fascinating things washed ashore. I'd found everything from unusual marine life to the occasional flip-flop, spending hours examining it with wonder. Where had each item come from? How far had it traveled? The fantasy of sailing around the world was one I still dreamed of.

The familiar sound of Amelia's voice pulled me from my reverie, echoing through the thick, salty air. I strained to listen, but the words were muffled by wind and waves. I couldn't see her, but she was likely visiting her Little Library just around the bend out of sight.

I hustled to the library over the aged wooden planks. A deep, guttural sound rattled through the air, and I faltered. "Amelia?"

She came into view as I rounded the curve. Seated on the boardwalk, back against her small wooden structure, Amelia looked as forlorn as anyone I'd ever encountered.

"What happened?" I asked, breaking into a jog. Amelia pulled her knees to her chest and rested her forehead on them.

I gave the structure behind her a closer look. This Little Library was my favorite and the prettiest by far, but I couldn't see the books through the small window this morning: someone had filled the entire structure with sand. "Oh no."

The library had once been a stout curio cabinet, four feet high and two feet wide. It was painted sky blue with white trim and covered in an adorable seashell motif. Amelia had swapped the glass face for a more durable clear plastic and repurposed it with love. Words like "Free Books" and "Take One or Leave One" were stenciled down the sides. *Little Libraries of Charm* stretched across the bottom, with her store's address beneath.

I circled the library. "How did they do this?"

"There's a little hole in the back," she mumbled into her legs. "It's where the wire for the display light used to go. They must have just poured it right in."

I took a seat at her side. "I'm sorry this is happening to you."

She turned her face toward mine. "Thanks." Her eyes were glossy with unshed tears. "I keep telling myself this isn't about me, but someone certainly seems determined to make me crazy, or at least ruin what I'm trying to do here."

I rubbed her back. "We'll catch them," I promised. "I can start tomorrow. My grand opening party is tonight, but tomorrow I have nothing on my evening schedule except busting the terrible person who did this." I offered her a crooked pinky. "Deal?"

She hooked her tiny digit with mine. "Deal."

I stretched upright and hoisted her up with me. "Let's get this cleaned up."

We opened the door to let the sand run out, shook off all the books, cleared the shelves, and restacked them before I waved goodbye.

With Amelia looking hopeful again, I took a direct turn onto Sand Street, skipping the longer, more scenic boardwalk route. I had no time left to dally. One block later, an unexpected face appeared at the corner: Lucinda Paine was collecting letters from a residential mailbox on Dune Street. She stiffened when she saw me. My feet carried me to her on autopilot.

"What do you want now?" she moaned. "Crashing my husband's funeral wasn't enough? Harassing me at my shop?" She closed the mailbox with unnecessary roughness. Her black blouse fluttered in the sticky breeze.

"I wasn't crashing the funeral. I was paying my respects," I said. "I'm so sorry about what happened to Mr. Paine. I told you that, and I never meant to make you feel harassed."

She matched my body language, crossing her arms and dangling the mail from her fingertips. "Well, I know who you are now, Everly Swan." She narrowed her milky blue eyes on me. "You didn't want to tell me earlier, but my nephew Martin filled me in on your one-woman crusade to find Benny's killer."

I rolled my eyes. "It's not a secret."

"Martin thinks you're innocent."

"I am."

We traded silent stares until I couldn't take it anymore. "What are you doing here, anyway?" I asked. "Don't you live in Duck? Whose mail is that?"

Lucinda tipped her nose in the air. "Not that it's any of your business, but this is Benedict's mail, and my house." She gave the small bungalow a loving smile. "We shared those walls for many years, and it was in his will that I should have it."

My jaw sank open. "Are you moving into Mr. Paine's old house?"

"*Our* old house," she corrected, "and yes. I prefer it here to Duck. I only wish it were under different circumstances. Benedict and I were trying to reconcile, you know. Before you poisoned him."

I furrowed my brow and bit my tongue so I wouldn't start a round of *Did not!—Did too!*

She glared back. "I know you're the tea-maker the cops are investigating, and I have faith you'll get what you deserve. Enjoy your freedom while it lasts, Miss Swan. My nephew may be a sucker for a pretty face, but I'm not. And don't come back here again, or I'll file a restraining order." She strode up the walk to her new home like it was a Fashion Week runway and disappeared through the front door.

I lifted my arms and looked for witnesses so I could project my astonishment: *Can you believe her?*

No one saw me, so I put my arms down. I was so rattled I couldn't even appreciate the fact that she thought I had a pretty face.

A big truck rattled up the road and pulled into her driveway before I could get my head together and walk away. A man in white coveralls and a matching ball cap jumped out and marched in my direction, wielding a clipboard. The patch on his chest said Modern Elegance and it coordinated with the logo on the side of his truck, painted above a picture of a fancy candlelight dinner. "Mrs. Paine? I need you to sign here."

I pointed to the house. "She's inside."

He grunted and turned away. I watched, dumbfounded, as he headed for her front porch. She'd just moved back in and was already changing the furni-ture? So much for nostalgia or just enjoying the senti-mentality of living there again.

Slowly, I pointed myself back toward Middletown Street. I had to keep moving. There was too much to do today, and I kept getting distracted. I'd have to replay our conversation and compose my theories while I shopped. The whole exchange had transpired so quickly, I'd barely had time to analyze her body lan-guage, even though I'd read to chapter three in body language book.

Currently, the only thing I could think of was more questions for Lucinda Paine. Had she really threat-ened me with a restraining order? Seriously? Did I look dangerous to her? Crazy? Homicidal? I looked at my outfit. It wasn't my best ensemble, but it certainly didn't make me look like someone who would hurt an old lady.

A restraining order! As if I were the criminal instead of the one constantly in danger. Hopefully, the mys-tery blogger wouldn't get wind of that threat.

I tried desperately to turn my thoughts back to the tasks at hand. Somehow I'd completely skipped the turn onto Vine Street and arrived instead at Blessed Bee on Main. I wandered inside, fixating on the way Lucinda had mimicked my stance. According to chap-ter two of that book, mirroring another person's pos-ture or facial expression was a way to connect, build a bond, or create understanding. Lucinda didn't seem interested in doing any of those things.

Soft scents of honey, lavender, and vanilla slowly enveloped me as I drifted through my aunts' empty store. Sounds of distant birds and rustling wind played on hidden speakers tucked in columns and corners overhead. For the first time I could recall, there were no customers' voices to break up the recorded nature sounds. I dragged my fingertips across colorful displays of lip balms, soaps, and face masks, getting angrier with each step. My aunts had a great store, and they loved what they did—they shouldn't suffer because of me.

Racks of Bee Aware T-shirts and accessories lined the walls. If the American honeybee population could be saved from the environmental threats facing them, I'd expect that ninety percent of the success could be linked back to my great-aunts. They loved bees like I loved iced tea. I hated knowing I was the reason their shop was empty.

"Everly?" Aunt Clara stepped out from the back room. Her fair hair was parted in the center and braided down both sides of her head. "What's wrong? Why the frown, darling?" The bell sleeves of her shimmery blue top slid up her arms as she pulled me into a hug.

"Any chance you've gotten wind of another suspect in Mr. Paine's death?" I asked, stepping out of her embrace. "I'm running low on resources."

Aunt Clara let her fingers trail over my face and shook her head. "No, sweetie. We've been too busy with your PR campaign. We're your personal cheer squad. Setting folks straight. Reminding them how special you are. And after that awful sunscreen incident, we thought it was best not to draw more attention by asking troublesome questions. There's no good reason to provoke another round of something as scary as that."

I rolled my head back and looked at the ceiling. "I have something else to tell you."

"Me?"

"Yes. You and Aunt Fran."

"Oh." She frowned. "Well, Fran's in the back with Hana. Why don't we go find her?" Clara slid one arm behind my back and escorted me around the checkout desk, then through a door painted to look like a giant hive.

"Fran?" Clara called.

Aunt Fran and Hana were seated at a table chatting over hot tea, goat cheese, and pita chips. The spread on the table was magazine-worthy: The teapot was yellow like the sun, set upon a blue braided trivet. Triangular chips were arranged around a mound of white cheese, like a pita chip sunflower with a marvelous and tasty center.

"Look who's here," Aunt Clara said, successfully interrupting the chitchat.

Hana beamed at me, a loaded chip caught between her fingers. "Hello. How is your day?"

"Super." I delivered hugs to her and Aunt Fran. "I thought I'd stop in and thank you for all your help with the party tonight."

"Anytime," Hana said. "We were just saying Everly wouldn't ask for this much help unless there was a problem. What is the problem?"

My aunts moved into position on both sides of me. I was trapped.

I gnawed the inside of my cheek. "After you left yesterday"—I swung my face toward Aunt Clara, then Aunt Fran—"someone went into my shop and tore it apart."

Their collective gasp pulled the oxygen from my lungs.

"It's fine now," I rasped. "The police dusted for prints and added my house to the nightly patrol. Detective Hays stayed to help me clean up, but a lot of things were broken, which is why I asked for the extra jars, flowers, and plates today. Plus, whoever made the mess threw most of my food on the floor, so I have a lot of cooking to do if I don't want to cancel the party."

Aunt Clara wrapped me in her thin arms and rested her head on my shoulder. "You poor dear. I'm so sorry this happened to you." She pulled back to shoot a pointed look at her sister. "What kind of monster would do this?"

Aunt Fran turned fuming eyes on me. "I don't know, but I'd like to. What did Detective Hays say?"

"He took the menu board in as evidence. The vandal left a message on it—'you were warned.'" I shivered just thinking about it.

"Mercy!" Clara squeaked and pulled me tighter against her side. "Was anything stolen?"

"No. And whoever wrecked the café kept the damage downstairs. My place was fine. No signs of any unwanted guests there."

"Well." She released me with a sigh. "At least there's that. You weren't hurt?"

Physically, no. "I wasn't even home." Emotionally? I planned to install an alarm system and twenty-seven dead bolts the minute I could afford them. "It's fine," I promised. "Detective Hays is on it."

Aunt Fran didn't look convinced. "And he helped you clean up?"

"Yeah, last night. I gave everything another scrub this morning, but it still feels icky, like I can't get the bad vibes off."

"It should feel icky," Clara said. "You were violated."

I didn't like the way that sounded. "I hate the way it feels in there now. A seaside café should be full of peaceful energy."

Fran nodded. "Just like the town's old slogan: *Relax. You're on island time now.*"

"Exactly." I liked that one so much better than the new one: *Carolina's buried treasure.* "I wish the new mayor would've left it alone."

"Well, there's good news on that topic," Fran said. "Looks like Mayor Dummy's retiring this fall. Thank goodness."

"Really?" I asked. "Mayor Dunfree is leaving office?" I guessed he was getting older, but was he already old enough for retirement? "Any idea who'll take his place?"

Fran lifted a narrow shoulder. "Maybe me."

"You?" Hana and I blurted in unison. A look of amusement bloomed on Hana's face.

Fran frowned. "Why not me? Henry says I have a commanding presence. As a four-star general, he would know. Maybe it's high time I put it to use."

I looked to Clara for guidance. She gave a wistful sigh. "Better Fran than that Mary Grace what's-her-name from your Outdoor Girl troop. She's such a goodie."

A bubble of laughter burst from my lips. Aunt Clara calling someone a goodie was a serious pot and kettle situation. "I don't remember anyone named Mary Grace what's-her-name." I did, however, remember every hike, campout, and Outdoor Girl adventure Grandma had taken our troop on. "Who is she?"

Clara groaned. "I think everyone called her Gracie."

"No." I slapped the table, my wide smile slipping into obnoxious territory. "Bracie Gracie? The one who wore Princess Leia buns and headgear all through middle school? Impossible. Her family moved away in ninth grade."

"Yeah, well, she's back, and she's not Bracie Gracie anymore," Clara said. "She's Mary Grace Chatsworth, and for the record, I still don't like you calling people names. It's mean."

"She was mean," I argued. "That's why no one liked her. It's *why* we called her names. She threw sand on us when Grandma wasn't looking. She kicked in our sand castles, and she told everyone that you and Grandma raised me because my real mom was a circus clown." I'd loathed Mary Grace. Learning she was moving away had been like an anvil off my shoulders. "Bracie Gracie for mayor," I whispered. "Wow. Whoever runs against her will have their hands full."

Fran made a face. "I just told you I'm running." Her pointed gaze lingered on each of our faces. "I hope you'll all get on board, because I'm going to need a campaign staff."

"Oof," I muttered. Her little sister, an accused murderer, and the Goat Lady. What a staff.

I kissed Aunt Fran's cheek and laughed. "Oh, why not? Whatever you need. Just let me know. Meanwhile, I've got to go make about one hundred mini quiches, finger sandwiches, and assorted desserts, then prepare ten gallons of sweet tea."

Hana launched to her feet. "All right. Let's go." She opened her arms to herd us toward the door. "We clean. We cook. We decorate. Teamwork. Let's go."

Hopefully the house would still be standing when we got there. The way my week was going, anything was possible.

CHAPTER

❦

FOURTEEN

I told my aunts and Hana I'd meet them at my place. I had to make a pit stop at Molly's Market for a few things first. We parted ways at Middletown and Main. They headed east toward the boardwalk and I turned west to Vine Street.

There was a line at the counter when I walked inside, and I waved at Mr. Waters. My canvas bag was heavy with flour, yeast, and sugar before I left the baking aisle; by the time I added a box of canning jars, my arm was nearly dragging the ground. I should've brought the wagon.

I stacked shrink-wrapped decorative bowls of sand and shells on top of the box of canning jars, wincing at the prices on things that were free in Charm and literally lying in piles outside my back door. If I had time, I could comb the beach for real shells that hadn't been whitewashed and shipped from China.

I piled dried starfish and sand dollars into one palm, careful not to crack them, then plucked a floppy hat from the wall and dropped it on my head. With a little luck, tonight's event would put me back on the path to owning a successful iced tea shop and squash the island hysteria surrounding it. It might even bring a little faith and goodwill my way.

I rushed to unload my booty at the checkout counter before I dropped the starfish—or my arm holding the heavy bag fell off. "I think that's everything." I rolled my aching shoulder, trying to restore circulation.

"What's with the shells?" Mr. Waters asked. "We got tons on the beach out there." He pointed in the wrong direction, toward the center of the island.

"No time." I shrugged. "My big party is tonight. I want to jazz the place up with an authentic beach vibe."

He squinted at the barcode on my hat. "All those flyers, pfft." He blew air against his teeth and wiggled one hand in the air. "Gone. Just like that."

"Someone stole them?" Was there no end to the personal sabotage?

My tummy knotted. What if I was spending all my money on a big party that no one would attend? I'd be further in debt and eating soggy finger sandwiches for the next two weeks.

"Nah." Mr. Waters pushed the keys on his ancient cash register. "The people took them."

"People?" I parroted, hope rising in my voice. "Locals? Do you think some will come?"

"Yeah, they'll come." He worked his way through another item's price code, then dropped it in my bag. "They're all coming. You're the talk of the town. That secret blogger can't stop going on about this event. Now everyone wants to see what you've got going on over there." He winked at me and his pink face lit up with a smile. "My wife bought a new dress."

My heart skipped and danced against my ribs. The *Town Charmer* had told people to come to my party? "Really?"

"Uh huh."

I rocked onto my tiptoes and bounced with enthusiasm. Whoever that blogger was, I could kiss them!

He finished ringing up my items and reached beneath the counter. "Here. It's for your beach décor. Part of my history in Charm. I want it back, though." He placed a clamming shovel in front of me. "The missus and I used to go clamming on our dates. We'd get all muddy, then take our time cleaning up." He wiggled his bushy caterpillar eyebrows and expelled a hearty laugh.

I shook my head at him. "Well, thank you for that visual," I teased. "I think it's great that you'd trust me with this. I'll set it out tonight." I pulled the shovel across the counter and paid my bill. "You're the best, Mr. Waters. See you tonight!"

I started home with my head in the clouds and the giant sun hat bouncing on my head. Its brim flipped and flopped with each step. I'd be a hit at the Kentucky Derby.

I can do this, I thought, a jaunty spring popping into my step. The town blogger might have encouraged folks to come to my party, but locals weren't lemmings. They thought for themselves, and maybe they'd needed a little push, but they were coming. A naysayer or two had made me erroneously believe Charm had turned against me, but the whole island hadn't assumed the worst. The larger, quieter, and more polite majority were keeping their thoughts to themselves. Thoughts like *Everly Swan isn't a killer.*

I shimmied my aching shoulders with glee. People were coming! My neighbors, old acquaintances, and friends were giving me a chance, and I was going to make them glad they did. I swung my hips and imagined twirling, if I could see past my hat and lift my bag far enough off the ground. I'd delight them tonight! Dazzle them! Awe them!

A figure in a fisherman's hat and trench coat at Amelia's little library took the wind out of my sails. He reached for the door. A metal pail sat at his feet.

"Hey!" I hollered. "What are you doing?"

The man turned toward me with a start and his mouth fell open. The wide brim of his hat shaded his eyes.

"Hold it right there," I said, picking up my pace, giant hat flopping.

He grabbed his bucket with both hands and hoisted it off the ground.

My stomach clenched. I couldn't let him trash the library while I stood and watched. "Stop!" I screamed, panic flooding through me. I refused to let Amelia down. She didn't deserve to be bullied and upset every day. "Don't you dare!"

I hoisted my shopping bag higher off the ground and broke into a run, waving my clam digger overhead. "Put that down!"

The man spun in place and speed-walked away, metal pail in his grip. He vanished around a neighboring home in the distance.

I was out of breath before I reached the Little Library. I bent forward and puffed for air. "Yes." I pumped the shovel overhead in victory, then wrenched myself upright. "Take that, vandal."

I shuffled the rest of the way home, good mood restored. I only wished I'd recognized the vandal— wearing a disguise had been a smart move on his part. By the time I reached my front porch, my heart rate had settled, but I was in desperate need of a shower.

The aunts were busy decorating when I arrived, and Hana was bopping around the room to Bobby Day's "Rockin' Robin." My broom doubled as her dance partner and microphone.

I stopped to watch and smiled.

Aunt Fran noticed me first. "Well, don't just stand there, get over here and tell us what you think."

I hefted my bag onto the counter and gave the whole room an appreciative whistle. "It looks amazing and smells like heaven."

"I'm baking you an almond pound cake," Aunt Fran said. "A gift to go with the rhubarb jam Hana made."

"Thank you." I pressed a hand to my heart. "That's perfect."

Aunt Clara dug into the canvas tote and examined

my purchases. "This is nice," she said, holding up a bowl of shells. She noticed the clam digger in my grip. "Oh, a shovel."

"Mr. Waters loaned it to me for the night." I handed it over, then drifted to a wall of new photos. My aunts had hung an array of dramatic black and white prints in coordinating mattes and frames, images of Charm over the years. Parades past, hot air balloons, and street parties. I should make sure Detective Hays and his makeshift family knew about this weekend's street party; Denver would love all the food and hoopla.

Aunt Fran adjusted the bottom row of photos, aligning them all perfectly. "We've been meaning to put these up all week. What do you think?"

I drew closer to a row of frames with my grandmother as a young woman, cradling my infant mother in her arms, carrying her through the waves and along the same boardwalk I navigated today. "These are amazing." I stretched a finger toward them slowly, afraid they might disappear. It was rare for my aunts to bring out any photos of my mother. I think they assumed it might make me sad, but I'd never really known her, so the loss I felt was a phantom pain. Missing something I never had was hard to explain. Fortunately, Grandma stepped in as my mother, father, best friend, and confidante until the day she passed.

I hadn't been there. I was at a rodeo.

I rubbed the tears from under my eyes. "Thank

you," I told Aunt Fran before enveloping her in a hug. "For everything."

"Of course," she said. Her gentle hand patted my head. "What is this monstrosity?" She peeled off the enormous hat I'd forgotten I was wearing.

I laughed through a sniffle. "I thought it would be pretty in a beach display with the sand and shells. It's a little much, huh?"

Fran made a droll face. "Not at all. It's the perfect size for an elephant." She carried the hat to the corner and staged it with the shovel and a pair of my flip-flops.

Clara hummed behind the counter. "The pasta is almost ready."

I hurried to my stove. "You're cooking?" Clara and the kitchen were a dangerous combination, and I couldn't afford another insurance claim.

"Heavens, no." She raised her brows. "I saw your menu on the fridge and thought I could save you some time by boiling the noodles. I've also organized the ingredients for each recipe on the counter and placed the corresponding recipe card on top. Hana washed, sliced, and chopped all the veggies before she started dancing."

Hana dipped the broom, then took a bow. "Thank you," she said, swiveling her hips as though she was an Elvis impersonator. "Thank you very much."

I clapped, and my aunts joined in with enthusiastic hoots and whistles.

Tonight would be perfect.

I worked steadily through the afternoon, prepping everything I could in advance and storing it inside the fridge for later, while my aunts set the counter buffet-style with empty bowls and trays as placeholders until I filled them with food.

"Did you know the *Town Charmer* encouraged people to come tonight?" I asked.

Aunt Clara nodded. "Well, yes. An anonymous source said you'd been eliminated from the suspects list. We even had a customer this afternoon."

"What?" My eyes bulged. "Why didn't you tell me there's finally some helpful news going around about me?"

She shrugged. "I already knew you didn't kill Mr. Paine. I figured you knew that too."

I rolled my eyes and wiped sweat from my brow, gagging at the whiff of body odor I got by raising my arm. "Lord have mercy." I caught sight of the time on my wristwatch. "Oh no!" I had one hour to transform my hot mess self into something resembling a human, preferably one who smelled good.

I stripped off my apron and made a run for the door to the upstairs. "I've got to hurry!"

"Take your time," Aunt Clara called after me.

"We've got this," Aunt Fran said.

And I knew it was true.

Thankfully, a hot shower did wonders for my appearance, untangling my hair and easing the tension in the muscles along my neck and shoulders. Afterward, I lathered my clean skin with peach lotion and doused my hair with Curl Keeper, the only thing that had any impact on my Medusa-esque mop, as long as I didn't venture outside for long.

I unloaded a tackle-box of makeup and pulled out every trick I knew for making it look as if I wasn't wearing any. Then I slicked red lipstick on and coated my lashes in mascara for pop.

My outfit was another issue all together. The only decent dress on a hanger was the one I'd worn to sign papers at the realty office and on the day after Detective Hays had announced that my tea might have killed Mr. Paine. Other than the dress I'd worn to Mr. Paine's funeral, I hadn't bothered unpacking anything less comfortable than T-shirts and sundresses.

I ripped into a stack of boxes in my closet marked Work Clothes and Special Occasion. The whole idea of buying a beach house and opening an iced tea shop was to kick back and dress down. The joke was on me as I ravaged the boxes in search of something perfect for a fancy party at the aforementioned tea shop.

Three boxes later, I unearthed a fitted cocktail dress, tags still attached. The heart-shaped neckline and halter top were made of satin to match a thick band at the waist. The glossy black was covered in sets of bright red cherries with thin green stems, and the look was so perfectly vintage I nearly swooned— which was why I'd bought it to begin with. I'd just never had an occasion to wear it.

I slid the dress over my hips and admired the way the cut made me look like a pinup girl. For the first time in a long while, I didn't feel plus-sized; I felt curvy and desirable, like Marilyn Monroe or Betty Boop. All I needed was a cute set of black heels and Grandma's pearls to pull it together, and I knew where to find those.

I strutted down the stairs and into the café, prepared to ask Hana and my great aunts what they thought of the dress, but they weren't alone. Hordes of guests stood in clusters throughout the room, chatting and smiling.

My heart clenched, and I made a run for the fridge.

Clara caught me by the wrist and shook her head. "It's all done, dear. We put everything out as soon as the first couple knocked." She leaned closer to my ear. "Folks were early and lined up on your porch."

"They came early?" I squeezed Aunt Clara's hand.

"Hello." I greeted guests with a broad and genuine smile. "Mr. and Mrs. Waters!" I pulled the older couple into my arms as a group hug. "I'm so glad you're here. Thank you for coming."

Mr. Waters straightened his jacket when I released him. "We wouldn't miss it."

His wife smiled brightly. "You've done a lovely job here. Everything looks amazing."

I winked at my aunts standing arm-in-arm behind the counter. "I had plenty of help, so I'll try not to take all the credit. I hope you'll sample a little of everything. Help yourself whenever you're ready."

I shook their hands again and turned to welcome another round of guests.

Sandy from the ice cream shop paused just inside the doorway.

"Come in." I waved, hustling over to meet him. "Welcome to Sun, Sand, and Tea. I'm so glad you're here."

"Thank you," he said, looking more at ease when a number of guests called out to him.

"I'll let you mingle," I said. "Help yourself to whatever you'd like."

I scanned the bustling café, full of smiling, chatting friends. Then I stopped to take it all in. *This* was what I'd dreamed of.

I made another pass at the buffet to be sure nothing was getting cold, or warm. Everything was disappearing fast.

Hana was positioned behind the counter, moving double-time on refill duty, topping off the bowls and trays as each ran low, while Aunt Fran manned the tea jugs, protecting them against potential poisoners and delivering fresh glasses to anyone who asked. People were eating *and* drinking.

I pressed a palm to my grateful heart. A fork clattered onto the floor, and I bent to retrieve it. A slick wolf whistle sounded behind me, and I turned to tell the culprit what I thought of it.

Detective Hays smiled back at me, only a foot away. His impish grin told me he knew exactly the sort of response to expect.

I forgave him immediately. He didn't just come to my party, he'd dressed for it. The simple black slacks and tie were perfectly understated. The cuffs of his crisp white dress shirt had been rolled to the elbows, exposing ropes of tan muscle in his forearms and making him look completely at ease.

Meanwhile, I felt a bit faint. "Detective Hays," I greeted, offering my hand.

He gave my palm a gentle squeeze. "I think it's probably time you called me Grady."

"Grady," I echoed, trying the name out on my lips.

He held my stare and my hand several moments longer than manners required. Then he let his soft gaze tour my body head to toe. "You sure clean up nice."

"Back at ya," I said, fighting a fierce blush and interlacing my fingers in front of me when he released my hand. "Are you here alone?"

"Yep."

"Business or pleasure?" I asked, feeling a little saucy. I blamed the dress.

"A little of both, I guess. I didn't want to miss your party, and given the day you had yesterday, I thought you might need a little emotional support. Clearly you don't."

I tipped my head toward Hana and the aunts. "I had a crew helping with the labor today. My emotional state is a whole other story."

He smiled back, flashing that dimple. "Are you happy?"

"Right now? Absolutely." I leaned in close, getting a delicious whiff of his cologne, and rose on my toes to whisper in his ear: "People are eating my food. They don't think it will kill them."

Grady laughed. "I'm glad, and I'm sorry I put that idea into anyone's head."

I stepped back. "Did you also know the *Town Charmer* claims that I am no longer on the suspect list?"

He gave me a wide grin. "I do."

"Any idea who leaked that information?"

His smile widened.

"You?" I asked, suddenly breathless. "So it's true?"

"After careful investigation," he said, "I've been unable to find any evidence suggesting that you had the intention, access, or ability to poison your tea for Mr. Paine in the way in which it was poisoned."

"You believe me." I grinned. I resisted the urge to say *I told you so*.

"Detective Hays?" A man with lobster-red skin and a deep scowl hobbled toward us.

"Mr. Coster. Nice to see you. How's the sunburn?"

"Hurts. I learned my lesson, though. Next time I go boating, I'll take sunscreen." His enchanting British accent stole the edge from his words.

"The sunburn won't last long," Grady said. "If you're hurting, then you've got to try to stay out of the sun while it heals."

"Yeah." The man nodded. "I wore my rain gear all day to keep the sun off my burns. Hot as Hades in long sleeves."

Grady smiled at me. "Mr. Coster moved here from Dorset last week. We met at the ice cream stand on Main."

"Ah." I smiled at the newcomer. "It's rainy there, I hear."

He huffed. "You don't know the half of it." Mr. Coster nodded at Grady. "While I've got your attention, I'd like to file a report," he said.

"Why?" Grady frowned. "What happened?"

"I was threatened earlier, and I'd like it noted in case it happens again. You never know with these things."

Grady crossed his arms. "Were you harmed in any way? I can take you to the station now, or we can meet there in the morning. Was it someone at this party?" He cast a questioning look in my direction and I shrugged.

"No." Mr. Coster shook his head. "It was earlier. I was too miserable to rest, so I tried to borrow something to read from one of those Little Libraries on the boardwalk."

"And?" he asked, folding his arms in irritation.

Uh oh. I gave Mr. Coster a closer look. *Add some rain gear...*

"And?" Mr. Coster snapped. "I had my eye on a historical romance, but some lunatic chased me with a shovel, yelling, 'Put that down!' I was nearly killed! Over what?" he squawked. "There's nothing wrong with men reading romance is there?"

Grady shot me an amused look.

I ducked out of the way.

"She had a hat about this big," Mr. Coster said. He mimed the size of my hat with both arms above his head.

I went to toss Mr. Waters's clamming shovel in the closet before I wound up on the town's list of homicidal maniacs again.

CHAPTER

❧

FIFTEEN

My café had reached max capacity by seven, and I hadn't stopped smiling for at least an hour. Grady ducked out early with a polite goodbye, leaving me to breathe a little easier. He made me nervous in all sorts of ways I preferred not to think about. By eight, I was sure I'd spoken with everyone in town. Folks would float in for a bit, then venture out as another round of guests arrived. I had a police detective and a mystery blogger to thank for the positive turn of my fate.

I plucked a date stuffed with Hana's goat cheese off the buffet and tapped my foot to an old Beach Boys song. Aunt Clara moved to my side and twined her arm with mine. "I'd call this shindig a whopping success, wouldn't you?"

"Absolutely." I scanned the crowd, searching for empty plates or glasses to refill and any new arrivals I hadn't greeted yet.

My eyes landed on Sam Smart, visible between a pair of women with oversized handbags. He was seated at the corner table, handing out business cards. I hadn't seen him come in, but I wouldn't let him leave without asking him a few questions.

"I'll be right back," I told Aunt Clara.

I nudged my way around the crush of bodies in the tightly packed room and tried not to question the structural integrity of my home's historic support beams.

I helped myself to the empty seat next to Sam as the music changed. "Hello." I forced a bright smile. "I'm glad you could make it. Are you enjoying the party?"

He lifted his tea glass with a strained smile. "Very much."

Tension rolled off him in waves. Had it been there before I'd arrived, or had I triggered it? It was hard to tell with Sam. He always seemed to be some degree of tense. Until recently, I'd assumed that was just his personality; now I didn't know.

Being accused of murder had opened my eyes in the worst of ways. If a detective, who dealt with criminals for a living, believed *I* could be a killer, then clearly anyone could be.

Sam scanned the room, determined to avoid eye contact. I tried to recall all the possible meanings behind his behavior, but the body-language book had been somewhat indeterminate on avoiding eye contact. One page suggested a person who wouldn't look you in the eyes was nervous, possibly hiding something, while the next page said the person might harbor a romantic interest and want to hide it. I didn't think romantic interest was the problem with Sam, but something was definitely going on. He'd looked me in the eye plenty of times before. "Am I making you nervous?"

His gaze snapped back to me. "No. Why?"

I folded my hands on top of the table. "You seem uncomfortable. Like when I stopped by your office a couple days ago. If it's something I've done, I'm really sorry. I've had a rough week."

"It's not you," he said. "I've got a lot on my plate right now. You understand." Sam checked his watch, his bouncing knee vibrating the table.

I might not have made him nervous, but *something* certainly had. "You know, I'd love to talk with you more," I said, offering up a warm smile. "How about lunch tomorrow?"

Sam wet his lips and cleared his throat, appearing to be suddenly rapt with interest. He leaned forward in his seat. "Are you having any luck with that thing you mentioned before? The one you were looking into?"

"I think so." I held back the part where I'd apparently gained the killer's attention but didn't know who he was, so now the lunatic was following me around making threats while I tried to keep the tail of my skirt out of my underpants. I matched his posture, leaning my elbows on the table. "Have you thought of something more to tell me?"

"Did you talk to Lucinda?" The words were barely audible over a group of women belting "Good Day Sunshine."

"I did," I said. "And did you know Mr. Paine was also in a verbal tussle with Mr. Metz over the colonial on Bay View?" I lifted my brows and waited for his response.

He sat back, putting distance between us and breaking the intimate bond of co-conspirators. "I had heard that, yes."

"Why didn't you tell me? I could've talked to him sooner."

He didn't answer.

I pushed further. "Is Mr. Metz a friend of yours? Is he a client?"

Sam's phone buzzed on the table; he turned it over and peeked at the screen. "I'm sorry, I need to get going. I have another appointment tonight."

"Wait," I said. "Just a few more questions."

The lines on his forehead deepened. "Lunch tomorrow, okay? Stop by my office." He stood and tucked his abandoned chair beneath the table. "Thanks for the tea and hospitality. I appreciate it."

Before I could respond, he'd strode out the door.

"See you tomorrow," I muttered to the empty threshold.

I made my way back to Aunt Clara in time to see her finish dancing The Freddie near my deck. The crowd had thinned out. "I guess this party is winding down."

She nearly fell into me, beaming with a goofy smile. "People don't dance enough anymore."

I nodded thoughtfully. I couldn't remember the last time I'd danced, in public anyway. My shower and bedroom were another story.

"It was such a nice turnout," Clara said. "Even better than I expected."

Hana pulled empty trays from the buffet. "Yes, and that's it for the sausage balls and cheese straws." She loaded the platters into my dishwasher, then wiped the counter. "Either your food was an incredible hit, or you invited some very hungry people."

I laughed. "Hopefully the first one."

Aunt Fran rocked one antique tea dispenser onto its side and emptied the dregs into the garbage can. "This one is cashed. Old-Fashioned Sun Tea was the clear hit of the night."

Warmth pooled in my chest and my spirits lifted impossibly higher. "This party was your best idea ever." I patted Aunt Clara's hand and smiled at Aunt Fran. "Thank you."

The last sprinkling of guests drifted toward the door.

"Thank you all for coming," I said, hurrying to see them off. "Come back anytime. There are still a few things on the buffet and I'd be happy to box something up for you."

They politely refused doggie bags, waving as they stepped out into the night. Mr. Waters and his wife were the last ones to the door.

"Mr. Waters!" I caught him by the sleeve. "Hang on. I want to send your shovel home so I don't forget it." I dashed to the pantry and back. "There you are. Thank you so much for letting me borrow a piece of your history for the night." I smiled, and his wife looked at the shovel and blushed.

Mr. Waters shook my hand. "Anytime. You know, we'd stay and help clean up, but it looks like you've got a nice crew here already, and we're running late."

His wife adjusted her little blue hat, the peacock plume in its band swaying back and forth. "Everything was delicious," she said. "Folks would've taken you up on the offer for leftovers if they were going home. Don't take it personally."

My gaze traveled from Mr. and Mrs. Waters to the mass of locals trailing down my front steps. "They aren't going home? Is something else happening tonight?" I strained to think of what it might be. The street fair wasn't for another two days.

"Sure," Mr. Waters said. "Lucinda's thing started at eight. A party to celebrate Benedict's life. I'm sure you've heard about it. She's been telling folks to spread the word."

I shook my head. "No." No one had told me much of anything lately.

"Well," he said, motioning to the café behind me. "You've been busy."

I doubted my busyness was the reason no one in town had told me.

His wife leaned against his side and grinned. "She says this party is about Benedict, but we all know she's just announcing her return to Charm."

"Kind of like she's throwing her own welcome back party," Mr. Waters said with an amused shake of his head. "But she's calling it a celebration of Benedict's life, so who can say no to that?"

The box truck and man in white coveralls blinked into mind. Modern Elegance wasn't a new furniture deliverer as I'd imagined, it was a party rental company.

I shot a look at my aunts, who suddenly seemed to be wholly absorbed in their cleanup and pointedly avoiding my gaze.

Mr. Waters held the door open for his wife. "Maybe we'll see you there, huh?"

"Maybe," I whispered, a fuzzy idea taking form in my curious mind. *I really shouldn't press my luck and risk that restraining order.* But the town had been on its best behavior here in my café, and maybe this was the perfect opportunity to make up with Lucinda. Maybe even make some progress on my fresh start now that there were no strikes against me.

I locked the door, then turned to my aunts and Hana. "I'm not going to ask why you didn't tell me about Lucinda Paine's party," I said. "So you can all stop trying not to look directly at me."

Clara lifted a timid face in my direction. "You're not mad?"

"Nope." I went behind the counter to evaluate the leftover situation and see if there was anything left fit to take to a party.

An uncut lemon cake was still in the fridge. "Perfect." I grabbed my purse and a sweater from the hall closet, returning for the cake. "I'd tell you to just leave this and go home to rest, but I know better. If I'm not back before you go, don't forget to lock up." I kissed my aunts' cheeks and hugged Hana tight, then I gave the trio a meaningful stare. "You know, I'm really glad I'm back home."

"Us too," Clara cooed. "We know where you're going, so be careful out there. This hasn't been your week."

I blew an air kiss on my way into the night. "Preach."

I stepped onto the boardwalk, cake in hand. Nerves twisted and pinched in my gut and a cool sweat broke over my chest and forehead. I didn't want a restraining order, but I also didn't like having an enemy in Lucinda. At least Grady had dropped me as a suspect. That should give me a little cushion if Lucinda didn't respond well to my appearance at her place. And worst-case scenario, I wouldn't be legally permitted within a certain distance of her, which I doubted would change my life. Once I proved I didn't hurt her ex-husband, she'd surely lift any restraining order, anyway.

The party would've been easy to find, even if I hadn't seen Lucinda outside the place this morning. Bistro lights hung in swoops along the wooden back-yard fence, only a few dozen feet from where I'd met her on the sidewalk. The measured notes of a waltz lifted gently into the air and couples streamed arm in arm up the cobblestone path to her home.

I filed in behind the ranks, heading for the front door.

A buffet had been set up in the room left of the foyer, Mr. Paine's furniture pushed against the walls or removed entirely to allow for rented tables and seating.

A man in traditional livery stood behind the overloaded buffet, hands clasped behind his back. "May I make you a plate?"

I blinked. Buffets were normally self-serve, but then again everything at this party seemed a little *extra*.

He smiled. "You have your hands full."

I followed his gaze to the forgotten dessert in my grip. "Oh," I said stupidly. "I brought a cake." My cheeks warmed at the obviousness of the statement.

I'd erroneously assumed this party would be a normal one, where the hostess hauled in extra seating and maybe linens if it was a big deal, otherwise everyone brought something to share—even if the invitation said dinner was provided. It was just customary. Courtesy. Good manners. Southern tradition.

"No one's eating," the man whispered. "I think it looks all right. Do you?"

I scanned the thoughtless spread: mini meatballs, tuna on rye slices, flat-bottomed spoons filled with garlic and mushroom mashed potatoes.

"Meh," I said. Hopefully Lucinda hadn't overpaid. I could've put this boring menu together on a dime—though I *wouldn't* have. Maybe I should offer catering to locals for events like this. Showers, graduation and anniversary parties… That would be fun.

The buffet man leaned closer. "Well, the food looks better than the desserts. I'm sure of that."

A table on the opposite wall held tiers of marshmallows, graham crackers, pretzels, and strawberries by an erupting chocolate fountain.

A balding man in a black polo shirt stuck a pretzel rod under the fountain, then bit into it with a smile; he did it again a moment later. Same pretzel.

"That's not a dessert table, that's a bacteria incubator," I said to the buffet guy.

I ferried my cake to the table and removed the cover. A guest took notice and pointed, whispering. I waved at some familiar faces, stepping away so folks could help themselves.

Most of the people in line at the open bar had been at my place earlier and nearly wiped my buffet clean. No wonder Lucinda's spread was virtually untouched—not to mention the fact that it was all unimaginative food in various shades of tan.

Lucinda stood among a cluster of women with champagne flutes and I backed away, suddenly uncomfortable with the possibility of being yelled at in public, accused of party-crashing or something worse. I kept assuming Lucinda would be cordial and behave the way I would in her shoes, but she hadn't so far, and I had no reason to think she would now.

I scolded myself internally for thinking that crashing her party was a good idea, blaming all the warm and fuzzy feelings from a successful grand opening. Lucinda hadn't come to Sun, Sand, and Tea tonight. She hadn't forgiven me, and asking her to do it publicly seemed beyond risky.

I longed to turn and run out the front door, but that would only draw more attention. Instead, I decided to slip out the back and try making amends with Lucinda later, in a more private setting. Putting as many guests between us as possible and attempting to look at ease, I made my way to the back of the house. It was comfortably full of friends and neighbors, chatter and laughter, with interesting conversations, but I didn't hear anything interesting about Mr. Paine's death. Also, praise the waves, no new gossip about me.

In the backyard was a string quartet playing Vivaldi from a stage. Tall bar tables draped in black linen stood on the small lawn.

It was the first party I'd attended in Charm that didn't feature margaritas, piña coladas, and barbeque—and if anyone had live music, it was karaoke or a bad Jimmy Buffett cover band. The whole setup Lucinda had going on was weird, over the top, and completely out of place in our little island community. I supposed fancy was the only available option from a company called Modern Elegance.

Maybe I was being a beach snob. Everyone seemed to be having a nice enough time, even if they weren't giving me any new information to work with.

"Lucinda," a woman called. She lifted her arm to draw the hostess's attention.

Lucinda moved through the back door, scanning the crowd and smiling. She waved as she moved gracefully across the lawn.

I stiffened, then ducked on instinct.

"Is that lemon cake?" Grady's voice cut through the night. His head bobbed above the crowd several feet away, a determined expression on his brow. *Oh sure. He left my party early to come to hers.* And just like everyone else I'd talked to before Mr. Waters tonight, Grady hadn't mentioned it, either.

Lucinda hugged several guests, before heading purposefully in my direction. "Well, Detective Hays," she called, "I'm so glad you could make it." She smiled demurely, an entourage of older women in tow.

I scooted behind a crowd of men who hadn't noticed me, unready to face her, and I couldn't talk to Grady without risking Lucinda's wrath.

Grady moved in a slow circle, sharp eyes hunting for me, before giving up to meet the woman of the house.

"Come. I have someone who wants to meet you." She locked her arm in his and led him back inside.

I inched toward the rear gate Mr. Paine had probably used to put out the trash. I wasn't in love with the analogy, but I slipped through the gate anyway and crept through the shadows toward the street like a ninja.

I did a double take at the line of bags and cans along the curb. Lucinda hadn't wasted any time moving herself in or Mr. Paine's memories out. Piles were prepped and tagged for disposal. A few were marked as donations. The rest was stuffed into lidless garbage bins: fishing rods, tackle boxes, pool cues, stacks of *Historic Home* magazine. It was sad to think the things that were important to him were so clearly unimportant to her.

I peeked into a box filled with rolled-up blueprints,

and the hair on my arms and neck stood at attention. I checked to be sure no one was around before thumbing through the contents. Maps of Charm were intermingled with the blueprints, and Sam Smart's company logo was stamped on the back of every document.

My mind raced with a new set of questions: Why would Mr. Paine have had all these maps and blueprints? Was he working on something that had gotten him killed? Something that had to do with Mr. Metz and his colonial renovation, perhaps?

I wanted to take a closer look, but could hardly have a seat near the trash and read by moonlight. I'd have to take the box home, so I hefted the box onto one hip.

Sleuthing was hard, frustrating work. No wonder Grady was grumpy so often.

A soft meow drew my attention to the neighbor's driveway, where my raggedy white cat stood, her bright green eyes eerie and luminous under the light of the full moon.

"Don't be judgey," I told her. "These could be important. Plus, they're on the curb. I'm allowed to take them."

She meowed again.

I took a few quick steps, struggling to balance the awkward box, and my fitness band trumpeted obnoxiously. *Good grief!* I froze, tummy clenched and heart hammering. As if a grown woman could simply vanish by holding still enough.

A long beat of silence stretched though the night. Even the band had stopped playing.

Applause erupted, and I sucked in fresh air. *Oh, thank goodness*. For a moment, I'd imagined a hundred faces peering over the fence at me. I dared a look at the closed gate as a new song began. My gaze drifted higher then, to Lucinda's home beyond.

A curtain dropped in an upstairs window. The whole town might not have seen me take the box, but someone had.

CHAPTER

SIXTEEN

I hightailed it home with the cat at my side. The night seemed darker than usual, though it could've been my imagination. It was after ten o'clock and well past the slivers of twilight that had struggled on the horizon as I'd made my way to the party. The stars and watching moon had tucked themselves in behind the dark velvet blanket overhead, and the air crackled with a strange new feeling, ominous and foreboding.

"I know what you're thinking," I told Maggie as she trotted along at my feet. "Someone saw me take this box, but there's a chance they couldn't identify me because it was dark in the alley."

She continued on without response, highly focused on our trip down the boardwalk, as if she knew where I was headed.

A brisk evening wind flipped the ends of my hair over my shoulders, sending shivers along my spine. I moved a little faster, hyperaware that most people on the island who weren't already in bed were probably at Lucinda's, which made it a prime time for crime everywhere else. I could be chased, kidnapped, or clobbered and no one would hear me scream. Even Grady would be none the wiser until a jogger found my body at sunrise. I held the box more tightly to my chest, prepared to use it in self-defense if necessary.

"Even if whoever I saw at the window knows it was me who took the box, I can always explain myself," I told Maggie. "I'll say I'm a map collector." Of course, then I'd have to run out and buy a bunch of old maps from another town and pretend I'd had them all along. So, maybe not. "Deceit is hard."

Maggie gave me a condescending look.

I sighed with relief as my beautiful, historic home came into view. Thankfully, the porch light over my front door was on, though the rest of the place was dark. My aunts must've called it a night at Sun, Sand, and Tea. I jogged up the front steps, maneuvering the box on my hip to free my hand for the key. The tumbler rolled easily, and I was instantly relieved that my aunts had remembered to lock up.

Maggie slid between my feet as I checked the street for stalkers before jetting upstairs without waiting for an invitation.

I followed her in, then kicked the door shut behind me and flipped the dead bolt back into place, feeling my way through the café without turning any lights on and stumbling up the stairs to my private quarters. By the time I reached my living room, I was ready to drop.

I lowered my burden onto the floor, then stretched out beside it. The soft fibers of my carpet cushioned my aching limbs. I'd walked more this week than I had in months, and my body felt it everywhere.

I stared at the elaborate crown moldings and painted tin panels on my ceiling until my eyelids drooped, grateful to be alone and safe in my house. Maggie leapt onto one arm of my thrift-store couch and gave a long, judgmental meow. She was right—I needed to get started.

"I'm glad you decided to come up here," I said. It was weird and a little funny that she had stalked me until I noticed her and fell in love, but I was glad for it. I'd heard of dogs following people home, but never a cat. Cats were picky. The fact she'd chosen me of all people to judge and ignore made me feel special.

I'd never had a pet before, though this particular animal didn't seem much like a pet. More like a college roommate who came home late and refused to answer questions about where she'd been. *Pet* also implied a certain amount of reliance on me, and this cat didn't have that problem.

"Did you live here before?" I asked, thinking back to Aunt Clara's crazy story about a raggedy cat as the embodiment of the two suicidal women who'd died here. "You can live here now, if you want," I offered. "I could use the company, and I have at least a million fish and tuna recipes."

Her eyelids drooped lazily.

"Must be hard being trapped in that cat body for a

hundred and seventy years," I said. "You want to talk about it?"

She flopped on her side and licked her paw, completely disinterested.

"That's fine. I have things to do anyway."

Apparently, rejection was my middle name tonight. First Grady slipped away from my appropriately relaxed and beachy party to attend Lucinda's over-the-top schmancy soiree, then Sam ran off on me while I was in the middle of talking to him, and now the cat wouldn't even look at me.

There were at least a dozen maps and blueprints in the box. I needed a pot of black coffee or gallon of sweet tea, because I hadn't slept well in a few nights—it had been a long day, and my eyelids felt as if someone had tied little weights to them.

I blew out a long breath. "First things first." I rolled the first map open and pressed it to the floor. It promptly rewound itself. I gave it another shot, this time concentrating on the corners and ends, but the paper spiraled back faster than I could stop it.

Narrowing my eyes at the uncooperative paper, I considered my options. There were bunches of maps and blueprints in that box, and I needed a way to look at them without having to hold them in my hands. The nearest bookshelf provided me with an armload of books, which I used to secure the corners.

The sight of half a dozen seminaked cowboys spread out on the floor made me shake my head in dismay. Despite my personal experience and the fact that no woman in my family ever found a lasting love, I was a sucker for happily ever after…especially if the hero wore boots and had good manners.

Not even knowing things hadn't worked out for sweet Amelia and her husband could keep me from dreaming about love. Somewhere deep down inside of me there was a tiny ember of hope that I would meet my soul mate, like in the books.

I shifted onto my hands and knees in front of the flattened maps and tried to make heads or tails of whatever I was looking at. "I don't suppose you can read these?" I asked Maggie. "There's a whole lot of blue with a bunch of white lines, plus a few curves and scribbles." And, of course, Sam Smart's company logo stamped on the back of each one.

I grabbed my phone to snap several photos. I wouldn't have to haul the box to Sam's place for lunch tomorrow if I had the pictures—I could just show him my phone and see what he had to say, and I congratulated myself for finally planning ahead.

Even if Sam wasn't involved in Paine's death, which I truly hoped was the case, he would be able to tell me what I was looking at.

Sam's troubled face came to back mind. He hadn't been himself tonight, and he was unquestionably weird at his office yesterday too.

It was probably a waste of time, but I opened the browser and plugged Sam's name in. Hundreds of hits came back, all of them applying to different people. Lawyers. Scientists. None had anything to do with the man I wanted to learn more about. I tried again, this time adding some other key words like "Realtor" and "North Carolina."

This time, the results were more interesting.

I curled against the couch and scrolled through the hits. Sam Smart wasn't just a high-strung small-town real estate agent—he was a thief! Article after article from newspapers and criminal justice websites popped up, dozens of cases of Sam Smart the Fraud all along the east coast.

I flipped through the headlines, mouth open.

ILLEGAL GAMBLING CHARGES FILED AGAINST
VIRGINIA BEACH REAL ESTATE AGENT

SUCCESSFUL ATLANTA REAL ESTATE AGENT
PLEADS GUILTY TO IDENTITY FRAUD

SAVANNAH'S FAVORITE REAL ESTATE AGENT REMOVED
ON FOURTEEN COUNTS OF EMBEZZLEMENT

I thrashed my head side to side, hoping to clear my brain Etch a Sketch style. Gambling? Fraud? Embezzlement? I pored over the articles with greedy eyes. Sam got the charges dropped just as often as he was found guilty and slapped with fines, community service, or both. From the looks of it, the fines must be adding up. I couldn't tell how much he'd paid off so far, but I was sure he didn't make enough selling homes in Charm to put a dent in the bill he had going.

Whatever amount of cash he'd accumulated from fraud and embezzlement couldn't have been worth the penalties. He'd practically have to keep up the illegal stuff just to pay the piper.

That thought got stuck in my head like barbecue on a spit. What if Sam had gone back to his old ways, forced to make bad choices if he wanted to pay the restitution installments and stay out of jail? What if he'd gotten into trouble again and Mr. Paine had found out? Would Mr. Paine have threatened to go public with Sam's past? Would he have blackmailed him?

Or what if Sam was plotting with Mr. Metz to turn all the massive old properties in town into exclusive bed and breakfast locations, or spas, or any number of things that would've made them richer, and Mr. Paine had protested? If Sam and Metz were in cahoots, it would explain why Sam had pointed a finger at Lucinda and not at Mr. Metz.

I rubbed my temples. The ideas came at me faster than I could accept or reject them. Sam and Mr. Paine were at odds the day Mr. Paine died. I'd noticed, but barely paid attention. I had assumed it was silly, like most of Mr. Paine's arguments. My imagination soon went from clever and creative to downright scary as it wove together endless scenarios that made Sam Smart a heartless killer.

Suddenly, lunch together in his office seemed significantly less appealing.

My phone buzzed, and I nearly screamed in

surprise. I swiped the screen to reveal a new text from Grady, a message as direct as the man himself.

Are you home?

The doorbell rang before I could respond.

Thank goodness! I'd scared myself half-senseless thinking of reasons Sam or Mr. Metz could've killed Mr. Paine and put me next on their hit list. I barreled down the staircase to the first floor, typing my quick response and nearly breaking my neck on the crazy cat who darted between my feet.

Yes! I've got something you'll want to see!

I flipped the dead bolt and yanked the door open. A cool gust of wind whooshed in. Maggie ran screeching into the night, and my heart rate accelerated.

There was no one at my door.

I poked my head carefully past the threshold, one hand on the doorknob, ready to slam it in the face of anyone who came near. Except Grady. "Grady?" I asked the air, hoping he'd stepped into the shadows along my porch.

I listened hard to the whipping wind and ocean waves, refusing to step foot into the darkness again without a Louisville Slugger or pepper spray.

Maggie trotted back into view and took a seat on my bottom step, tracking something with her shiny green eyes.

My phone buzzed, pulling my eyes down: a new message from Grady.

I probably misunderstood that, but I'll be right over.

As I read his words and smiled, a blast of blinding

light flashed in my eyes, and my knees wobbled. Searing pain short-circuited my brain, and my legs gave out as the world went dark.

CHAPTER

SEVENTEEN

"Everly!" The sound of my name rattled painfully in my head. "Everly!"

Warm fingers pressed the tender flesh of my throat, and I struggled through the thickness of unconsciousness.

I groaned, wishing to be left alone. My body ached, and my eyes rolled helplessly behind sealed lids.

"You're going to be okay. Thank God," the voice said. Strong arms ran beneath my hips and shoulders, hoisting me in the air.

"Grady?" The word came from my mouth, but I wasn't sure how I knew it.

His chest bounced with a humorless chuckle. "You're easily the most danger-prone person I've ever met. The good news here is that it looks like you'll survive this time. You want to fill me in on what happened?"

I rocked and floated in his arms. The intoxicating scents of cologne and night air clung to his shirt and skin. I locked my arms around his neck in appreciation. "I don't know."

He set me upright on the couch, prodding my head, neck, and arms. "I don't understand what happened. It hasn't been ten minutes since your last text, and you were laid out on the floor at the bottom of your steps like you were dead. There's a goose egg the size of Texas on your head, but no other injuries that I can see. Did you fall?"

I pried my eyelids open. "Ow."

Grady rested his hand on my arm. "What hurts? Is it just your head?"

"I feel like I was struck by lightning." I did a quick inventory of my body. Nothing hurt specifically, aside from my forehead. I just felt achy all over.

He lifted his hand. "Is your vision blurry? How many fingers am I holding up?"

"Two." I pushed his hand down.

His hand popped back up, one digit pointed at the ceiling and he moved it slowly back and forth. "Can you follow my finger?"

"Stop it," I said, swatting his hand away once more. "I'm fine."

He stared back, lips downturned. "You could have a concussion. I'm a trained medic, now stop fussing and start cooperating, or I'll take you to the hospital."

"A medic?" What was this, World War II? I piped down and let him check me over. I'd been a regular patron of emergency rooms while following Wyatt and his friends with the rodeo, and I'd taken several first aid courses to prepare myself for assisting injured cowboys, so I knew Grady was right. I also knew what a concussion looked like, and I was pretty sure I didn't have one.

When he finished his exam, he relinquished his too-close stance by an inch. "Then tell me what you remember."

I rubbed my forehead. "I remember you were at the door."

"Wrong."

I dropped my hand. "You weren't at the door? Someone was."

"No. When I got here, the door was open and you were on the ground. I thought you fell down the steps and broke your neck." He rubbed a heavy hand over his face. "It wasn't me at the door. What else can you remember?"

I forced my addled mind to recall something else, any detail that might be useful. "There was a bright light. And pain." I wrinkled my nose. "A ton of pain, and it still hurts." A tear slid down my cheek.

Grady's face went from red to eggplant-colored. "So you didn't fall. Someone did this to you." He reached for me again, running his broad hands over my head, face, and neck. He moved a palm to my torso and I winced. "Did that hurt? Can you take a deep breath? You might've bruised your ribs in the fall. Can I take a look?"

I chewed my lip. "This feels like a game of doctor I played once in middle school."

He rolled his eyes. "Just let me see."

"That's exactly what he said." I took a deep breath to clear my head, wincing from the pain. "Okay, but don't look."

Grady made a face. "What? How can I see but not look?"

"I don't know. I can't think straight."

Grady dialed his phone and stood up, pacing the floor.

I watched him until a tidal wave of anxiety hit, and I tipped forward to place my head between my knees. This was the worst day ever. Bad. Bad. Bad.

"She was attacked," Grady barked into the phone. "Right inside her front door. Where the hell was that patrol I asked for?"

Attacked. The word brought everything together. "I was attacked?"

Grady shot me a look.

"Someone attacked me," I said, covering the goose egg with both hands.

Grady finished his call and returned to the couch. "Stop saying that. I get madder every time I hear it. Try to remember what happened, because I sent you a text when I was leaving Lucinda's to make sure you got home safely. Then I got a response saying you had something you thought I'd like to see. Ten minutes later you were out cold."

"I remember that," I said. I hadn't until he said it, but I knew it was right. "I don't know what it was that I wanted to show you, though."

"I didn't see any signs of a break-in downstairs," he said. "This place is as neat and tidy as mine ever is, and I've got someone tending to it. Your door wasn't damaged. Your television and computer are here. I don't think it was a robbery. I suppose that even you don't have that bad of luck."

I stared at his boots resting on my soft carpeting, and a fuzzy memory took shape. "My maps!"

I jolted to my feet, then sat immediately back down, palm on forehead.

"Sit still." Grady went to my kitchen and filled a glass with ice water. He set it near the fridge and took a bag of frozen peas from the freezer, handing it to me. "What were you playing doctor for in middle school? Didn't you know better by then?"

I put the peas against my forehead. "I was a late bloomer."

He pushed the glass of water in my direction with a lazy half smile. "Drink up. Hydrate."

I sipped gingerly at first, then gulped the glass dry.

Grady's expression turned sad. "I can't believe I let this happen to you."

I set my hand on his arm to comfort him. "It wasn't your fault."

He searched my face with keen cop eyes. "Let's start again."

"Okay," I agreed, pulling my thoughts back together.

"This doesn't look like the scene of a robbery, but you said something is missing? Your maps?"

Oh, right. I moved my hand away. Being knocked over the head was rough on a brain. "There was a box of blueprints and a few maps of Charm outside Mr. Paine's house, so I brought them home. I swear they were with the other trash and donations. A totally legal find."

Grady pinched the bridge of his nose with his thumb and forefinger. "I knew that was your lemon cake at the party. That's why I texted you. When I couldn't find you, I assumed you'd left. Just marched out into the night like some lunatic hasn't been tearing up your café and making threats on your life all week." He dropped his hand and leveled me with a pleading stare. "Why would you even go over there? Lucinda told me she wanted a restraining order against you. I told her she had insufficient grounds, so now I'm on her blacklist too."

A flimsy wave of guilt swept through me—mostly for crashing her party. It was just bad manners.

I wasn't even sure where to begin explaining why I'd gone to Lucinda's. I had about a dozen reasons in my head and heart. "For starters," I said, sighing, "I wanted folks to know I hadn't done anything wrong, and I wasn't afraid to show my face at Mr. Paine's life celebration. I even brought the cake as a show of goodwill. And if I'm being honest, I was angry that Lucinda would have the nerve to threaten me when I haven't given her reason. I've never given *anyone* reason to threaten me. I hate bullies. So what if I found her ex-husband on the night he died? That's all I did. It wasn't wrong, it was happenstance. Also, I tend to do things without thinking. *Sometimes*. I'm working on it."

Grady moved his head in slow deliberate nods. "So going to Lucinda's had nothing to do with snooping or eavesdropping?"

"I listened a little," I admitted.

He circled a wrist in the universal symbol for *move it along*. "Keep talking. Tell me the part where you stole out of the trash."

I gave him a grade-A stink eye. "You can't *steal* trash. I brought that stuff home and unrolled all the maps and blueprints on my floor." I gave the expanse of empty carpeting a long look. All that remained of my elaborate setup were the romance novels scattered across the floor. "I used those books to hold down the corners."

I took a few cleansing breaths to clear my mind and moved the bag of peas from my pounding head to my aching side. "Everything feels like it happened in a dream." I caught Grady's eye. "This was my fault, not yours. I'm stubborn, and impulsive, and I can't listen to a proper warning, apparently. It has nothing to do with you."

His eyes bulged. "I'm the town's only detective. This is the town's only homicide investigation. In what twist of reality is this not about me?"

"First of all"—I flicked a finger in his direction—"stop yelling at me."

He ground his teeth.

"I had no way of knowing any of these awful things were going to happen, okay? I started out trying to do the right thing. I wanted to clear my name because you implied that my tea was poisoned on the night Mr. Paine died, and I wanted to get him justice because he didn't deserve what happened to him, so I started asking my own questions. You"—I paused for dramatic effect—"were only looking at me as a suspect. How could you find the real killer like that? Within twenty-four hours I was getting shoved into marshes and threatened with cryptic messages written in sunscreen. I couldn't quit then. If the killer already knew what I was up to, it was only a matter of time before I would end up like Mr. Paine. So I pushed harder, figuring once I knew who the killer was and had them put in jail, I'd be safe. That part isn't going as fast as I'd hoped. Trust me. I'd like to let this go, but I'm already in past my knees."

Grady looked at my knees. "I've already told you you're off my suspects list, so you can strike that one from your excuse arsenal. As for the marsh, the sunscreen, and the break-in at your café, I'd say being attacked at your front door is a clear escalation and continuing to pursue this is going to land you in the hospital, or worse. So, you need to back off." He rolled his shoulders and massaged the muscles there with a grimace. "I don't even know why you mentioned your knees."

"In past your knees," I repeated the phrase more slowly, waiting for him to get it. "You know." I patted them for clarity.

"I know what knees are." He lowered himself onto my couch and dropped his head over the back.

"It's a water thing." I folded my legs beneath me and twisted to face him. "At first you just want to get your feet wet. Test the temperature. No big deal, but it feels good, so you take a few steps and the waves get the bottom of your dress or your rolled-up pants wet, so you figure, oh well. And you stand there while the waves pull the sand from beneath your feet until the next thing you know, you're wet up to your knees, and at that point, you're already halfway in. So, you might as well dive headlong through the next wave and just enjoy it."

He turned his tired face in my direction. "That was very descriptive."

"Thanks." I considered my situation. "Are you any closer to knowing who did it than you were when we met?"

"Yes." He answered without hesitation, and there was no doubt in his tone. He locked his gaze on mine. "I can get this case wrapped up if you'll let it go. What I can't do is solve a murder and look after you at the same time. After an attack like this, I'm going to have a hard time not looking in on you as much as I can. You have no idea what it was like to see you lying there at the bottom of the steps like that." Emotion flashed in his eyes.

"How about we strike a deal?" I offered. "I'll do my very best to stay out of this from now on, but I just remembered I have something you'll want to see."

"How can I know you'll keep your word?" he asked.

I drew an X over my heart.

"Not good enough."

"I came back to Charm for a new start, and I've got stuff I want to do with my life. I won't do anything to mess it up."

"What kind of stuff?"

"I'd like to make Sun, Sand, and Tea a success," I said. "I want it to be one of those places that tourists tell other people about. Like, 'Oh, if you're anywhere near Charm, you've got to stop for some sweet tea at this little shop on the boardwalk.'"

He smiled.

"I'd also like to find my soul mate and get married on the beach, surrounded by wild horses."

His gaze darted to the array of cowboy-covered books on my floor.

I kept going, lifting one hand to tick off my list with my fingers. "I want to host my own cooking show and teach people how to make authentic Southern sweet tea. Maybe have a couple of daughters. And a dog. Maybe a cat." *Where was Maggie, anyway?* And why was I telling Grady such personal things? My mouth opened again before I could stop it. "I want to grow old rocking my grandkids on that porch and telling them crazy stories about how I met their grandpa and how wild their mother was as a child."

Grady furrowed his brow. "You don't want a son?"

"Swan women usually have girls," I said. It was an unintentional, unrehearsed, knee-jerk response that had been drilled into my head for nearly thirty years. I shrugged through a blush. "That's silly. I know. My family has all these crazy ideas. Legends. Unusual history. And I say I don't believe it, but you ask me something simple like that, and I tell you exactly what I've always been told." I groaned, moving the peas back to my head. "I've never considered having a son because I've always assumed I won't. Swan women have daughters. We're also cursed in love, so my dreams of growing old with my husband are just that—dreams. I guess I'll have to be content with a successful business and a cooking show."

Grady stretched long legs out in front of him. "Don't most people have nice family stories? Tall tales of amazing feats designed to teach younger generations something like perseverance or morality?"

I smiled, realizing for the first time that all the Swan stories were new to him. "It gets worse. We aren't cursed to never find love. That would be too easy. No, we always find it, and we're blissful for a while, until the unlucky man succumbs to an untimely and occasionally gruesome death, or leaves us forever." I pulled my phone from my pocket and opened up the photos.

Grady pulled his chin back. "Wow."

I shot him an I-told-you-so look and changed the depressing subject. "Here." I pushed my phone in his direction with a picture of an unrolled map center-screen. "The blueprints were all stamped with Sam Smart's company logo, and I just learned that he's a fraud and embezzler. I think he might have been working with Mr. Metz on something and Mr. Paine got involved."

Grady didn't respond to my revelations. He swiped through the collection of photos I'd taken, enlarging some, bypassing others. "I need copies of these." He accessed my Share feature without asking and emailed the files to himself. "So, what happened to your dad?" he asked, daring a glance in my direction as he worked. "Was he a victim of the Swan curse?"

"Sudden, massive heart failure. Age thirty-six."

Grady cringed. "I'm sorry."

"I wasn't born yet."

"Your mom?"

I'd nearly forgotten I'd already told him about my parents. "The doctors said it was postpartum depression. My great-aunts say it was a broken heart."

His expression crumbled further.

I clamped a hand over my mouth. Why couldn't I stop talking?

Grady returned the phone to my lap and gave my other palm a squeeze. "It's like I always say. We can't choose our families." The thick, gravelly tone in his voice made me think there was a heavy meaning behind those words. What was wrong with his family?

The defrosting peas began to drip down the front of my pretty dress. "Do you mind if I shower and change before you leave? I'm not ready to be alone."

"Take your time." He drew his phone from his pocket and tapped the screen to life. "I've got plenty I can do from right here."

"Thanks." I returned the peas to the freezer, then headed for my room. I stood under the steaming hot shower until my skin was pruney. Afterward, I dabbed a little lip gloss on and gave the mascara wand a couple swings before leaving the bathroom. I stepped into my comfiest pajamas and went to find Grady.

He was already on his feet when I reemerged. He did a double take and smiled. "There are ponies on your pants."

"I like ponies."

His smile grew wider. "You'll have to come by the house after we get the stables built."

"The what?" I stammered.

"Stables. It's where we keep the horses. Stop me if it starts to sound familiar." He broke into a gentle laugh.

I tried not to imagine him on horseback. Grady was not a cowboy or a potential love interest. He was my new friend, of which I could use plenty. "Are you buying horses?"

"No. My family raises and trains them. I grew up in the saddle, and Denver misses his colt. I figured I'd bring him and a couple of our others to Charm. Do you ride?"

I nodded woodenly.

"You look pale." Grady strode to my side and grasped my elbow. "Maybe you'd better let me help you into bed."

I made a strangled sound, but followed him to my room and shuffled toward my bed, another thing weighing on my mind. "Grady?"

He grunted softly.

"I'm truly sorry about your wife."

He waited while I climbed in to bed, sizing me up for another long moment. "I didn't handle her loss well. Not at first. Not for a long while. That's why I'm here. When I finally got it together, I realized I had to get out of our house, out of Charlotte. I needed a big change, one that would serve Denver, because nothing else mattered. I might be hurting, but it's not about me." The cost of his words was etched in the lines on his forehead. I knew this was information he didn't give freely, or to anyone he didn't trust.

My heart bled for him, and in that moment, the mysterious new detective seemed impossibly human.

"Get some sleep," he said, before turning and walking out.

I stared at the open door behind him.

He returned a few minutes later with another glass of water, a bottle of aspirin, and Maggie at his feet.

She leapt onto the foot of my bed and purred.

"He makes a good guard cat, huh?" Grady said.

"She," I corrected, tossing back a couple pills. I downed the water, then slid further under the covers. "And if she plans to stay here often, she's getting a bath."

Maggie hissed. I stuck out my tongue at her.

Grady gave me a peculiar look. "I'm going to walk through the house, check all the window and door locks, use the dead bolt on my way out. I'll return your house key tomorrow. I found it on the floor beside you in the foyer."

"Okay," I said sleepily.

"I'll patrol the perimeter before I leave, and I'll send a car to sit watch tonight. No one will bother you while you sleep. That's a promise." He slipped into the hallway, pulling the door shut behind him.

I listened as he walked from room to room, then outside across the wooden beams of my porch. Finally, I heard the engine of his vehicle rev to life and grow quiet in the distance. I was facing dreams of Grady Hays on horseback, and I knew it.

I would rather have taken my chances with the killer.

CHAPTER

❧

EIGHTEEN

The next morning was long and slow, bogged down by confusing memories from the night before. The knot on my head reminded me, with every quick twist or turn, of the danger I'd been in. The danger I was likely *still* in.

Now that my box of fancy clothes was open, I'd chosen a knee-length, A-line sundress and dug out a pack of those silicon stick-on brassiere cups to avoid unnecessary pressure on my tender ribs. So far, the cups were earning their keep, though I wasn't sure how. Sorcery came to mind.

Luckily, the only thing on my schedule today besides the usual café stuff was putting on a brave face, avoiding another tussle with whoever I'd peeved off, and eventually making my way to the police station. Grady had texted me after he left the night before to say I needed to file a formal report about the assault, and he offered to take me to see a doctor. The report would help him with his investigation, but the checkup would ease his mind.

He'd suggested I spend the day in bed to try to clear my head, but the definition of "clear" seemed extremely subjective this week.

I'd briefly considered closing the café for a few days while I recovered and Grady, hopefully, found my attacker, but that seemed unwise after the wonderful turnout at my party. No need to risk giving folks the impression something was wrong after spending the whole week trying to prove everything was fine. Besides, perseverance was the key to success, or at least that's what the poster hanging in my advisor's office said when I went to drop out of culinary school.

I stepped back to admire my morning's work and adjusted the rolled paisley bandanna I'd tied around my head, which struggled to wrangle my hair while hiding my goose egg.

In ninety short minutes, the thrift-store bicycle had gone from drab to fab thanks to a little love and attention. I'd used the rest of my light-blue spray paint to cover the frame, then stenciled my café logo along the center with some happy pink and yellow flowers where it had once said Schwinn. The braided vinyl basket had cleaned up nicely and the ruined weave was easily righted. The small bin would have to be enough for now, but I had plans to get a larger, metal-framed basket soon. I wove two dozen plastic flowers into the front as a finishing touch. I couldn't wait to ride it again.

I patted the newly bleached, bright-white seat and smiled. "You look like my wagon's big sister." The revamped Radio Flyer stood at the Schwinn's side—they were adorable together.

A soft meow drew my attention to the open garage door.

"Good morning, Maggie," I said. "Are you ready for your bath?"

She arched her back.

"I'm serious. I don't need you filling my house and café with sand fleas or anything else. You've got to get groomed, pretty lady. Also, thank you for sitting with me until I fell asleep last night. That was nice."

She walked away. Story of my life.

I left the bike to dry in the morning heat and followed the pretty cobblestone path from the carriage house to my home. There was plenty to accomplish before I needed to open the café in an hour.

I unlocked the café's entrance door, taking my time at the window to enjoy the heavenly beach view. Families and couples were already out, kites in the air and blankets on the sand. Scents of last night's storm hung in the already humid air. I kicked sand off the boards, then went to set up for lunch.

Three cucumbers in to a veggie-chopping marathon, I remembered my lunch appointment with Sam Smart. My knife stilled in the air. I wanted to know what he knew about Mr. Metz, but I didn't want to be alone with someone who may or may not have recently brained me.

Also, I'd promised Grady to let my independent investigation go, and I didn't break promises.

I dried my hands on a kitchen towel and dialed Sam's office; voicemail picked up after the fourth ring.

"Hi, Sam," I began in my cheeriest voice. "It's Everly Swan. I was just calling to confirm our lunch plans today. Here's the thing. I own a café, so I'm not sure why I thought I could get away at lunchtime." I gave a little laugh. "However, I feel terrible breaking plans last minute, so why don't you stop in here for lunch again? I'll fix you whatever you'd like. No charge. Sound good?" There would be witnesses here in case Sam was a murderer. If he wasn't a killer, then the offer to feed him for free would make up for my changing the plans last minute.

"If I don't hear back from you," I told his machine, "I'll assume you accept the invitation. No need to call if you're coming. See you soon. Have a great day!"

I hung up, praising the sun, moon, and stars for voicemail. That would have been a horrendous conversation to have with a human. What could I have said if he'd insisted on eating at his place or rescheduling for after-hours? "No thanks, I know you're a criminal and fear you're a murderer. Let's only get together in public places from now on." Hopefully, the quiver in my voice wasn't as perceptible over the phone as it was in my head, because the entire time I was keeping my voice perky, my brain was imagining Sam on the other side of that dropping curtain at Lucinda's house or standing in the shadows of my porch, a blunt object poised to swing at my head.

Shivering from my shoulders to my flip-flops, I

texted Aunt Clara. She promised to come right over and stay as long as I needed. Aunt Fran would cover Blessed Bee for the day.

After I washed my hands I got back to menu prep. Hana had brought enough produce to the party to keep me cooking for a week, and I needed to turn some of her greens into meals before they weren't so green anymore.

I rolled a pair of lettuce heads on the counter and whacked them through with a cleaver. In my inventory of leftovers and unused ingredients I found enough quinoa to bury myself alive. "Salads it is."

Summer soups and salads were personal favorites of mine, anyway, so I counted the insane amount of quinoa as a blessing. I smiled as I wrote the salad and soup names on my new menu board.

> *Berry, Arugula, and Quinoa Salad with*
> *Lemon-Chia Seed Dressing*
> *Apple and Arugula Salad with Maple Tahini*
> *Dressing*
> *Chilled Asparagus Soup*
> *Chilled Strawberry Soup*

And for the guests who somehow managed to not like cold soups and salad, I added two of my almost-always-available café staples.

> *Crisp Cucumber Sandwiches*
> *Salmon Cucumber Boats*

I cleared some space beside the food list and added some big bubble letters with today's specialty tea flavors, starting with my personal favorite.

> *Iced Carolina Chai*
> *Blueberry Watermelon*
> *Peach Basil*
> *Sparkling Mint Lime*

Perfect! I sliced, diced, and pureed until Aunt Clara appeared at the door half an hour later. "Come in!" I rushed over the wide, whitewashed floorboards to hug her, wincing as her arms wrapped around me.

"What's wrong?"

I considered lying, but that was a waste of time. "Someone attacked me last night. I'm fine, but I'm officially ducking out of the private eye business. Would you like some strawberry soup?"

She flung her arms up, hands flailing overhead. "You were attacked?" she wailed. "You should've called me. Have you seen a doctor? Let me take you now, or make you a poultice. Oh my stars!"

I waved her off. "I'm fine. I don't need a doctor or a poultice. I'm just a little sore. What's important is that I'm going to keep my curious nose right here"—I poked my nose with one finger—"where it belongs. And focus on making this iced tea shop a huge success."

She fanned her face and went to pour a glass of ice water. "Glory."

"Promise." I made a show of stirring my bright pink

soup. "This business is my new distraction from Mr. Paine's murder, my attacks, the break-ins, and every other scary thing I'm done worrying about. In fact, I'm thinking of buying a mini chalkboard for outside the door and more deck furniture. With pillows."

Aunt Clara liberated an apron from the metal hook on my pantry door and strapped it around her tiny middle. "This is awful." She shook her head and took long exaggerated breaths. "You were always interested in facts. From the youngest of ages. You wanted to know why, when, and how about everything. I could hardly tell a story without interruption. For a while I thought you'd become a neurosurgeon or a rocket scientist, something that took a decade of schooling just so you could stuff as many facts into your head as possible."

I rolled my eyes. "Rocket scientists don't really live up to the hype, you know. It's just an engineering degree."

"See?" She raised her eyebrows. "Who else would know that?"

"Everyone knows that."

"I didn't." She hip-checked me out of the way, then took over stirring my pureed soup. "Sit down and relax. I'll do this."

I moved on to tossing salad ingredients into an extra-large serving bowl. "I appreciate you coming, but I really am fine."

"I'd do anything for you," she said. "I love you very much, you know that, right?"

"Of course I do. I love you too."

She returned her attention to the soup. "I wondered a little. Since you were nearly killed last night and didn't call me. It leaves room for doubt, and I think maybe my efforts as an aunt are failing."

I shut my eyes so they wouldn't roll. Clara was a truly gentle soul, but the downside with that was that her feelings were perpetually being hurt by someone—far too often, me. "I didn't *not* call. It just never crossed my mind."

She made a gasping sound, then touched the pad of one thumb to the corner of her eye.

"Don't cry," I pleaded. "I was confused afterward, but Grady checked me out and put me to bed. He wouldn't have left if I needed more help. He secured the house, and I fell asleep. I honestly didn't have another clear thought until this morning." If she counted four fifteen as morning, when I woke up with all sorts of crystal-clear thoughts, mostly designed to scare me to death.

"I just wish you'd called me or Fran to take care of you, that's all. When you push us away, it makes me think you don't trust us to help you, and then I worry I've done something to cause a rift."

I abandoned my salad prep to wrap her in my arms. "I trust you both implicitly. If Grady hadn't shown up, I might have called you. I can't honestly say, but if I didn't, it wouldn't have been meant as a slight." I didn't know what would've happened if I'd woken up on the floor by myself. I hadn't even realized I was attacked until Grady told me.

I rested my head on her shoulder. "I've made a mess of my return to Charm."

"You haven't."

"I have. First I hid away from everyone because I had so much guilt for leaving and shame for the epic way I tanked that adventure. Then all of this happened. It's no wonder people felt iffy about me."

She patted my puffy hair. "I promised Hazel I'd take care of you. I just want to make sure I'm living up to that."

My eyes stung at the sound of Grandma's name. "I should've been here when she died. I never got to say goodbye."

Aunt Clara kissed my head. "You said goodbye when you left, darling. No one could have known she wouldn't be here when you came home."

"I should have visited more often."

"She understood. More than any of us, really. After all, she left Charm once too."

I snapped upright, peeling myself away from Aunt Clara's embrace. "What?"

"Her and your mother both. Your particular line of Swan women is filled with rebels. Even my mother was a bit of a tart. She didn't leave Charm, but I hear some of the women around here wished she would have." Clara nodded, a slow smile creeping over her face. "Fran and I always admired our sister for being brave enough to go."

I took a few steps back to process. My mind raced with questions. Why had no one ever told me this? Why hadn't Grandma? "Where did she go? Grandma, I mean."

"Hollywood."

"Hollywood!" Good grief! A gigantic smile stretched my lips.

"She always had a flair for the dramatic and a desperate love of cowboys. Back then western television shows were all the rage: *The Cisco Kid, Maverick, Gunsmoke.* She said she wanted to be an actress, or at least get a job on one of those shows. She told our mom that being a part of something that grand was a life experience worth having. Even if it meant upsetting her for a while. Hazel was gone more than a year before she came back, and she was awful at keeping in touch while she was away. Who knows what she was up to all the way across the country. Well," she paused, "we know a little about what she was up to. She got to be an audience member on the *The $64,000 Question*, and she came home pregnant with your mother, so." Aunt Clara tipped her head left and right, a small, prideful smile on her lips. "Her adventure wasn't a total bust. Without that side trip down life's path, we would never have had your mother, or you." She crept forward to set her soft palm against my cheek, then hooked some flyaway hair behind my ear.

The concept rocked my already shaky idea of who I was. Every story I'd heard of Swan women before that moment was to say they toed the line, played according to the rules of silly legends, and accepted their confined fates. I was more like my grandma than I'd ever realized. The warmth of pride filled my chest, for grandma's decision to challenge what she was told, and for my mom's and mine as well. I imagined it was infinitely harder to leave when they had. Times were tougher then, money tighter, transportation options fewer. Today I could be in L.A. before dark. I couldn't begin to imagine how Grandma had gotten there or how long it had taken her to save the money to go.

Clara unloaded the dishwasher. "Fran and I think your grandfather was an actor named Jack Randall, but your grandma would never say. He went by Allen Byron for a while too. Very popular cowboy. She had a thing for chaps and spurs, I guess. Anyway, after all those years of being a Hollywood cowboy, he just falls right off his horse one day during a shoot. Dead." She snapped her fingers for effect. "Hazel wore black for a month. She claimed they were only friends, that he was the nicest actor in Hollywood, but he died suddenly at thirty-nine, and she was torn up over it. I don't think that's a coincidence."

I stored that information in the back of my reeling mind. Aunt Clara's stories always had a way of messing with my mind. She gave the perfect blend of provable fact and questionable theory.

The wind chimes jingled over my door with the arrival of my first customers. I'd have to think more about my possible television cowboy grandpa later.

"Welcome to Sun, Sand, and Tea," I said, rounding the counter to greet my guests. "I'm so glad you're here."

Business was steady from eleven until one. Everyone seemed satisfied with the menu options, and a few out-of-towners thought it was magnificent that I changed the menu from day to day and totally at will. I served while Aunt Clara cleaned. The process was a gloriously simple dance. Summer soups and salads climbed higher on my favorites list as I filled orders in seconds. The no-prep, no-wait scenario was something my guests seemed to like too.

By one fifteen, I was coming off the high of victory and feeling a little miffed. Yes, I'd had a successful day, proving the well-attended grand opening hadn't been a fluke, but Grady still hadn't shown up with my key, and Sam had stood me up.

I tapped my fingers on the counter beside Aunt Clara. "I specifically asked Sam to call if he couldn't make it. He didn't call, and he hasn't made it. It's almost one thirty. What if he didn't get my message? What if he thinks *I* stood *him* up?"

"Or," she said, interrupting my spiral, "maybe Sam got tied up with a client. This is the time of year people start drifting over the bridge and thinking they should relocate to Charm permanently. I've known him to show a tourist the same house every day for a week without making a sale. The visitor goes home happy anyway, telling big stories to their mainland friends about the time they almost bought a house on an island."

She was right, that did happen.

"I'm going to call him." I turned my phone over and dialed. My jaw clenched in irritation. "Voicemail." I disconnected. "Do you think he's intentionally ignoring my calls? Why would he do that?"

Aunt Clara flicked a polite look in my direction. She'd already told me what she thought. "I really don't know, dear."

I dialed Molly's Market. I had other ways to do things. "Hi, Mr. Waters, it's Everly Swan. I was just wondering if you've seen Sam Smart this morning."

Sam's realty office was right next door to Molly's on Vine Street, and Mr. Waters took enough cigar breaks on the bench outside the market to know if Sam was in, and how long he'd been there.

I hung up, feeling provoked. "He says the realty office hasn't opened today."

Aunt Clara stilled, apparently mulling that over. "Maybe he's been out showing homes."

My torturous mind had already worked up a dozen more sinister reasons. *He attacked me last night* was at the top of my list. "What if it was Sam who hurt me and stole those maps and blueprints? They had his company stamp on them."

"I don't really think Sam is a violent fellow," Clara said, looking terribly distraught at the idea.

"I'm calling Grady." I walked toward the rear deck for some privacy. Aunt Clara thought I was losing it, I could see it in her eyes.

"Hays." Grady answered on the first ring.

"It's Everly," I said, "Swan," I added. As if anyone had ever known another Everly.

"This isn't a good time," Grady said. "Let me call you back."

"No, wait!" Now that I had him on the phone, I

wasn't sure how to broach the subject without making it seem as if I'd continued poking into his investigation, when I hadn't done anything at all. "I was supposed to have lunch with Sam Smart, but he never showed, and Mr. Waters says he didn't open the office today, so I'm a little worried."

"You're worried about Sam Smart?"

"I'm worried he might've been the one who attacked me, and now he's fled town to escape Mr. Paine's murder charge because I had all those blueprints and he knows I was on to him."

Grady groaned. "We talked about this already."

"I'm not getting involved. I'm only speculating based on previously gathered information."

"Where are you?" he asked.

"Sun, Sand, and Tea. It's been a busy morning."

"Stay there. I'll be over later."

"Wait!" I said again. "Don't hang up on me. Aren't you going to at least say something about what I just told you? Did you know Sam has a slew of fraud and embezzlement charges? I looked him up online last night."

"Yes," Grady snapped. "And I know, not because you told me, but because *I'm* the detective. And no, I'm not addressing your wild theories, because I've got bigger problems right now. I told you this isn't a good time."

I bristled at his awful manners. What happened to the gallant savior I'd had last night? *Men.* I threw my head back and straightened my spine. "Well, I hope you'll at least look for Sam when you finish doing whatever it is that's so important right now."

Grady's breath puffed through the line in long, measured bursts. I imagined him silently counting to ten. "I don't need to look for Sam Smart, because I know where he is. I'm standing twenty feet from him, trying to get off the phone with you."

"Well, if you're not arresting Sam for murder or for assaulting me, can you please tell him I'll be at the café all day if he wants to come by?"

Grady chuckled darkly, his patience clearly at its end. "I would, but he's floating in his pool. Face down. Right where the gardeners found him before they called me."

CHAPTER

✦

NINETEEN

Lou stared at me through the glass door I couldn't tear myself away from, cell phone still clutched in my hand. He fixed one coal-black eye on my panicked face, seeming to understand.

Sam Smart was dead.

I'd spoken to him last night. He'd sat in my iced tea shop handing out business cards and watching the time. So, what had happened to him after he'd rushed off to his "prior engagement" that ended with him face down in his pool? Where had he gone? Had he made it there? Who would've killed him? Was it the person he was in such a hurry to see—or someone else?

I strained my brain, trying to recall Sam's face at Lucinda's party, but the night was a little fuzzy due to the nearly incapacitating fear still clinging to my skin. An unsettling chill climbed the back of my neck whenever I gave last night any serious thought. It was a psychological defense mechanism, no doubt, my mind's desperate attempt to keep me out of the loony bin.

I took slow, measured breaths and refocused on the café behind me. The sound of gently sloshing tea over ice. The beloved sighs of satisfied customers and the clink-clink of forks and spoons on salad plates and soup bowls. Sun, Sand, and Tea wasn't busy, but it wasn't empty, either, and I still didn't know who the town gossip blogger was, so I couldn't afford a breakdown. I definitely didn't want to give any ammunition that could be used to try to sink my ship again.

Clara met me halfway to the counter, near an empty set of tables. Her worried expression crumbled into despair as I relayed the heartbreaking news.

"Oh my," she whispered, rubbing my back as we made our way to the prep area. "This is awful. Two murders in a week. It's unheard of."

Time crawled by until the wind chimes jingled over the front door again, and my heart danced with hope that Grady had gotten away long enough to fill me in on the details of Sam's death. Plus, I needed my key back—with a lunatic trying to silence me at every turn, I preferred to know where all the keys to my house were.

Mr. Metz thundered inside, growling into a tiny cell phone pressed to one big ear. Clara's eyes widened.

I hustled over to meet him.

"Today!" he barked, stopping me in my tracks, his voice nearly rattling the windows. "I don't care how you do it. Just make it happen!" His striped dress shirt was open at the collar, as if his thick neck had popped a button. I tried not to stare at the blue vein pulsating at the side of his throat.

The other customers gawked openly. I gave them my least terrified smile.

Mr. Metz dropped his cell phone on the counter with a clatter. Dark stubble covered his ruddy cheeks, and curly black hair peeked through his open collar. "You." He snapped, finally making eye contact with me.

"Me." I did a little wave, hoping he'd heard all good things, and knowing he hadn't. "What can I get you?" I pointed to the menu board. "Today's selections are up there, and we have a number of iced teas on tap. You're welcome to sample before you choose."

He scowled. My gaze dropped to a bandaged hand at his side: white gauze wrapped the palm and knuckles, dark spots seeping from beneath.

Clara sneaked out from behind me and went to stand at my side. "The Old-Fashioned Sun Tea is always a good choice."

"Fine," he growled. "Give me that." Metz lowered himself onto a stool at the counter and rested his injured hand on the marble.

I placed a napkin and straw beside the massive white bandage while Clara poured the tea. "What happened to your hand?" I asked. It hadn't been injured two days ago when we'd first met.

I couldn't help wondering if Sam Smart had any defense wounds when Grady found him.

Metz's cheek lifted with a smile that looked more

like a sneer. He raised the bandaged hand and made a show of bending and stretching the scraped-up fingers. "I did this bustin' heads at the job site. Got to keep them in line or they run all over you."

"The heads?" I asked.

Clara nudged me away and pushed the tea toward him on the napkin. "There you are. Enjoy."

I shifted nervously. "Can I get you something to eat? Salad? Sandwich? Maybe a light dessert?"

He looked over his shoulder at the door. "Maybe. I'm supposed to meet someone here."

"Who?" The word was out before I realized it might be rude to ask. "I can help you keep watch," I suggested, hoping to seem less nosy.

He glowered. "You're from here, right?"

"Yes." I looked to Aunt Clara. If I couldn't answer his question, she surely could. "Why?"

"What's your mayor's problem?"

"Mayor Dummy?" Clara asked, hurrying into the conversation.

"Mayor Dunfree," I corrected, breaking the name into syllables. "I don't know him very well," I admitted, but then something occurred to me. "Is he giving you a hard time about the B&Bs?" Mayor Dunfree had been Mr. Paine's biggest advocate when it came to petitioning the rest of the town council to keep me from opening Sun, Sand, and Tea. Maybe he had taken up Mr. Paine's torch for stopping Metz's renovations on Bay View.

"Yeah," Metz groused, bending and stretching his

bandaged fingers. "I thought I'd finally gotten rid of all my problems."

I stifled a shiver, hoping Mr. Paine and Sam Smart hadn't been two of Metz's problems.

Twenty minutes later, Metz had yelled at two more people via cell phone and taken his tea to go, having apparently been stood up.

After that, I counted the minutes until closing time. I needed to talk to Grady, and I'd promised to file an official report about last night at the station. The way I saw it, he couldn't accuse me of interfering with his case when I showed up—I was only going because he asked me to make the report. And if the topic of my workday happened to come up, I might be inclined to mention the angry, injured man who scared the tea out of me every time I saw him.

❧

I called it quits at seven, satisfied that everyone planning to stop in for a glass of tea or a bite to eat had already done so. From here on out, the big winners in town sold ice cream or alcohol. I sold neither, but I could use a little of both.

Aunt Clara had left a few minutes before six for dinner plans with Aunt Fran, so I was on my own to lock up, change clothes, and head to the police station.

I didn't want to be caught walking alone after dark again, so I swapped my sundress for my most comfortable jeans and a flowy maroon tank top, then saddled up on my newly painted bike.

Each time I tried to think about what I would put in my official statement, my brain went blank and refused to bring anything relevant to mind. Instead, I found myself focusing on why Grady had told me to stay put because he'd be over when he finished at Sam's place, but he never showed. That just made me mad.

I decided to think about tea instead. Tea made me happy. Once I got home from the station, I would spend my night prepping a few new tea jugs that could steep in the sun tomorrow. My old-fashioned sweet tea was a favorite, and it made a nice base for several other flavors folks loved, like my Strawberry Basil. If I wasn't careful to keep plenty in stock, I'd run out. I'd also need a few gallons of black tea for my Raspberry-Mint blend. And maybe just one green tea. I hadn't decided what to do with that yet.

I imagined each finished drink in the perfect jar, stuffed with fruit, herbs, and ice. Oh, and I wanted to make an Earl Gray Cocktail, which was basically Earl Gray with a dash of lavender, honey, and fresh-squeezed lemon. I'd stick a sprig of lavender in for aesthetics and pizazz.

I fell into an easy rhythm as I pedaled and dreamed of customers' awed faces when they experienced the beauty and simplicity of a perfect iced tea escape. Tomorrow, I'd add some sweets to the menu.

Police station first, then tea-making.

But before I could do any of that, I had two stops to make on my promised patrol of Amelia's Little Libraries. I pedaled toward my first stop, soaking up the gentle warmth of a late spring evening.

Laughter floated on the breeze as a couple stepped and sank, repeatedly, through the thick, dry sand near public parking. They leaned against one another's tanned frames to stay upright in their current state of bliss.

Beyond them, a line of gray-haired men spilled from old pickup trucks parked along the road. Aluminum-framed chairs hung over their shoulders like weird rectangular purses, and tackle boxes, coolers, and fishing poles were clasped in one hand, the rusted handles of little beach wagons pulled along by the other. Their hats were heavily laden with whirligigs and doodads as they made their way to the water's edge, buzzing with anticipation of the night's big catch.

I slowed my pace to a crawl, letting the beautiful twilight view settle in. Before I'd left town, I'd thought of Charm only as a daytime playground, but since returning home, the island had looked different to me in many ways. For one thing, I'd become highly aware of how much folks enjoyed the nights here. At least once a week, there was a bonfire on the beach after dark; sometimes I could see the flames and hear music from my deck. And I knew from personal experience that the ice cream shop stayed busy until well after ten, as did many restaurants and cafés. People had house parties or cruised the main strip along the bay, going nowhere and in no hurry. I'd done many of those things myself, but I'd only thought of them abstractly. Nothing about the island had seemed quite as lovely or extraordinary to me then, the way it did now. I supposed time and life experience had made the difference, peeled away the youthful blinders and revealed a much deeper and more fascinating world that I'd been able to see before.

I slid off my seat and walked my bike up to the first Little Library. Everything looked perfect. I opened the door and moved a few books around. No sand. A lovely literary selection. My work there was done. I snapped a picture on my phone and sent it to Amelia so she'd know I'd kept my promise and wouldn't have to make a trip to the boardwalk tonight.

Climbing back on my new ride with a satisfied smile, I picked up a little speed as I headed for Little Library number two, and I soaked in the warm, salty wind and steady thunk-a-thunk of my tires as they moved over the historic boardwalk. I tried in vain to imagine my mother or grandmother riding her bike in my place decades back. Were they happy then? What would they have thought of me today—would they be proud? Maybe I hadn't accomplished much yet, but I had hope that I could make them proud in time.

A pair of boys stood in front of the next library, laughing and looking around suspiciously.

Suddenly, I remembered that I hadn't chased away the vandal last night, only frightened a guy who didn't understand sunscreen or how to care for a burn. "Hey!" I hollered, pedaling faster.

The boys caught sight of me and started.

"Hold up!" I called, determined to look seminormal in case they weren't up to no good.

The duo turned and fled, banging into one another and toppling two big red buckets of sand onto the boardwalk.

It was them!

"Stop!" I screamed, leaning forward over my handlebars and standing up to pedal.

They only laughed louder and changed direction, diverting from the clean, even boardwalk to a rugged dirt path behind the public changing rooms.

I gave chase like a small-town superhero until my front tire hit a loose rock, and I went careening toward the public restrooms. I dropped my bike and floundered, trying to get a footing on solid ground. "Come back here!"

The boys doubled over in laughter, having stopped precariously in front of a small trench masked by seagrass. They watched while I untangled my feet to regain pursuit. Neither kid was more than fourteen years old and both were rail-thin, with miles of freckles and mounds of wavy, sun-bleached hair.

I slowed down and limped, feigning an injury and waiting for them to turn away. A moment later they toppled into the hidden trench with dual yelps.

I took my time closing the distance between us. That ought to teach them to laugh at a lady who'd lived here twice as long as they'd been alive. I braced my hands on my hips and tried not to look as out of breath as I felt. "You guys have filled your last Little Library with sand. Now, give me your names so I can tell your mother, the police, and the owner of those libraries. What you've been up to is absolutely rotten."

"Yeah, right," the taller kid said, pulling to his feet. "Give you our names so you can turn us in? What do we look like to you—morons?"

I held my tongue.

"Oh snap!" The shorter hooligan popped up beside him. He covered his mouth and raised one knee in a dramatic bout of laughter. "No way!"

"What?" I asked.

The boy pointed an obnoxious finger at me. "It's her, man. She's the one." He mimed falling on the ground, laughing hysterically.

I got the feeling these two weren't taking my authority very seriously.

"Noooo." His friend dragged the word out for five long seconds before offering his friend a hand up. "Shut. Up! For real?"

"What?" I repeated, more aggressively this time, internally fuming that I'd lost the upper hand.

They straightened and put on a matching pair of cocky faces. "We saw you get pushed into the marsh," the first one said.

"Yeah, like a fool," the other added.

My hands slid off my hips to hang loosely at my sides. "You did?"

"Yeah, dude. We remember because we were digging your hair, you know? We were on the beach getting sand."

"You were?" I touched one hand to my silky headband. "I remember seeing two boys on the beach that night."

"Us," they said in unison, patting their narrow chests.

I turned my face toward the surf, bringing the memory of their silhouettes to the forefront of my mind. I'd hoped then that they wouldn't have seen what had happened, much less recognize me, but now I wanted to hug them. They must have seen my attacker! And if they recognized me from that distance, maybe they recognized the other party too. I was ready to make a trade—their anonymity in exchange for my assailant's name and a good faith promise never to mess with Amelia's libraries again. I spun back to them. "Can you describe the person who pushed me?"

Their footfalls beat a rhythm in the distance, already several yards away.

"Hey!" I took off after them. "Stop! Don't run!" I sprinted for at least ten seconds, then jog-walked until spots danced in my peripheral vision and one calf cramped up.

"Jeez," I panted, bending forward to brace sweaty hands on shaky knees. I gulped air through a tight, painful windpipe, bending my knees and lowering myself to the ground, trying to convince myself not to roll onto my back and die.

I am in terrible shape.

No wonder my Git Fit was usually so disappointed in me.

I shifted to one hip and worked my phone free from my pocket, dialing Amelia. In between raspy pants, I provided her with the description of her vandals and regaled her with the story of my grand, heroic attempt to capture them. We laughed until I was in tears, and she agreed to pick me up because there was no way I could walk or bike home. Plus, she said she'd join me at the police station. Thanks to my partial success tonight, she now had a report of her own to file.

CHAPTER

ॐ

TWENTY

I met Amelia on Ocean Drive, across the marsh from the boardwalk. I'd collected my abandoned bike and walked it to the road. She stuck the Schwinn in the backseat of her convertible and headed for the police station.

"Thanks," I told her, checking my face in the visor mirror. I'd laughed my mascara down to my teeth and my lipstick was smudged all over my hands from trying to shut myself up as I'd snorted in hysterics.

Amelia turned onto Sand Street at the light. She slid a mischievous gaze in my direction while I wiped the lipstick onto a tissue from her glove box. "You really asked for their names so you could turn them in?"

"Yes!" I started laughing again. "I don't know what comes over me sometimes. I don't think, I just act, and it gets me into so much trouble. You'd think I'd learn."

"I don't know," she said. "I like that you can just *do* things." She sounded as if she thought impulsivity was a goal and not a curse. "I get all paralyzed with fear and anxiety until I can't decide what to do, so I usually just go read a book."

"Reading is good."

"I guess. What do you do when you get upset? Probably charge into battle."

"Ha. I cook. Then I eat." I gave her a sad smile. "We all have our things."

We passed Charming Reads, and Amelia slowed. "The light's still on at my shop. Do you care if we stop? Sometimes Dad falls asleep and people just keep coming in."

"Not at all."

A familiar SUV was parked at the curb outside Blessed Bee.

My aunts closed up at five most days, so the curbside parking was mostly for Sandy's Seaside Sweet Shack at this hour: Grady was getting ice cream.

He'd stood me up at Sun, Sand, and Tea, and hadn't returned my key. And now that I was on my way to find him, he was out having fun.

When Amelia climbed out of the car, I joined her. "Hey," I said. "I'll be right back."

She shrugged. "Meet you back here in ten?"

"Perfect." I marched along the sidewalk, propelled by purpose and partially carried on the scent of fresh-baked waffle cones and homemade hot fudge. I stood at the patio's edge, scanning faces and preparing what I wanted to say.

A thin hand popped into the air and waved. I

followed the arm down to a pretty young blond I recognized as Denise, the au pair. "Everly!" she waved.
"Come! Sit!"

I suddenly understood what Amelia had been
talking about when she said she got too nervous to
speak. Grady wasn't there, and I had no idea what to
say to Denise.

I peeked behind me, hoping Amelia was done
already and waiting at the car, giving me an excuse to
turn around and leave. No such luck.

"Everly!" Denise called again. This time she
stood, in case someone on the block hadn't noticed
her. Soft blond hair tumbled over her shoulders and
covered the top portion of her flimsy tank top. It
was cornflower blue, an exact match to the color
of her perfect eyes. Her white skirt was pleated and
her long, tan legs led the way down to little designer
tennis shoes.

I felt four hundred years old.

Forcing a big smile, I pretended to finally see her.

She sighed in relief, then pushed the empty seat
beside her away from the table so I could sit.

As I crossed the crowded patio, I spotted Denver
sitting beside Denise, his big gray eyes fixed on a
pile of sprinkles sliding down a strawberry river.
Vanilla iced cream puddled in the bowl around his
melting sundae.

I couldn't bring myself to sit. "How's that ice
cream?" I asked Denver. I would've asked Denise, but
all she had was a bottle of water.

"Good." He positioned his face over the cup and lapped at it like a dog.

"Oh." Denise leaned over the table. "Careful now. It's good to eat, but you probably don't want to wear it."

Denver froze, his expression full of wonder. "You can wear ice cream?"

"No!" Denise laughed. She crumpled a napkin and tossed it at his sticky face. "Silly." The love she had for him was written in her gentle smile.

"You're really good with him," I said. "It's nice."

She beamed. "Well, Denny and I've been pretty tight since he started preschool. We go way back."

Denver threw the napkin back at her, a little more chocolatey than it had arrived. "Don't call me that. I hate Denny." He made a face. "It's a restaurant. I'm a man."

Denise leaned away and crossed her arms. "Well, that's true, but I wish we could find you a nickname. Every sweet, adorable boy needs a cool nickname."

"How about Bruce?"

I laughed and squatted beside him, immediately drawn in. "I like it. Just like Bruce Banner."

His mouth fell open. "Yeah," he said. "No one knows Hulk's real name."

I didn't argue, because I liked the awestruck look on his face too much. "I know a lot of his secrets."

Denver quirked a sun-lightened eyebrow. "You're Daddy's friend."

I glanced at Denise. "I think so." Though Grady

could have at least called me today, knowing it was after eight and I still hadn't given my statement at the station. What if something else had happened to me? I mean, wasn't he just going on about how keeping me safe was a huge distraction? "I'm Everly."

"I remember," he said. "Where'd you get a name like that?"

"It's a family name," I said. "Where'd you get a name like Denver?"

"It's my Grandma's name, and she's a giant big deal."

"Your Grandma's name is Denver?" That seemed unusual, but kind of quirky and interesting.

Denise sat forward, wiping his face with sudden gusto. "Look at this. You've got a little something."

He spat at the napkin roving around his mouth. "Stop!" He wiggled and fussed until she relented. "Yuck!"

Denise gave him a pointed look, then turned a smile on me. "Are you going to get something? You're welcome to sit with us if you are. We could talk about horses," she suggested. "Denver loves horses."

"Me too," I said. "I really can't stay. I'm headed to the police station with a friend, and I'm supposed to meet her in a minute." I checked the street again, in case Amelia was already waiting.

Mr. Metz came into view, strolling casually along the sidewalk with a rolled blueprint in his hand, waving it at a man I knew from his construction crew at the colonial on Bay View. Thankfully, he wasn't yelling as loudly as he had been earlier. Then again, the white noise of fifty sugar-buzzed people helped cover most sounds.

He turned and looked in my direction, so I dropped into the previously rejected seat. "Maybe I could sit for a minute," I said, smiling brightly at Denise.

"Great." Her brows tented as she scanned the area to see what had changed my mind. "Grady's supposed to meet us here soon."

"What?" I asked. "When?" I couldn't be caught having ice cream with Denise and Denver. It'd look like I was stalking Grady, or prodding them for information. Grady was sure to have an opinion about me running into them, and his opinion was guaranteed to be negative.

I stood up again.

Denver stopped his spoon halfway to his mouth. "Where are you going now?"

I glanced in Metz's direction. I still hadn't had a chance to tell Grady about the injury Metz had from all that head-busting.

Metz was gone, but Grady was making his way through the crowd on the patio.

"I'd better get back to my friend." Hunching down, I hoped Grady wouldn't see me and squeezed past a table of teenagers. "Talk to you soon," I called. I fled the crowded patio by way of an access gate, landing gracelessly in the alley the shop shared with Blessed Bee.

I watched as Grady greeted Denise with a smile and Denver with a giant hug. The boy stood on his chair and leapt into Grady's arms. My heart did a nonsensical flip. A moment later, Grady looked in my direction and so did Denver and Denise.

Someone had tattled.

I ducked and crouch-jogged back to the road where I'd left Amelia and her car and rounded the corner to safety—only to come face-to-face with Mr. Metz, climbing into his car.

His thick brows bunched together.

I waved. "Hello again."

"What were you doing in that alley?" he asked.

I forced myself to look natural. "Nothing." I moved past him, turning my back to Blessed Bee in an attempt to put a few more inches between the irritable giant and myself.

"Were you eavesdropping?" His voice was low and thick, an unspoken threat slicing through the words. He slammed his door shut, then took a step away from the car. "Are you following me?"

"I was just getting ice cream," I told him over one shoulder as I picked up my pace. "I'm meeting a friend. I have to go." I turned and ran for Amelia's car at the end of the block.

Thankfully, she was already behind the wheel. "Go!" I yelled, jumping into the car and yanking the door shut behind me.

She looked up from the book she was reading. "Why are you all sweaty again?"

"Fear." I swallowed hard. "I saw Mr. Metz yelling at some of his men and waving a blueprint. Then he saw me sneaking out of an alley, and now he thinks I'm stalking him. What if he's the killer and I just made him really mad?"

Amelia dropped her book on the console, jamming her car into drive. She headed back down Main Street to Middletown, breaking the posted speed limit all the way to the police station.

The officer behind the desk put us in separate rooms to complete our reports. I asked for more paper twice and stuffed the sheets I'd scribbled on into my purse, thankful they couldn't see every version I'd written.

I'd had no idea how hard it was to state only the facts, especially when I didn't have any. Mostly, I wrote three pages of personal observations, things like what I'd taken from the curb outside Lucinda's house, and how it felt like someone followed me home, but I couldn't substantiate that. I admitted the feeling might've been because I'd seen someone in the upstairs window when I left the party, but I couldn't say who they were or if they could identify me from that distance.

Mine was a useless report, more or less. *I got home. Got a text from Grady. Thought he was at the door, but instead I blacked out.* Maybe Grady could at least use the time frame I gave; it was the only thing I was certain of. Once he had a suspect, the information might at least help pin them with my assault.

Amelia was in the waiting room with a book when I got there. "Finished already?" she asked.

"I've been more than an hour."

She looked at the clock on the wall in confusion, then back to her book. "Wow. Okay. Let's go." She tucked a slip of paper between the pages and hopped to her feet. "I am really loving this book."

I felt lighter when I climbed into her convertible. We'd made our reports. The police would do the rest, and soon our troubles would be solved.

Amelia reversed out of the lot, humming along to a country song playing softly on the radio. I watched her cheerful expression. She made life look easy. "I know it's shameless," she said, "but I love this car so much."

I laughed. "Who wouldn't? It's adorable, and it fits you perfectly. Every beach babe needs an open-air ride."

Amelia's eyes went wide and her smile became jubilant. "When you get your golf cart, we should paint it to match your wagon and bike."

I loved this woman. "That sounds perfect. I was thinking of making delivery an option so folks who can't get away from their desks could still have something good for lunch."

"Better get two carts, then," she added matter-of-factly. "You'll need one for emergencies and another for your driver."

Right. I'd have to hire a driver.

I didn't have the money for one golf cart yet, let alone a second and an employee. "I'll have to put a pin in this until business picks up."

"It's fine," she said, motoring carefully through town. "Business goals are supposed to challenge you.

They seem like impossibilities until suddenly they aren't. It's then that you'll realize how awesome you really are by seeing how far you've come. Trust me, I've been there a couple of times." She turned onto Middletown Street, and my attention drifted out the passenger window.

Lucinda's home, the one I'd fled from less than twenty-four hours ago, was silent and dark now, no evidence the big shindig had ever happened. "Were you at Lucinda's last night?" I hadn't seen her, but it had been crowded.

"No. I wanted to finish my book."

"No luck?" I asked. The book riding between us was only about three-quarters of the way read.

She gave me a puzzled look. "No, I finished."

I lifted the book up. "Are you rereading the end?"

She laughed. "Yeah, right. I started this book at breakfast."

"No way." I dropped it back on the console. "I'm only on chapter seven of the book I borrowed from one of your libraries two days ago."

"Well, reading is practically my job, and you've been busy. Speaking of that, where are you on the investigation? I meant to ask earlier when you jumped into the car, but I thought we were being chased to the police station."

I heaved a sigh. "I'm nowhere, and I promised Grady I'd leave it alone." I filled her in on every theory I had before we made it to my place.

We rocked to a stop in the grassy area beside my

house. "Jeez Louise," she gasped. "You could write a novel with all this crazy! You can't make this kind of stuff up. You've been home three months and this town has seen more action than it has in a decade." She unlatched her seat belt and swiveled to face me.

I frowned. "I just hope no one thinks any of the recent chaos has anything to do with me."

It would be interesting to look up local articles from the months following Grandma's return from Hollywood and see if she'd also triggered a crime spree. If so, I might be inclined to think harder about my aunts' theories.

"Some of it is a little your fault," Amelia said. "Not Mr. Paine's murder, but the threats against you. No one else would've gotten involved, but you've been deep in this from the start." Amelia dug into her purse and produced a pink stun gun.

I nearly rolled out my door. "What are you doing?" I stumbled back in the grass, putting several feet between myself and the weapon. How could Amelia be the murderer? It wasn't possible! "Don't do this!"

Amelia looked as if I'd slapped her. "I'm going to walk you upstairs," she said. "It's dark, except for your porch light. Do you seriously think I planned to hurt you?"

I pursed my lips and rocked my head side to side.

She raised her hands, palms out, then put the stun gun into her glove box. "Sorry. I should've told you what I was doing first, and I should've known you'd freak out. You've been through a lot."

I waited, unsure of whether I could trust her.

"You should probably leave a television and some lights on when you go out so people will always think someone's home. At least, that's what all the cops in my novels tell women."

"Is that what you do?" I asked, regaining my nerve slightly.

She shrugged. "I live over a bookshop, so I'm not in any real risk of a break-in. Readers are generally pretty honest people." She turned her phone over and dialed 911, then hovered her thumb over the call button. "There. Now we can at least call for help if there's trouble."

I followed her to my door in body, but my mind was back at her car—specifically in her glove box. "How long have you had a stun gun?"

"Since college. I upgraded from pepper spray after a girl was assaulted outside the campus gym."

"Where did you buy it?" Were they available everywhere? Could I pick one up at the gas station?

"Are you thinking of getting one?" she asked. "If so, we could see if my dad has some advice. Truthfully, mine's getting old and it's probably not charged."

I let us into the house and locked the dead bolt behind. "Are you kidding? I'd probably stun myself. I was just curious." I smiled, feeling a little guilty for thinking Amelia would hurt me.

She followed me up the private staircase to my living area, then wandered into my kitchen. "Do you have any ice cream? I've never had to go to the police station before, and I'm kind of upset about it."

"Of course I have ice cream. Why are you upset?"

She leaned against my kitchen island. "You'll think it's silly, but I have massive guilt for giving out the description of those kids. They're just kids, and what were they hurting, really? They were only putting sand into the libraries. Stay on the island long enough and there's no place you won't find sand."

"Amen to that, but those kids need a good scaring. It's not like they'll get into any real trouble. The cops will probably just tell their parents and let it go, but I definitely want them found. They probably saw the maniac who pushed me into the marsh." I opened the freezer and waved one hand to showcase my stash of frozen dreams. "Lady's choice."

"Butter Pecan," she said, helping herself to a spoon on the drying rack. "No bowl necessary."

I followed her excellent example and picked out a pint of Mint Chocolate Chip.

Amelia leaned against the counter and gazed around my small kitchen. "Your house is amazing. Have I told you that? I've loved it all my life. There's nothing else like it in Charm. Maybe not even in all of the Outer Banks." She moved to the window over-looking the ocean. "Gorgeous."

The cat slunk into view on the deck outside, green eyes flashing in the night, and Amelia jumped. I opened the sliding door to let Maggie in.

"How did she get up there?" Amelia asked, walking out onto the deck and peering over.

"I have no idea. I think she's the reincarnated ghost

of a woman, or maybe two, who died here." I stuffed a hunk of Mint Chocolate Chip into my mouth. I was warming up to Aunt Clara's hooey about the mistress and the scorned women. Plus, *ghost cat* would explain a lot about Maggie's mysterious appearances.

Maggie wound around Amelia's legs, and Amelia scooped her up, nuzzling her face into the ragamuffin's fur. "She's not a ghost cat. She's a princess. Aren't you?"

"Fine, she's a homeless germ-fest who's getting a bath if she keeps coming up here." Maggie gave me the stink eye.

"Aww." Amelia stroked her head. "Maybe I could take her home with me? People love to see cats in bookstores."

"No." I almost spit the ice cream out of my mouth.

Amelia grinned.

"I think she lives here," I said hastily. "That's all."

"You love her," Amelia sang. "You think she's sweet." She lifted the cat's paw and waved it at me.

"I do not." I smiled around my next spoonful of minty heaven. "But Lou would miss her if she left. I think they're friends."

"The gull? Sure. Sure." Amelia let Maggie jump down on the deck and went back to the ice cream she'd left sitting on the railing. "I think you've got the best view in the world." She tipped her head back, letting blond hair fly over her face. "Standing here, I feel like I'm in another era. I feel like a wealthy land-owner's mistress waiting for his arrival."

"What?"

Amelia laughed. "Just kidding. Clara told me all about this home's history."

"That was mean." I chastised myself for being so gullible.

"I think the stories are neat. A little gruesome, but cool. It doesn't even matter if any of it is true. Having a story to go with your home is just so *Charm*."

I hadn't thought of it that way. I'd never known a life without my aunts' wild tales. My whole life had a back story.

I spooned ice cream into my mouth and let the wind throw my hair everywhere at once. Watching dark waves roll in, I dared voice the question that had been on my mind for days. "Who do you think has been threatening me?"

Amelia gave me a sad smile. "I don't know. Based on personality, I'd say the angry contractor is the most likely islander to lash out, but I don't know why he would exactly. There's definitely something fishy about his beef with Paine, and the real estate aspect would also tie him to Sam Smart." She frowned. "I think this is all about the three of them—Metz, Smart, and Paine. I just don't know how."

I wasn't convinced of anything anymore. I just hoped it would soon be over.

CHAPTER
TWENTY-ONE

The next day was quiet. I woke with a sugar high from the late-night ice cream and worked on pins and needles through lunch, but nothing remotely scary or interesting happened. Unless I counted Lou carrying his still-live catch onto the deck and tearing one of the poor crab's claws off in front of my lunch crowd. A table of men and women in golf gear cringed. Everyone else exchanged knowing looks. Survival of the fittest was a common theme for wildlife in Charm, right alongside proper use of sunscreen and community spirit for the humans.

I knew I was back in the town's good graces when a patron asked if he could leave a flyer advertising the annual street party on my counter. I agreed to the request and asked for a second copy, which I proudly displayed in my window—just in case anyone wandering in for tea or a snack was still unclear about my full public pardon.

At closing time, I headed upstairs to change, wishing I'd remembered to tell Grady about the event.

I locked my front door around eight and headed down the boardwalk toward Main Street. Warm wind off the ocean whipped my hair into a frenzy and fluttered my flowy off-the-shoulder blouse. I tipped my head back and held out my arms, feeling ten years younger in my faded jeans and flip-flops. The pale gray color and light fabric of my top reminded me of Aunt Clara—except that her entire wardrobe screamed *mystical hippie*. An apt description of both my great aunts, now that I thought about it. I could only dream of being half as peaceful and centered as either of them tonight, but maybe someday.

I faced forward and watched where I was going as the boardwalk went parallel to Ocean Drive. A dark pickup approached, so I waited. When it slowed, I stepped back, fear jumping all over my skin, tearing me out of my happy place.

The driver's-side window rolled down and Grady peered out. I pretended not to notice him, certain I was in trouble for hijacking his family's ice cream party last night.

He stopped the pickup before me and hung an elbow over the open window frame. "Good evening, Swan." His voice was tight and his expression unreadable, but his pale gray eyes were as unfairly attractive as usual.

I lifted a hand in greeting. I couldn't tell if I was in trouble.

He pushed the truck into park. "Where are you headed?"

"Main Street. Why?"

"Alone after dark?"

I smiled and tried to keep my voice light. "You don't think I'm safe to walk a mile these days?"

"I'm starting to think you're not safe waking up in the morning."

"Ha, ha."

A small smile formed on his lips. "It just so happens I'm headed your way. You want a lift?"

I dithered for a moment, feeling certain this was some sort of ambush. "I don't know."

Grady leaned out the window, giving me one hundred percent of his attention. "I have a confession."

"Yeah?" I took a step forward.

He dipped his chin in affirmation. The vibe around him was charged and strange. "I was on my way to see you."

"Me?" I asked, utterly baffled. "Why?" I shuffled closer to his door. I supposed it wasn't about Sam Smart, even though Grady had said he'd come over after that mess yesterday and then never showed. My heart rate spiked. What if someone else was dead? We'd have to change the town name if people kept dropping every few days—Charm wouldn't really be appropriate anymore. "What happened?"

"Nothing." His blank cop face turned a little vulnerable. "I was going to invite you to the street party."

I rolled the words over in my head, trying to make sense of why he wanted to do that. "Why?" I asked again, this time with a blush. *Seriously. Why?*

He worked his jaw. "I heard some folks saying it's a good time, but I don't know anybody. Not really. Feels like everyone I've met this week has been in an official capacity. They're starting to look at me funny. I figured you could show me around, introduce me to folks as your friend, not just the new detective. Teach me how this place works. You might not believe this, but I've never been anywhere like Charm."

"You need me," I said with a fresh smile.

"I just thought it would be nice to go together."

I cocked my hip and crossed my arms, gloating a little. "So, I'm not always a big pain in your keister. Admit it."

Grady narrowed his eyes. "Get in, Swan."

I rounded the hood of his truck and climbed into the passenger seat, feeling unreasonably victorious. "Are Denise and Denver meeting you there? Denver will love all the junk food. And there will be live music and lots of light-up toys and glow sticks and stuff like that."

He waited while I buckled in, then pulled carefully away from the curb. "They're there now."

I gave him a cursory look. "Without you? Why?"

He slid his eyes my way. "I was coming to get you."

A strange new idea formed in my head. "Is this a date? I'm just asking so I know."

"Do you want it to be?"

I twisted toward him, evaluating his expression. He hadn't answered my question. He just asked me a new one, as if I wouldn't notice the evasion. "I thought you didn't like me," I finally said.

"What?" He widened his eyes in what could only be faux shock. "Why?"

"I don't know. I'm a clumsy mess. Butting in to your investigation. Being a distraction. Making your job harder. Stuff like that. Or so I hear." It was confusing, and I felt half nauseated by an attack of middle school-type butterflies. I pried my tongue off the roof of my mouth. "Basically, I make trouble everywhere I go."

"True." He grinned.

I got comfy in my seat and watched the scenery rolling past my window, enjoying the fun twist my evening had taken.

We rode in companionable silence for a bit until we reached Main Street. The street had been blocked off with wooden barricades. Ropes of white lights swooped between streetlamps over the pedestrian-filled roads.

Grady parked in the grass a couple of blocks away, as close as possible to the festivities. We'd have to walk from there. Music and chatter floated on the evening breeze as I slid down from his cab. He met me on his side of the truck and cast me an appreciative gaze. "You look nice tonight; did I tell you?"

"No." Did I also look floored, rattled, and at a complete loss for words? Because that's how I felt.

"Well, I meant to," he said.

"Thanks." I fought a goofy blush.

A pair of little girls ran through the grass beside us, sparklers flaring, bare feet flying, and pigtails streaming behind them. Their parents were lost in conversation several steps behind them, carrying two pairs of pink flip-flops and two half-melted ice cream cones.

"What must that be like?" I wondered, recalling all the times I'd brought my grandma and two great-aunts to Parents' Day. "Two normal parents, making regular family memories."

"I wouldn't know," Grady said. The sadness in his tone reminded me that he'd had a normal life once.

I let my eyes slide shut for a quick beat. "Sorry. I didn't mean…" He'd lost his wife too soon, too harshly. He could've known what it was like to raise a child with a partner, if fate hadn't been so cruel.

"It's fine."

"No," I said, stopping to look at him with determination. "What happened to your family isn't all right. It sucks. A lot, actually."

He nodded. "You're right."

I nodded back, then fell into step at his side.

"Thank you," he said softly.

I walked a little closer to him after that, feeling strangely protective of a man who clearly didn't need protecting. We joined the crowd inside the first wooden barrier. Families filled the sidewalks, wiping their children's sticky mouths and bouncing babies on their hips. Couples laughed and leaned against one another, lost in private moments no one else could understand.

Grady nodded toward side of the street lined with vendor stalls. "Where should we start? Funnel cakes? Ice cream? Maybe a little steak on a stick?"

"I'm not eating anything that comes on a stick," I said. "You could put your eye out."

He nudged me toward a vendor cart with his elbow. "How about some delicious fried butter?"

"No." I laughed. "Just. No."

"Fried pickles?"

"How about a lemonade?" I countered. A drink with a lid and straw seemed like the way to go. It would be significantly harder to spill on myself or get stuck in, my teeth.

Grady raised his eyebrows at the lemonade line. "Look at all those people in line for a drink. You need a booth at this event."

I smiled. The town council had settled the street fair plans long before I'd finished unpacking and months before I'd had time to open up shop. "I missed the deadline for vendor applications this year, but next spring, Sun, Sand, and Tea will be represented."

He lifted a palm, and I gave it a high five.

"Everly." Mr. Waters came in our direction, pulling a cart of light-up toys and glow sticks from Molly's Market. There were flashing necklaces around the brim of his hat.

"Hi, Mr. Waters." I gave him a squeeze. "Love the new look." I took a blinking pinwheel from the cart and blew on it to see the petals spin.

"Who's your friend?" he asked.

"Him?" I turned to be sure no one else had joined us. "That's Grady." Had he not met Grady?

Grady lifted a hand and they shook. "I'm Detective

Grady Hays. I'm new to Charm. Miss Swan here has agreed to show me around and introduce me."

Clearly, I was off to a poor start.

Mr. Waters's lips parted in apparent shock. "Aren't you the one who insinuated she poisoned the tea?" He stared at me. "That's him, right?"

"Yep." I puffed again on the pinwheel. "I'm surprised you haven't met."

"Why would we meet?" Mr. Waters asked. "I'm not in any trouble. Unlike you," he added with a teasing smile.

"I'm not in trouble at the moment," I informed him.

Grady pulled a money clip from his pocket and extracted a business card. "I'd actually planned to drop in on you and your wife tomorrow. Would you give me a call when you have some time?"

A group of kids with cash in hand giggled their way up to the blinking cart of toys so Grady and I stepped away, allowing him to handle the crowd.

We moseyed to the end of the lemonade line. "Why do you want to talk to Mr. Waters and his wife?"

Grady stared ahead at the menu board. *Small, medium, large*. Not exactly worth studying.

"Hey." I batted his hand, which was dangling at his side. "What was that about back there?"

"I'm just following a lead," Grady said, attention still fixed on the three-item board.

"Yeah, right."

A couple carrying hot popcorn and cotton candy drifted past, and my mouth watered. The rich buttery scent tickled my nose so delectably I nearly forgot what I was saying.

"I went out today, looking at the area around the Little Libraries after reading Amelia's report."

I softened my expression. Grady had news, and he was going to share it.

"I found a new frying pan in one of the public beach trash cans between the library where you confronted the kids and your place. The tags were still attached, and there was blood and hair on the back."

My heart skittered and my hand flew up to touch my barely concealed goose egg.

"So I ran the numbers from the tag and learned it was in a shipment sent to Mr. Waters's store. I'd planned to talk to him tomorrow about it. Plus, the Waterses have been in Charm for thirty-five years and run the busiest store in town. I hoped they'd have some personal insight to offer."

I gave him my most serious face. "When were you going to tell me about the frying pan?"

"Tonight." He sighed. "I'd hoped you'd consent to a DNA swab so we can match the blood and tissue on the pan to you. Until we know it was the weapon used to attack you, it's not worth anything."

My stomach bucked and rolled. I couldn't tell if it was because Grady had found the weapon used to assault me or because he apparently only asked me to come to the street fair to fill me in on the details. A man in a paper hat leaned over the lemonade stand counter. "Can I take your order?"

Grady pushed me closer to the window and ordered two lemonades. I was still trying to figure out when we'd gotten to the front of the line. Grady paid and handed one bright yellow cup to me.

"Thank you." The icy sweetness loosened a wad of bunched muscles along the back of my neck. "You can do the DNA test. If that pan was the weapon used to hurt me, then I want its owner found."

He sipped and nodded. "Good. Thank you. We couldn't pull any fingerprints from it, but I know where it came from, so this isn't over yet. With Waters's records, we might be able to find the buyer through credit card receipts. If the purchase was cash, we can use the timestamp on the register tape to check surveillance footage from nearby shops and look for shoppers leaving the market." He bumped his cup to mine. "Tossing the pan in a public trash receptacle was a sloppy mistake. Here's to soon-solved cases."

I tapped my cup to his with a pang of disappointment in my heart. I'd hoped I was right about this being a date. Still, I was thankful for the progress on his investigation. Whoever had knocked me out with a perfectly good frying pan should be punished.

We headed back into the mash of people, my tummy flipping for new reasons now. Grady had a lead that could take him to my attacker. It was the thing I'd been praying for.

Amelia's laugh caught my ear and turned me around. I bounced on my toes, looking for her outside her bookshop. She was surrounded by a half-dozen familiar faces, all smiling wildly.

"Come on," I said, hooking one of my arms with Grady's. "There's my buddy Amelia with a bunch of your new neighbors and friends."

He put on a brave face as I dragged him into the little crowd.

Two hours later, I was exhausted from laughter, having run into everyone I'd ever known in Charm and loving the blessed nostalgia. Grady was witty and pleasant, but clearly distracted. No one seemed to notice but me. Standing beside him, I felt each twitch and thread of tension. He was never in the moment, seemingly hyperaware of everything. He continually scanned the area, for what I couldn't say, but it made me feel safe for the first time in days.

Afterward, he walked me to my house, leaving his truck in the grass along Ocean Drive, where he'd been boxed in by others who'd come out to have fun.

"I had a good time tonight," I told him.

"I'm glad. Me too. I can't say I'll remember half those names tomorrow, but I'll try."

"I wouldn't be surprised if you can't. You were only half there," I said.

Surprise crossed his face. "It was that evident, huh?"

"To me."

Amelia's Little Library caught my eye. Instinct told me something was wrong. "Hold that thought," I said. "I want to peek in on this so I can report back to Amelia."

The window was dark and I couldn't see any books inside. Had they all been borrowed?

I inched closer, bending at the waist and peering inside. "Oh!" I growled, yanking the door open. A flood of sand and seawater washed out, splashing onto my tank top, jeans, and feet. "Ah!" I tried to shut the door again, but the water kept coming, and Amelia's books fell onto the ground in a ruined heap. "Jerks!"

Grady handed me a handkerchief before pulling out his phone to capture a couple of pictures.

A bubble of laughter rocked through me as I examined the crisp white hanky. What could I possibly do with the tiny scrap of material when I looked like I had just washed up on the beach?

"What?" He tucked his phone away.

I opened the little cloth in front of my ruined outfit and held it near the dark smear of sand and water for comparison.

Grady began to laugh, and I started all over again. "Right. Sorry."

I linked my arm with his and groaned. "This week has not been my best."

He tipped his face down toward mine, glancing at me sincerely. "It hasn't been my worst."

I turned away with a smile. Another round of giggles caught in my throat over my ruined outfit versus his perfect hanky. We continued on in snatches of laughter, though it wasn't funny at all.

I used the handkerchief to dry my tears. "We should take a look at the other boardwalk library just in case."

"Deal."

A hundred yards later, a pair of puffy-haired silhouettes appeared, toting buckets toward the next Little Library.

I lifted a finger in their direction. "Look! I think those could be the boys I chased last night." I took a step forward, debating whether I could reach them before they saw me coming this time. At least with Grady, I wouldn't be outnumbered.

"Wait." Grady held a hand in front of me and turned his phone over. "Let them go. I'll have someone meet them at their next hit."

My eyes went wide. "Grady. I think they saw who pushed me in the marsh. They could know who the killer is."

He froze for a second, then burst into action, running full speed toward the little vandals. I couldn't have caught him even on my bike.

I walked to my porch steps, torn. On the one hand, I wanted to see him take down the little creeps. On the other hand, I didn't want to still be covered in sand and seawater when he came back.

Pride won.

I hurried up the steps, prepared to do a fast wardrobe change and de-sanding. A shadow moved on my front porch, and I started.

It only took a moment to recognize Lucinda Paine, carrying my cake pan and wearing a frown. "I believe you left this at my house."

I squinted at Grady's now-tiny figure in the

distance. He'd be right back. Then he could see it was *her* that approached *me* this time and not the other way around. Hopefully, my cake pan appearing at her home wasn't grounds for that restraining order. "How can you be sure that's mine?" I hedged.

She flipped it over to showcase my name written in marker on a patch of masking tape.

Labeling dishes—my signature move.

"Oh, right." I climbed the front porch steps and opened the door. "Won't you come in for a glass of tea?"

Maggie screeched up the front steps and into my shop with a hiss, and I pressed a palm to my racing heart. "Ignore her," I told Lucinda. "She's just mad that she's getting a bath." I announced the second sentence extra loudly into the empty room.

Lucinda didn't look like she cared. In fact, she kind of looked like she'd rather push me down the steps than enter my shop.

I took the empty cake pan. "I hope you weren't waiting long."

"No. The walk was hard on me. I figured I might as well wait if leaving meant I'd have to come back."

"I'm sorry," I told her with utmost sincerity. I'd had a great night, and I didn't want to ruin it. This was my fresh start. "I'm sorry for attending your party uninvited and for rubbing you the wrong way since we met. I wish we hadn't gotten off on the wrong foot, but we're going to be neighbors now, so…" I let the sentence hang. "How about some tea?"

Her shoulders drooped and her furrowed brows

rose with defeat. "Fine, but only one glass, and no funny business."

I rolled my eyes as I flipped the lights on inside and let her pass. "Deal. That goes for you too," I joked.

Apparently, I'd be wearing my sand-crusted outfit a little while longer. Making up with a crotchety old lady was not exactly how I'd hoped my night would end.

CHAPTER

TWENTY-TWO

I set a pair of napkins on the counter. Lucinda looked at them with visible skepticism. "You'll understand if I'm hesitant to try your tea."

"Sure." I bit back a grimace. "But I assure you there's no reason to be nervous."

I filled two jars with ice, setting the cubes afloat with a flood of strawberry tea. I stuck a sprig of fresh mint in each, then set the jars on the napkins. "Maybe you'd like to hear about the history of my iced teas," I suggested. "It might help you understand why I'd never use my recipes to cause trouble."

Lucinda didn't answer, but remained just inside the door, clutching her necklace in one hand and pressing her big, quilted handbag against her chest with the other.

I could almost sympathize with her. *How would I feel in her shoes?* I opened the fridge and stared at the contents. Good food and great tea fixed many things; maybe it could become the foundation for a middle ground between two women at odds. "How about some fresh fruit salad?" I asked over one shoulder. "It's fantastic with the sweet tea. Might be even better with my Strawberry tea."

She shuffled forward reluctantly, but eventually climbed onto a seat at the counter and arranged her purse on top. All in all, it seemed like acceptance to me.

I prepared two bowls of fruit and joined her. "You see, my family has been on this island for generations, and the recipes I make today come from them. The foods and teas are part of our legacy. Some say the women of my family have been in Charm since the town was settled. Can you believe that? In three hundred years' time, there has always been a Swan woman here."

"Not really, no."

I chuckled at her unbridled snark. "Me, either, sometimes. Other times," I tilted my head left, then right, "I think, *maybe*."

Lucinda fiddled with her necklace. When she caught me waiting for her to say something more, she waved at the stove. "I like hot tea," she said.

"Okay." I filled a kettle with water and set it on the stove, before turning around and smiling. "Earl Gray okay?" Honestly, I could use the additional caffeine. I was as tired as I'd ever been, and my week had taken a hard toll.

Her eyes were wide, as if I'd startled her. "Yes. Now go on. You were telling me about your family history here."

"My great aunts like to say we moved here from

Salem following the witch trials, which were simply too heartbreaking to bear." I frowned, imagining the horror. "They'd tried to stop the drowning and burnings, but the will of a scared community was stronger than the power of a good cup of tea. The Swans couldn't stand the tension, animosity, and accusations, not to mention all those young women tortured and lost. For what?" I felt my chest swell with pride as I told the story. Maybe there was a little of Aunt Clara in me after all. "Accusations are powerful weapons, don't you think?" I tossed a meaningful look in Lucinda's direction. "I learned that lesson recently."

"Detective Hays said the poison was in your tea."

"I know." I gave a noncommittal shrug. "And maybe it was, but I don't know who put it there. It wasn't me. Detective Hays knows that now. He said so."

"He did?" She raised her brown, penciled-on brows. "Who do you suppose he's looking at as a suspect now?"

"I don't know." I pressed the tines of my fork into a slice of orange, dodging the little spray of juice. "I didn't ask, and he didn't say." Did he have a new suspect? I'd been so thankful to hear my name was cleared, and so torn up by Sam's death, that I'd forgotten to ask Grady who could've done it.

Anyway, that was off-topic. "What's important here is that you know I would never do anything to harm another living creature or damage my family's name." I lifted my glass in a single-sided toast and sucked the contents down by a quarter.

The taste smacked on my lips and tongue. Something wasn't right. Did the mint and the fruit salad create too *much* contrast? It wasn't like me to be wrong on these things.

"Is something wrong?" Lucinda asked, lifting her drink for inspection and giving it a jostle.

"No." I took another long drink to prove it. Then I slid off my stool and went to find something that would go better with the tea. "Do you like almond pound cake?" I asked, hoping she wouldn't try the tea and an orange slice combo like I had. "I made this to go with Hana's rhubarb jam. Do you know the Goat Lady?"

She sniffed her tea, then took a reluctant sip, eyes locked on me. "Not really. She's a farmer, right? That's not really my thing."

I bobbed my head. Lucinda wore the high-maintenance look like a medal of honor. Which was possibly the way I wore my flip-flops.

I set a slice of pound cake before her. "Another family recipe. The water will be ready soon, if you'd prefer a hot cuppa."

"I'm diabetic," she said, pushing the cake away. "Hot tea will be fine."

"Of course." My throat tightened with memory and emotion as I recalled arguing pointlessly with Mr. Paine. "I'm sorry. Excuse me."

I shook my head, trying to clear my thoughts.

"What's wrong?" She leaned away from the counter, as if I might be highly contagious.

"Mr. Paine always asked about the sugar content

in everything. I'd assumed it was him who watched his diet."

"No." Sadness drew a path over her tired face, pulling and tugging at the corners of her eyes and mouth. "That's me." She wiped the corner of her eye. "He was always fussing about my health, thinking I didn't take good enough care. It's part of what broke us up a few years ago." She drew lines in the condensation on her glass. "I've been doing better. He knew, and we were working things out. I was taking care of him more and more instead of the other way around."

I pushed my napkin to her, and she dabbed at another escaping tear.

"Was Mr. Paine unwell?" What did she mean by saying that she had been caring for him?

Her milky eyes snapped back to mine, grief replaced by distrust once again. "How are you feeling?" she asked.

Honestly? Not my best. The night, maybe the whole week, had taken a toll, and fatigue tugged incessantly at my limbs and eyes. My heart rate hadn't settled since finding Lucinda on the porch, and my thoughts were more blended than my smoothies. "Fine."

"Your cheeks are red and your skin is pale." She circled a finger at my face. "And there's some sweat on your forehead."

I checked. She was right. I couldn't see the redness, but I felt the heat then, and my fingertips camp back damp from beneath my bangs. "Tough night, I guess."

My phone buzzed with a text from Grady. I grabbed it off the counter and carried it across the room to see what he learned. "Will you excuse me? I just need to check this." Steam puffed from the kettle on the stove as I passed. "Looks like we'll have tea soon."

I swiped my thumb over the screen, bringing his message front and center, leaning against the far wall on the opposite side of my counter from Lucinda, careful to shield the incoming information.

Caught the boys. Stay put. I'm headed your way.

I frowned at the lack of detail. "Just one more minute," I told Lucinda. "That was Detective Hays."

I dialed his number and waited. He'd caught the boys, but who were they?

Lucinda's expression was peculiar, but I couldn't place its meaning. "I hope everything's all right," she said, stroking the large blue bauble on her necklace. "Maybe you should lie down now and talk to him later," she suggested.

My knees wobbled.

The phone connected. "Hays," Grady barked.

"Hey," I started. "You can't tell me half a story. What did they say?" My speech slurred slightly, and I ran a hand over my numbing lips. "Sorry. I'm feeling weird."

A drop of sweat slid along my temple to my jaw, then dripped onto my shirt. I braced a hand on the counter in an effort to remain upright. My hazy mind dimmed, and my tongue attempted to double in size.

"Are you home now?" he asked.

"Yeah. Lucinda stopped by and I made a snack, but now I'm wondering if last night's events are catching up with me. I'm so tired."

He swore under his breath. "Don't move." An engine roared in the background. "I'm three minutes out."

My raggedy cat crept along the counter in Lucinda's direction. Her lips pulled back in a hiss.

My knees wobbled. Spots danced on the periphery of my vision. "Grady," I whispered, fear striking against my tightening heart, "something's wrong with me."

"Dammit, Swan," Grady snapped. "Lucinda Paine shoved you in the marsh that night."

CHAPTER

❧

TWENTY-THREE

I turned slowly back toward Lucinda, who was still seated quietly at my counter, a small smile on her puckered lips. "Everything all right?"

"No," I answered breathlessly. The phone tumbled from my hands. I knelt down and swept it off the floor with bumbling fingers. "Grady caught the kids filling Amelia's Little Libraries with sand." The call had disconnected.

"And he called to report that to you?"

I nodded, my chest constricting with each move of my chin. Lucinda had pushed me into the marsh. Did that mean she'd also killed her ex-husband? And Sam Smart? Why?

Was she the one threatening me all along? The one who hit me with a frying pan? I touched the wrap covering my bump.

"I didn't realize the two of you were so close." She clucked her tongue in distaste. "Calling you at home, at this hour. That man has only been in town a week. It's not very professional."

My tummy rolled and pitched. I knew in my core that it was all true. Lucinda had been behind everything from the start.

She'd killed her ex-husband, and she'd let the town blame me for it while she played the victim. She'd even had the audacity to be mad at me. Now she was sitting in my café, pretending she was afraid to taste my tea and judging Grady for our friendship.

I shuffled toward her on sheer indignation. "He's a nice guy," I said. "We got to know one another while I was being investigated for murder."

She pulled her chin back, clearly appalled by the bluntness of my statement.

I opened my mouth to tell her Grady was on his way for a visit, but the floor tilted and my stomach lurched. I grabbed for the counter with sweat-slicked hands. My head dropped forward and my eyes pinched shut, waiting for the world to stand still again. "You did this to me, didn't you?"

Lucinda scooped Maggie into her arms. "I think you're confused. Why don't you finish your tea?"

The sight of my nearly empty jar sent a tidal wave crashing in my gut.

"You poisoned me with my own tea?" The words were like tiny flares suddenly illuminating the obvious. No wonder the flavor combination had been so off. I never make mistakes like that. I'd been poisoned!

I tried to raise my eyes to hers, but my gaze caught on her necklace. An age-spotted hand wrapped around the blue bauble.

I forced my gaze to hers. "It was your necklace that I saw at the water's edge," I said, the pieces coming slowly together in my addled mind. She must've dropped the locket and gone back to retrieve it, then shoved me in before I saw her there or got my hands on evidence that would have connected her to the murder.

Lucinda gave a low and hearty laugh. She stroked Maggie's dingy fur. "You think you're so smart," she said. "Everyone thinks I'm so dumb."

"What did you put in my tea?" I struggled to clear my thoughts. Maybe the effects were reversible. Maybe there was an antidote.

"Insurance," she snarled. "Now drink up or I hurt the cat."

"What?!"

She repositioned her hand, suggestively, around Maggie's throat.

"No! Stop!" I raised my hands in surrender. The world blurred and spun around me. "Don't hurt her," I begged. "I'll drink." It was a terrible idea, but I couldn't run. Couldn't fight. And Grady was on his way. Supposedly. How long was three minutes, anyway? Hadn't it already been an hour?

Maggie struggled, knocking Lucinda's hand off her neck and swinging the necklace over her chest.

I gasped. "Is that where you keep it?" I was

suddenly unsure what was more shocking: my recent poisoning or her cavalier behavior. "You just wear it around your neck like jewelry?"

"That's right," she quipped. "Benedict wasn't meant to get a double dose, but Sam Smart certainly was, and when I realized you were getting close to the truth with your ridiculous pursuit, I loaded the locket up again. Can you blame me?"

"Yes!" I squeaked.

Maggie wrestled free with a hiss and flew past me with an indignant roar.

"Yeow!" Lucinda shrieked. Blood streamed from fresh claw marks on her thin arm. "Finish the tea." Her voice turned cold and demanding. "Just drink up. It will help this go faster."

"This what?" My voice ratcheted another octave. "My *death*?" Who would want to speed up their death?

The teakettle whistled in my ear, and I spun toward the stove with a scream. A fresh flood of panic and adrenaline washed through my system. I jerked it off the burner and turned back, kettle in hand, unsure where to set it or why any of this was happening. "Why are you doing this?" I cried.

I'd let her inside my café, thinking we could make friends. I'd wanted to make up for offending her—meanwhile, she'd come to kill me!

Lucinda turned her enraged expression on me, plowing forward at a tilt. She swiped the cleaver off my knife rack and charged me. "Drink it!" she screamed, lifting the knife overhead. "Or you're about to have a ghastly kitchen accident, and I'll still end the cat. I'll find that grubby thing and I'll—"

The sound of my steaming kettle colliding with her forehead was gruesome. It reverberated up my arm and in my ears as she fell to the floor in a heap, a red kettle imprint over one eyebrow.

I yelped. The rage that had bubbled in my limbs for everyone she'd hurt had overcome me in a burst, moving my arm to stop her before I'd had time to think better of it. I released my weapon, scalding water streaming across my floor in a tiny flood that washed against Lucinda's crumpled frame.

As I stared at her, the too-familiar flash of red and white emergency lights registered through my windows.

I sobbed with relief, slipping and sliding across the splattered planks on weird noodle legs, and wrapped weak and trembling arms around my middle. *Had I killed her? Was she dead?*

The steady thump of footfalls on the stairs outside my door echoed through my head and heart. "Grady?"

"Everly!" His strong form came into view a moment before my world slanted.

"I'm sorry," I whispered through the cotton filling my mouth.

"Medic!" he yelled.

I ached to tell him everything, to see his face and know things would be okay, but my brain had been disconnected, unplugged, no longer in control of my limbs or tongue.

"Everly?" Grady's hands were on my face and neck. "You're going to be okay, Swan. You hear me?" He heaved me into his arms and began to move. His words were barely a whisper against the blast of fresh sea air.

I pulled in a series of shallow breaths, sipping the beloved ocean breeze and relieved at the flutter of hair across my face. Humidity clung to my skin, and the treasured scents of sand and salt air seemed to pull my eyes open. Dual carousels of emergency lights lit the darkness. A pair of ambulances blocked the path to my front porch, and Grady set me on a gurney outside the first. His truck was practically parked on my porch.

He kept a hand on my shoulder as a new face drifted into view.

An older gentleman wearing a stethoscope snapped a mask over my nose and mouth, the sweet taste of oxygen poured into my lungs. "I'm Tom," the man said. "How are you feeling?"

I looked at Grady and struggled to swallow. "She has poison in her necklace," I choked through a tightening esophagus.

The men exchanged looks.

Grady removed a phone from his pocket and barked orders across the line.

Tom flashed a light in my eyes and took my pulse.

Fear swam in Grady's ethereal eyes. "How is she?"

"BP is sixty-six over fifty, dilated pupils, shallow breathing. I'd like to know what was in that necklace."

The ponytailed woman from Mr. Paine's crime scene appeared, as if on command. Her black jacket had a Charm PD logo over the pocket, and her face was all business. She lifted a plastic bag in Grady's direction. "Lucinda's awake. This is the necklace. Traces of the medications are available for testing, but she claims it's the remnants of a prescription her late husband discontinued using last year."

"Which?" Tom asked.

The answer was completely unfamiliar and slightly garbled by my ringing ears.

"I don't know how you're still conscious," Tom said, presumably to me, though his eyes were fixed on the needle he pressed into my vein. "This will help." He attached a tube and bag of fluids, then popped a clip on the end of my finger and wiggled it. "You're going to be just fine, Miss Swan."

The gurney began to move. My head rocked side to side.

"I'm coming with her," Grady said.

My eyes slid closed before the ambulance doors had time to shut, and I drifted to sleep with the warmth of Grady's hand heating my shoulder.

CHAPTER

TWENTY-FOUR

I swiped a wrist against my forehead, moving a bead of sweat into my hairline before it could drip onto my tray.

The lunch crowd at Sun, Sand, and Tea had grown steadily in the two weeks since a lunatic woman had tried to kill me. News had traveled fast, and I seemed to be cleared of any lingering suspicions before my aunts had taken me home from the hospital. Thankfully, I hadn't killed Lucinda, but her mug shot had wound up on the gossip blog, and I was certain she wished I'd gotten the job done after seeing that photo. The goose egg and kettle burn/imprint combo was enough to give viewers a sympathy headache—as was the resulting black eye. For a woman who'd worked so carefully on her appearance, I imagined that was its own kind of corporal punishment.

I, on the other hand, had overdosed on Mr. Paine's sleeping pills. Luckily, Grady had arrived in time—even if Lucinda hadn't managed to stab me to death, the pills could've finished me. She'd mashed half a bottle into dust and dumped them into my tea like sugar. I'd been appreciating my life in new ways since then, mostly during every breath I took.

I set my tray on the table between two tanned girls. "Two fruit salads and two Old-Fashioned Sun Teas. Is there anything else I can get ya?"

The girls shook their heads and dug in. They'd chosen the right ensembles for my sun deck, bikini tops and jean shorts. They looked cool despite the rising mercury, unlike myself in capri pants and a T-shirt that clung to my every humidity-dampened curve. I didn't care what the calendar said: it might've only been the middle of May, but summer had officially arrived in Charm.

The wind chimes over my front door jangled, and I spun my way back into the café. My heart leapt stupidly at the sight of my personal hero. "Welcome to Sun, Sand, and Tea," I said, tugging the screen shut behind me.

Grady sauntered to the counter, a trip he'd made almost daily since saving my life. Today, the collar of his dress shirt was tugged open, and his tie hung loosely around his neck like a scarf. "Not an empty seat in the house," he said, a twinkle of pride in his eye.

"Or on the deck." I set a napkin in front of him. "What can I get you?"

"How about a few minutes?"

I cast my gaze around the room, checking the levels on the tea jars and making certain all my orders had been filled. "Y'all," I called, drawing the room's attention. "I'm going to have a walk on the deck. If you need me, I won't be long."

"Police business," Grady added.

Some folks nodded, the rest went back to their conversations.

I poured Grady some tea, then stripped off my apron before following him to the rear deck. "Well?" I asked, stopping in the corner farthest from my customers. "How did it go?"

Wind swept through my hair, tossing it against him. I stuffed as much of it as possible behind one ear.

Grady released a heavy sigh. He turned his back to the sea and hooked both elbows on the handrail behind him. "I met with both attorneys for more than an hour. The defense is trying to avoid a trial, but that won't happen. This was more like a Hail Mary."

"Was she there?" I asked, still unable to say the name *Lucinda* without flashbacks.

"Yeah." He grimaced and sucked down some tea. "She won't be able to avoid jail time after what she did to her ex-husband and Sam Smart. Not to mention what she did to you." His eyes darkened for a moment after that last line. "She admits to all of it, though she's calling Mr. Paine's death accidental. Regardless, she's going away for a while."

I guffawed. "How does she suppose Mr. Paine's death was accidental? She drugged him." I crossed my arms in defense against the slew of terrifying memories begging to be relived, prepared for a colossal tale.

"Apparently," he began with a roll of his eyes, "she was slipping Benedict doses of her old diabetes medication in an attempt to keep him slightly ill so he'd need her again. She wanted to reconcile, but he didn't, so she decided to give him a little push. The drug she gave him was dangerous for someone with a heart condition and the medicine he took for it."

"How romantic."

He laughed. "From what I gathered, her jewelry business was failing, and she needed a lifeboat. She was on my radar long before she showed up that night. The lab sent lists of the medications found in Mr. Paine's system, and we knew that either he or Lucinda had taken each of them at one time or another, but he'd overdosed on painkillers and sleeping meds. We had no way to prove that she had been the one to put them in his tea, but we knew they met that afternoon for lunch. Without proof of her involvement, it could have easily been an accidental situation."

"I wish you would have led with that at the crime scene," I deadpanned. "Possible accidental overdose sounds so much better than 'the poison is in Everly's tea.'"

He wrinkled his nose. "I suppose it does."

"You saved my life, so I'll let it go." I smiled. "So, he didn't eat anything at my place because he was meeting his ex-wife for lunch. Then she rewarded him by slipping a fatal dose of crushed-up old pills into his tea? And all because she wanted his money? What a waste. Lucinda could have come back from financial troubles. I'm not so sure about two murder charges."

Grady squinted against the sun. "Lucinda had more debt than she could manage on her own, and a reunion with her ex would've saved her. Instead, he died and ruined her life. Her words, not mine."

I cringed. "That's awful." I'd thought I'd wanted to be there and hear the details firsthand, but maybe getting the information this way was good enough. I pressed a palm to my anxious tummy.

"I almost feel bad for her," Grady said. "Clearly, she's touched." He tapped his temple. "She had no idea what she was doing. We found her old pill bottle for the diabetes medication stuffed inside a coffee can and tossed in a dumpster behind her store. An entire ocean all around, and she left the pills she killed her husband with right outside a business she owns." He shook his head in wonder. "When she wanted to shut Sam Smart down, she went back to her medicine cabinet and made him a whiskey and oxycodone cocktail. She tried a little harder to pull it off with Sam—the extra pills and half-emptied whiskey bottle were left on a patio table. I suppose that was meant to make it look like he got doped up and went swimming. I mean, he was fully dressed, but like I said." He made a tiny circle around his ear with one finger. "The whole thing is a mess. She ought to plead insanity. Nothing she said today indicated otherwise."

"I still can't believe she killed Sam too," I said, my heart breaking all over again. "*Why* did she kill Sam?" That puzzle had eaten away at me, leaving me up at night for two weeks straight. I understood the concept of drama within couples and between exes, but

I couldn't fathom a reason for her to kill Sam Smart. "What was the connection there?"

"Sam saw Lucinda on the boardwalk with Mr. Paine on the night of his murder, so he attempted to blackmail her over it. He hatched a plan to make Lucinda his voice on the city council, promising to help her get Benedict's old position and keep his mouth shut about whatever he saw as long as she helped him get a few new real estate situations past the council. That's why the Paines had all those blueprints. Those were projects Sam wanted approval on."

"Shameless." *What a partnership.* Two crooks motivated to commit crimes for the sake of money. "I doubt Sam could've even gotten her on the council. That's a big deal around here, and the positions aren't filled willy-nilly." Maybe Mr. and Mrs. Waters had been right, and Lucinda's big party to "celebrate Mr. Paine's life" was just her trying to reintroduce herself to the community, and hopefully score her murdered husband's spot on the council.

I felt icky just listening. I tightened my arms over my chest. "So, she's the one who hit me with the frying pan?"

Grady's gaze traveled to the place on my head where Lucinda had clobbered me. "She never expected someone to take the maps and blueprints from the trash. When she saw you making off with them during her party, she had to go after them, and grabbed the first thing she saw on her way out to use as a weapon. She'd just bought some new things for her home that afternoon. I've got the records to prove it."

So it had been her watching from the upstairs window. I shivered.

Grady rubbed a broad palm up and down my arm. "Lucinda said she couldn't trust that Sam's blackmail would end there, so she had to silence him. Plus, she didn't want to be on the council." He dropped his hand away and smiled. "Then she pointed out that blackmail is a crime, so maybe Sam deserved what he got. The prosecutor reminded her that murder is a capital offense, and she started crying."

"Yikes."

"Pretty much." He rubbed both hands against his face and into his hair. "That wasn't the worst of it, though."

I failed to imagine how something so convoluted and horrifying could possibly get worse.

Grady dipped his chin sharply and locked his breathtaking gaze on me. "She accused me of only pursuing and apprehending her because she'd gone after you."

"Oh." I struggled to concentrate through the charged silence between us. "That was bad for you?"

"It implied that I didn't care about the murders until you were in danger. So, yeah. Not a great look for a new detective."

I smiled, recalling something I knew about Grady that crazy Lucinda did not. "But you aren't new at this. I've read all about you online. You would've found the truth, regardless."

"Undoubtedly."

I laughed. "See? Everyone knows it had nothing to do with me."

Grady didn't smile. He clenched and popped his jaw. "I *was* more motivated once you were in danger."

I did a slow blink. "Because you knew me personally," I suggested.

"Maybe."

I fought the urge to fan my face. Had we always been standing so close? I flicked my gaze away from him, trying to unscramble my thoughts and assure we were still alone.

Dozens of faces stared eagerly back. Patrons had moved to the window where they openly gawked. A few had cell phones. Even Lou peered judgmentally from the roof's peak.

"It's what you do," I said. "You solve things. Save people."

A low chuckle rumbled in Grady's chest, turning me back in his direction. An impish grin had broken over his face and he'd loosened his stance, falling back by an inch. "That's not what I was trying to say, but we seem to have an audience, so maybe we can pick this up later."

"We can try, but I've told you. Charm *is* an audience. You can't escape it."

Maggie trotted into view before stopping to watch Grady and me. Her fluffy white fur had been scrubbed spotless and blown out against her will, her nails trimmed and a pink bow tied in her hair. She pretended to hate it, but I was sure the bow would have been shredded to bits by now if that was true. Our local pet groomer was clearly part magician.

She batted luminescent eyes at me and an invigorating wave of boldness overcame me. I covered the back of Grady's hand with mine. "Have I told you about the free food and tea for life promotion? It's a special I offer to detectives who save my life."

"I accept."

"Good." The intimacy of the moment suddenly seemed too much. I moved my hand away with a smile. I'd spent enough time being featured on our local gossip blog lately.

I turned on my toes and headed back to the café's interior, desperate for the frigid air conditioning to cool me down; Grady followed. "Do you think it works like that with everyone who owns a business around here? Maybe I'll get free stuff everywhere soon."

I waited while he slid the patio door shut behind us. "Planning to save us all, are you?"

"At least you and the ice cream guy. Denver would love that."

I laughed. My phone buzzed, and I freed it from my pocket, expecting a message from Aunt Clara, who liked to help with the lunch crowd.

Multiple limousines spotted on Middletown Street. Celebrity visit?

I showed the notification to Grady. "I registered for the *Town Charmer*'s newsfeed."

He frowned.

"Finally, I'll be in the loop," I said.

The wind chimes jingled again, and two familiar silhouettes swept inside. The short one ran directly into Grady's arms. "Daddy!"

Grady raised Denver overhead like an airplane. "Buddy."

The closing door balanced the lighting, and I smiled at Denise in her perfect Tiffany-blue sundress. "Water?" I guessed.

"Yes, please." Her smile was unusually tight and her voice mildly strained. "Grady? Can I speak with you for a moment?"

He lowered Denver onto his hip. The smile he'd worn at first sight of his son was gone, replaced by the blank cop face that made me nervous. I guessed he'd heard the fear in her tone too.

I took my time getting two new napkins, a water, and a lemonade, my newest recipe created just for Denver Hays.

A woman at the counter waved to me. "What's in your Honey Vanilla Tea?"

I pulled a fully laminated menu from the pile behind me and ferried it to her fast. "The teas are in alphabetical order. Ingredients are listed to the right of each." Mr. Paine had been right. Folks wanted to know what they were consuming, and I'd needed to let go of all the secrecy. How I made my products was. proprietary, but what went in them shouldn't be.

The door opened again, and Aunt Clara walked

inside, waving a handkerchief dramatically overhead. "Hello!"

Half the patrons stopped eating to welcome her.

I returned to Denise and Grady with ears primed for whatever news had made the most beautiful girl on earth look like she'd seen a shark. She stood so close to Grady that only Denver's small frame separated them. "She's here," Denise whispered.

I inched closer to the pair sharing a secret. "Grady?" I asked, suddenly willing to give up a prime eavesdropping situation for his benefit. "Do you want to talk privately?" I asked. "If so, I bet Denver would like to meet Lou the seagull."

"Yeah!" Denver swung his body toward mine, nearly plummeting from Grady's grip. "Seagulls are cool!"

I hoisted him onto my hip and moved to the deck again, the warm weight of a sweet boy in my arms and a deep sense of gratitude in my heart. Denver had taken a liking to me the day Grady had brought him over for a visit after I was released from the hospital. We'd talked about horses, and I'd shared some local legends about the Spanish galleons that had crashed against our shores centuries ago, spilling mustangs onto the land. Those same lucky horses' ancestors ran wild here today. Denver had eaten up every word exactly as I had when Grandma first shared those stories with me.

Aunt Clara stopped me short of making it to the rear deck. "What's with the line of limousines outside? I half expected to find Rod Stewart in here."

I turned for the café entrance. "First let's see some limos," I told Denver.

He rested his cheek on my shoulder. "Boring."

Grady and Denise were already on the porch when I got there.

I gave a long whistle. Aunt Clara and the community blogger were wrong: there wasn't a parade of limousines, there was one limousine and convoy of government SUVs out front.

"What's going on?" I asked Grady and Denise, hefting Denver higher. I fixed Grady with a curious stare. "Are those vehicles here for you?"

He and Denise exchanged a look. Grady had been a big deal at the U.S. Marshals Service. It was plausible this was about him, wasn't it? Maybe they wanted him back? "If you'd like, I can prepare something for everyone. Invite them inside. It's no problem." Heck, I'd make Thanksgiving dinner if he wanted, anything to know who was behind the black tinted glass and how they were connected to Grady. "Denise?" I asked, pressing the weak link. I doubted this was about her, but she knew exactly what was happening. I could see it on her face and in her rigid stance. She'd come here to warn him, asking to speak with him moments before the caravan arrived. "What's happening?"

She shot her arms out for Denver. "I'll take him to her," she said, putting up a bright but very fake smile. "Ready, sweetie?"

Denver went to Denise without a fuss. He turned

happy eyes back to me. "First Grandma, then I meet Lou, right, Everly?"

"Absolutely," I agreed, completely befuddled. "Maybe we can even find something to feed him."

"Cool!"

Denise squared her shoulders and descended my porch stairs with the enthusiasm of a funeral procession. Grady shifted his weight and locked long tan fingers over narrow hips.

"Did he say 'Grandma?'" I asked, eyeballing Denise and Denver from behind. *Whose grandma comes with an escort of government SUVs? And why wasn't Grady going with them?*

"Yep."

"Your mother?" I guessed. It would explain his wild success at the marshals service.

Grady mindlessly thumbed the space on his left ring finger where a wedding band had briefly lived. "No."

"Your wife's mother?"

Grady groaned. "She's a story for another day." He rubbed his palms against his thighs, then made the same slow descent Denise had made before him.

I craned my neck for a look inside the limo when the door swung open. A pair of thin legs appeared, complete with black heels and a pair of reaching hands well-appointed in diamonds. The woman never leaned forward as she helped her grandson and his au pair inside.

Grady gave me one last look before joining his family

inside the vehicle. A moment later, the convoy purred to life and pulled away in a strangely formal parade.

I wandered back into Sun, Sand, and Tea with a head full of new questions.

Aunt Clara looked up from a table near the window, a sweating pitcher of tea poised in her hand. "What was that about?" she asked.

"A story for another day," I said, repeating Grady's words.

A story I planned to get to the bottom of as soon as possible.

I smiled my way through the crowded room, thankful for a bustling café, wacky, loving aunts, and our tight-knit seaside community.

It was probably too soon to think it, but I was thankful for Grady in my life too.

Mostly, I was glad for a future where anything was possible and all my best adventures were still ahead.

Summer Strawberry and Peach Tea

Nothing complements a hot summer day like this Swan Family Favorite, so dive in and enjoy!

Prep Time: 20 minutes
Yields: 16 servings

10 cups cold water, divided
1 cup strawberry preserves
8 herbal peach tea bags
12 fresh strawberries, cored and sliced
Ice

Using a medium saucepan, add 4 cups of water, strawberry preserves, and peach tea bags, and bring to a boil. Remove from heat, and steep 15 minutes.

Pour in remaining 6 cups of cold water. Remove tea bags and let cool completely. Then, add strawberry slices, and stir.

Refrigerate until ready to serve. Pour over ice.

Iced Chai Latte

Time for a midday pick-you-up? Try Everly's Iced Chai Latte. Caffeinated tea with a latte to love.

Prep Time: 20 minutes
Yields: 10 servings

10 cups milk, 2 percent or skim
5 tablespoons refined granulated sugar
10 chai tea bags
½ teaspoon cardamom
Cinnamon, ground, for garnish
Ice

In a large saucepan, bring the milk, sugar, tea bags, and cardamom to a boil, stirring often. Remove from heat and steep 5 minutes. Remove tea bags and chill in the refrigerator until ready to serve.

Serve over ice and garnish with cinnamon.

powder, celery salt, and Worcestershire sauce until well blended and creamy.

Arrange two slices of the pumpernickel bread on your work space, and spread a thin layer of the mixture onto each slice.

Cut the slices into circles with a cookie cutter. Center a cucumber slice onto each sandwich, spritz with lemon juice, and dash with pepper, to taste.

Serve open-faced.

Carolina Cucumber Sandwiches

Need something light and refreshing after a long day at the beach in the sun or something to serve at your next garden party? Try Everly's Carolina Cucumber Sandwiches for the perfect summer fix.

Prep Time: 20 minutes
Yields: 48 sandwiches

1 cucumber, seedless, peeled and thinly sliced
1 (8-ounce) package cream cheese, softened to
    room temperature
2 tablespoons fresh dill, chopped
¼ teaspoon garlic powder
¼ teaspoon celery salt
Dash of Worcestershire sauce
1 loaf pumpernickel bread, thinly sliced without
    crust
Splash of freshly squeezed lemon juice
Pinch of freshly ground black pepper, to taste

Line cucumber slices on paper towels to drain. In
a medium bowl, mix the cream cheese, dill, garlic